n05

DATE DUE

AUG 0 2

OCT 0 7 2002			
JUN 10 03			
GAYLORD			PRINTED IN U.S.A.

Heart
and
Soul

Also by Sally Mandel
in Large Print:

Out of the Blue
Portrait of a Married Woman

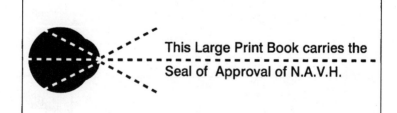

This Large Print Book carries the
Seal of Approval of N.A.V.H.

Heart
and
Soul

Sally Mandel

Thorndike Press • Waterville, Maine

Published in 2002 by arrangement with The Ballantine
Publishing Group, a division of Random House, Inc.

Thorndike Press Large Print Americana Series.

The tree indicium is a trademark of Thorndike Press.

The text of this Large Print edition is unabridged.
Other aspects of the book may vary from the original edition.

Cover design by Thorndike Press Staff.

Set in 16 pt. Plantin by Myrna S. Raven.

Printed in the United States on permanent paper.

Library of Congress Cataloging-in-Publication Data

Mandel, Sally.
    Heart and soul / Sally Mandel.
      p. cm.
    ISBN 0-7862-4271-X (lg. print : hc : alk. paper)
    1. Large type books.   2. New York (N.Y.) — Fiction.
  3. Women musicians — Fiction.   4. Pianists — Fiction.
  I. Title.
  PS3563.A446 H43 2002
    813′.54—dc21   2002020262

In memory of
ELIZABETH TROUT
with love and gratitude

ACKNOWLEDGMENTS

The completion of this book would have been impossible without the kind assistance of many people, including Mark George, Gino Rafaeli, Harold Schonberg, Jerome Lowenthal, Jean Bernard Pommier, Patty Kopec, Cipa Dichter, Francoise Davis Mallow, Tony Regna, Blake Rowe, Fouad Salloum, Delana Thomsen, Gino Francesconi, Richard Clark, Cindy Belt, Jim Murray, Jacob Lateiner, Alexei Kuznetsoff, and most especially the generous and gifted Sandra Shapiro. I am indebted to my invaluable agent, Andrea Cirillo, and to the Ballantine team, especially Shauna Summers, Charlotte Herscher, Linda Marrow, Kim Hovey, and Gina Centrello. And thanks as always to Barry, Ben, and Sarah, who fill my life with music.

CHAPTER ONE

When I turned eleven, my major goal was to grow bigger breasts than Pauline Sabatino. At that point, I could still ignore my need for music, and what was definitely not on my list was the notion of performing in Carnegie Hall with the great David Montagnier in front of 2,802 people, not counting standing room. If you had told me it was going to happen, I would have said you had your head stuck someplace where the sun didn't shine and we all would have had a good laugh, except for Pauline who didn't know what Carnegie Hall was. Anyhow, the media is always wanting to know how I got from a crummy neighborhood in Nassau County, Long Island, to a world-famous two-piano partnership. Being Bess "the Mouth" Stallone (no relation), I used to hand out the old flip response: "Practice." But given the way my life has turned out, I decided it's time to try to make some sense out of it all.

First of all, I never thought of myself as some kind of girl wonder, unless you count a genius for dreaming up creative excuses for why my report card didn't show up in my parents' mail, or how come the family laundry — my responsibility along with the rest of the housework — had blue stains all over it. But there was always this thing inside me that made me different. When I was little, I thought everybody had it, but once I figured out it had to do with the piano, I knew I was really on my own. I mean, there was nobody else in Rocky Beach who flipped out over Mozart, or if they did, they sure as hell kept it a deep dark secret. I know it's supposed to be impossible to run *at* something just as fast as you're running *away* from it, but that's the way it was for me with music.

My earliest memories are of sound: my mother's voice singing "Bela Bambina" in the darkness as I fell asleep; the opera of dogs yapping to each other on the street outside my window; sirens, car alarms, and always, always music. I can give you the theme songs of every TV show all the way back to 1968 when I was two years old. My visual impressions of childhood are pretty hazy, but the sounds stuck with me.

Then in sixth grade there was a recital at school. Mostly, it was selections by the band which sounded pretty much like a bunch of elephants with intestinal distress. Ray Zilenski kept pulling my hair from the seat behind me and Pauline was crying because she got gum stuck on her new blouse. I was cranky from the pain in my ears. But then the band clattered off and Amanda Jones sat down at the piano and began to play "The Happy Farmer," by Robert Schumann. Talk about being bonked over the head. Nobody was paying attention except for Amanda's parents and me but I'll never forget that first clumsy little classical ditty. I hung around after everybody left the auditorium and went to the piano. It was a beat-up old baby grand with dirty yellow keys but to me it seemed like a holy relic. I started fooling around until I'd figured out more or less how the keyboard was organized and then I worked out the tune I'd heard Amanda play. Bess Stallone Meets the Piano — it was like being born.

My parents didn't quite see it that way. When I pleaded for lessons, my father said, "Sure, Liberace. I'll just hand you the mortgage money and you can serenade us when we're living out on the street." Nobody in my family knows from a simple yes or no answer. There always has to be drama.

I kept my mouth shut, but all the time I was scheming. I'd saved over fifty dollars

9

from doing chores in the neighborhood, which I figured was good for a couple of lessons, and a few times a week I snuck into the music room at school and tried to reproduce stuff I heard on the classical radio station. I was eleven years old when Mrs. Fasio caught me trying to work out Chopin's *Raindrop* Prelude, which I liked even more than Wild Cherry's number one tune, "Play That Funky Music." Mrs. Fasio was the chorus teacher who also gave piano lessons. The kids called her Olive Oyl behind her back on account of her having popped-out eyes and being so skinny.

"Who are you?" she asked me as I was trying to make a run for the door. She was quick, and grabbed hold of my elbow before I could squirm away. I remember noticing that her panty hose hung off her ankles, she was that thin.

I slumped back down on the bench, knowing I was in deep shit — (a) because I had given the gym teacher a phony excuse about being sick so I could practice the piano, and (b) I'd figured out how to pick the lock Mrs. Fasio attached to a clamp on the piano lid.

"Your name," she said.

"Bess Stallone."

"How old are you?"

It's funny how I remember every detail of that first meeting. It's like when I first met David. Even at the time, I must have sensed how important it was. Anyway, I told her I was eleven.

"Good." Mrs. Fasio sat down beside me. "Then maybe it's not too late."

I had my first lesson right there in the music room that had the sharp metallic smell of spit from the brass instruments. We didn't hear the bell that signaled the end of gym class and the next thing I knew the assistant principal was banging on the door. The way he looked at Mrs. Fasio, I was scared she'd get fired.

"I'm not going to gym anymore," I told him. "I'm doing this instead." Not the most sensible remark I could have made to a guy who thought sports was what God did on his day off, and it didn't sit well, especially when Mrs. Fasio backed me up. The guy was on my butt for months after that, sending demerit slips home to my parents and docking my privileges. Funny thing, he showed up backstage at Lincoln Center years later and asked me and David to sign his program. I was thinking, okay, Bess, here's your chance: *Dear Asshole, If I'd listened to you, I'd still be bagging groceries*

11

in Rocky Beach. But I took the high road and even though I spelled his name wrong on purpose, I scribbled *Best regards.*

I finally got my parents to pay for lessons by agreeing to baby-sit my sister every Saturday night. Mrs. Fasio found me an old junker upright piano. It lost a few of its keys right away when my cousins fell through the top screwing around but I was crazy about it and called it Amadoofus. Nobody wanted to listen to scales and when I played Chopin, my father would start yelling, "What the fuck is this, a fucking funeral? Can't you play something with a fucking beat?" I loved the guys at the firehouse where he worked, but the vocabulary was kind of limited. Anyhow, Dad finally took an axe to Amadoofus, but I don't want to talk about that.

So Mrs. Fasio taught me some pieces that I was supposed to play at her semi-annual recital. That's when I learned about fear. One time when I was little, my cousin dangled me by the ankles over the side of a bridge. I thought that was pretty scary at the time, but it couldn't compare to the way I felt about Mrs. Fasio's recital. I phoned her the night before, pretending I was my mother with some bullshit story about how Bess couldn't attend the recital because she'd come down with pernicious anemia, a disease Pauline found in the encyclopedia. Naturally Mrs. Fasio double-checked, so not only did I have to show up for the recital but I caught hell from my mother for lying. Since I was slated for last, I had to sit there sweating through my party dress and tasting Fruit Loops from breakfast in the back of my throat while everybody else waltzed up and did their thing without so much as a twitch. Anyhow, time marched on and it was my turn. When I sat down on the bench, my right knee started bouncing and my fingers were slimy and cold. All I can remember thinking was *Oh, God, somebody kill me kill me kill me.* I must have stumbled through my Mozart Sonata because I somehow arrived at the last chord, but when I stood up, everything went black. Well, no, not black, everything *but* black. Every color exploding at once in front of my eyes. I passed out and broke my nose on the keyboard.

After that experience, it didn't matter if there were ten or ten thousand in the audience, I was scared shitless, and that is a reasonably accurate term, I can tell you. I didn't realize it then, of course, but right there in Mrs. Fasio's living room I had taken the first step on my journey to David Montagnier.

So after that I became a teenager with this totally weird need to be listening to the local classical music station twenty-four hours a day. There was only one person in the world who didn't seem to think I was nuts and that was Mrs. Fasio, which was pretty scary in itself. If I followed her lead, I figured I'd wind up a lonely old maid who was half-fermented from the buckets of bourbon she started guzzling about four o'clock every afternoon.

I suppose most adolescents feel alone, like nobody understands their own special problems. On the one hand, I was ashamed of my obsession and felt like there was something seriously wrong with me and I should just study computer technology like my father said. On the other, there was a tiny kernel of conviction way down deep that God had slipped a special gift into my packaging and I'd damn well better honor it. Talk about confused. I tried distracting myself with things like sex and drinking, but the bottom line was I still couldn't stay away from the keyboard. It's like the piano was a person to me. The way Pauline was hung up on Billy Joel, our Long Island piano man, I was mooning over a photo of Vladimir Horowitz that I kept hidden under the junk beside my bed. I'd get it out just before I turned out my light and stare at it despite the fact that even in the picture he was probably at least a hundred years old, listening in my head to the passionate pyrotechnics of his recordings. For me, Horowitz's rendition of a Scriabin Étude inspired the same intense "if only" mix of longing and joy that "Just the Way You Are" produced in Pauline. I don't know if anybody's ever done the research, but it seems to me that music and love occupy the same hunk of real estate in the brain. It's all hooked up, at least for women. So imagine what happened to my head when music and love collided: David Montagnier, Mr. Cosmic Fusion.

I know that's what everybody is really interested in, me and David. We're getting there, but it won't make any sense if I start with that summer day in 1994 when we finally met. I must explain that Mrs. Fasio got me to the Juilliard School through her connections. (Her father was the famous violinist Max Pantani, and how Mrs. Fasio wound up in a dumpy little town like Rocky Beach is another story and has to do with a man. Don't they all?)

So at Juilliard, I was completely out of my league socially and intellectually. I wore tight clothes and my hair was so big that other students would compete to sit behind me so they could sleep through class. Except for the secret vice of classical music, my idea of culture was *Rambo: First Blood*. What did I have in common with these smart-ass Manhattan kids and foreign students who were mostly Korean? The only other Italian student came from Milan, for Christ's sake. Anyhow, the fact that I made it there was a major miracle, which is why I'm still always chasing off to the boonies to listen to some third-grader with talent.

I commuted into the city for classes and music lessons with the legendary Harold Stein. He scared the crap out of me, with a voice that thundered when he didn't think I was trying hard enough and beady eyes that glared out from under a thicket of eyebrows. I knew I was way behind the others who'd been studying nonstop since they were seven years old. But Professor Stein kept telling me that if I worked my butt off, I could catch up. He also gave me pep talks about living up to my heritage. Up to that point, I was still under the impression that Italians didn't have much of a musical culture unless you counted my uncle's old Perry Como recordings. Professor Stein understood that introducing me to compositions by Scarlatti would be inspiring for me. It would never have happened except for the professor, but two years after graduating from the conservatory, I was on a par with some of the top students. The only problem was, if I was going to be such a hotshot pianist, I was expected to perform. And I wanted to, desperately.

I don't know what it is, exactly, that need to share your music. I mean, what the hell, if you love it so much, why shouldn't it be enough to just sit alone in your apartment and make pretty sounds for the dust balls under the sofa? But it isn't. Keeping your music private is like having your mouth taped shut, which I must say is a frustrating prospect for somebody like me. On the other hand, all those years later I could still resurrect the sour taste of fear just by thinking about Mrs. Fasio's ivory keyboard, the one that broke my nose.

Jake Minello, who for most of my life shared billing with Pauline as my best friend, could never understand why I'd get so scared. "You're not going to die out there, Bess," he used to tell me. "The worst that can happen is you make an ass out of yourself in front of a couple thousand people. It's not fun but it's also not a plane crash." I know it's hard to believe, but facing a performance made me long for death. I would hope for any kind of disaster that would prevent my going out onstage. I'm ashamed to say that one time my mother was hospitalized just before I was supposed to perform a concert at the Church of the Heavenly Rest and they had to find a replacement for me. I was ecstatic. Now how sick is that? But ask anybody who's got a bad case of stage fright and they'll tell you the same thing.

Suffice it to say, I built up quite a rep at Julliard. If I was listed in the program, they had to keep a bucket in the wings because I was definitely going to need it. Twice, I just sat there with my hands stuck over the keyboard like they had rigor mortis. I never played a note. Professor Stein tried everything. First, he sent me to a shrink who told me I'd been so freaked out by my father that it was a bloody miracle I could play at all. I went on beta blockers but first of all my betas refused to be blocked, and second, I had some unusual reaction that made me itch so much I couldn't stop scratching long enough to perform.

Drinking relaxed me a little but then I couldn't remember the notes. Professor Stein kept telling me not to give up, that every pianist suffered from this problem and it was the ones who conquered their fear who succeeded. He said he was sure I would be one of those, but once I graduated, I could see that even he was beginning to feel defeated. It was looking like it was time to give up my dump of an apartment and my three jobs, and get myself a gig at the supermarket back in Rocky Beach.

I knew about David Montagnier, of course. Everybody did. He was part of that small group of respected artists who somehow managed to cross over into popular culture, like Pavarotti or Isaac Stern or Baryshnikov. It didn't hurt that he was beautiful, with his shiny black hair, brown eyes, and a smile that was half sexual promise, half little boy. *People* magazine loved him. By the time I graduated from Julliard, everybody knew that David and his longtime two-piano partner, Terese Dumont, had split up due to some unspecified illness of hers. The last I'd heard, he was pursuing a solo career.

I started running into him around Juilliard, where I was continuing my lessons with faithful frustrated Harold Stein. Once, I was waiting for the bus on Broadway and he got into a cab right in front of me. I recognized him instantly, of course — who wouldn't? Twice, I came out of a practice room and he was walking past. Finally, I was hurrying to my waitress job and I literally slid around a corner and into his arms. Now, I'd spent years listening to recordings by Montagnier and Dumont (music students called them the Twin Peaks) and I had a lot of respect for them. Furthermore, I will never, ever forget the wattage of that first smile David flashed at me. So that's my defense.

"Shit! Oh my God, I almost killed you!" Pathetic, I realize, but at least I didn't say *Fuck me!* which tended to slip out when I was flustered. (I was no stranger to my father's firehouse.) "Bess Stallone, no relation," I said, and held out my hand.

"Yes, I know," he said, wrapping long, muscular fingers around mine.

"Shut *up!*" I said. David Montagnier knew my name! Jesus! He had a fabulous accent, sort of nonspecific European. He could make the menu from Schmuel's Kosher Deli sound romantic. I know, because one time I made him read it to me just to test it out. *Salami, pastrami, gefilte fish, and flanken*. It was like a Puccini libretto.

"Are you hurt?" David asked.

"I'm okay," I said. "Just abashed." I felt quite pleased with myself over that one. "Abashed" happened to be my vocabulary word of the day — my effort at self-improvement — and it wasn't often I got to use the selection *du jour* to such terrific effect.

Meanwhile, David still had me by the elbow, and even though I was blushing to my roots, I was self-possessed enough to be pleased that a student from my old Music Theory class had spotted us and almost went into cardiac arrest from envy.

"The Ruggiero's coming along well," he said. David smiled again — whoa, fetch me my shades. "I heard you practicing," he explained. "Would you possibly have time for a cup of tea and some pointers?"

What if I'd said no? Not that it ever would have happened. But here it was, the major crossroads of my life.

"Sure," I said. Sure I can not show up for my shift waiting tables at O'Neals. A lifetime of food stamps was a small price to pay for half an hour with those eyeballs.

We went to a café on West 68th. I was annoyed that it was off the main drag where we couldn't be seen by the entire

Lincoln Center community. David ordered us herbal tea, which I hate.

"I approve of what you're doing with the phrasing in the Ruggiero," he said. "You know, Bess, your playing makes me think of diamonds."

I didn't know what to say. On the one hand, I was flattered that he'd been eavesdropping, but I was also wary. How long had he been listening to me, anyway? The tea came. I started to reach for the sugar bowl, but David covered my hand. "It's so bad for you. If you must use sweetener, I'll ask for honey."

"Healthy food gives me hives," I explained. But I put my spoon down and sipped at my tea. It wasn't so bad. I was thinking back to that diamond remark. I felt as if, from under my mother's hand-me-down turtleneck sweater, I was glittering like jewels in a Tiffany's window. "About the Ruggiero . . ." I said, not wanting to lose my chance at words of wisdom from the Man Himself. Besides, the composer was so contemporary and weird that there was hardly anybody around who knew how to play her stuff.

He leaned forward across the table, took my hands in his, and started examining my fingers. "Yes, excellent," he said. "Beautiful."

I wanted to close my eyes so I could concentrate on the sensations he was producing in my body. Maybe as a pianist I had extrasensitive hands, but I suspect that even somebody with heavy-duty calluses would get a buzz from that kind of exploration. I recommend it in the foreplay department. In fact, the impact of David's total physical presence was something you couldn't begin to imagine from the photographs in a magazine. His thick dark hair had just the right amount of wave at the ends, with maybe six threads of gray, a harbinger (vocab word from two weeks ago, thank you very much) of the distinguished way he would age. When he looked up from the table, those brown eyes fastened on you and didn't let you go.

"In the second movement," David said, "the left hand should dominate. It must be ferocious, not wempy."

I smiled. "Wimpy?"

"Yes. And don't allow the tempo to accelerate so precipitously. It must be like a clever thief escaping from the house he has just robbed. First creeping away, stealthily, then picking up the pace until he is running headlong into the darkness. It must have drama."

Suddenly the section made sense. I felt

my fingers twitch with eagerness to try it out.

"You need more time with Chopin," he went on. "Especially the Études."

"I did those when I was a kid," I protested, and felt myself getting red in the face. Any idiot knows you can always learn something from good music.

"Not properly, I would guess," he said. "The Professor fully agrees with me. You play magnificently, Bess, but there is an emotional restlessness in your work. Chopin will help you with that."

"You've talked about me with Professor Stein?" I was beginning to get pissed.

He gave me a smile and a charming shrug, which I tried to ignore. "Lookit, Mr. Montagnier, you want to tell me what's going on?"

"Please, it's David. I wonder if you'd ever consider experimenting with the two-piano repertoire?"

"I guess it never occurred to me." Hard enough to find one piano in my old neighborhood, let alone two. I had just noticed that practically everyone who came into the café stopped to stare at us. It made me feel like I was in a play. It couldn't possibly be real life.

"I've never even done duets," I admitted.

"I think you might enjoy it. Could I convince you to take a look at the *Scaramouche* by Milhaud? It's lively and fun and I think you could play the daylight out of it."

So what was I supposed to say? Correct him on "daylights" and tell him I had better things to do right now, like giving up my career? I'd actually been scanning the want ads over breakfast. "Sure. I'll get a copy from Patelson's," I said.

"I took the liberty of giving one to the Professor."

There were a couple of things I liked. One was that he offered me a sheepish grin when he said this, which acknowledged how pushy he was, and second, he called my teacher "the Professor" instead of "Harold," which I thought was respectful. I recently overheard another female student complain that Professor Stein was getting too old to teach and she was lucky to escape with her life.

Montagnier waved at the waiter. "I wish I didn't have to rush off, but I have a rehearsal in a few minutes."

I happened to know that he was due to perform at Lincoln Center that night with the Oxford Harmonia Chamber Orchestra. I had cheap seats up in the nosebleed section so I could catch an hour of bliss in between jobs.

"So what happens next?" I asked as he paid the bill.

"Here's my number." He scribbled it on a napkin. "Call me after you've had a chance to work on the Milhaud." He glanced at his watch and stood up. "A pleasure to meet you, Bess Stallone-no-relation." Then he hurried out and left me sitting there panting. A couple of groupies were standing by the cash register and when they turned to look at me enviously, I tried to look casual, like David Montagnier and I were in the habit of hanging out.

At the concert that night, I tried to concentrate on the music, but don't ask me what they played because I kept drifting into the most ludicrous fantasies about David and me. I was going to knock him on his ass with my fabulous rendition of Part Primo of the Milhaud and then he'd take me on as the replacement for Terese Dumont, and I'd be *so* much better than she ever thought of being. The two-piano scene would be in demand in the U.S. like it had always been in Europe, and of course, David would fall madly in love with me and we'd get married and have half a dozen kids. We'd go on the circuit like the Von Trapp family, with each kid playing a different instrument, and every day right after lunch David and I would go straight to bed. Oh, I was on some trip.

Naturally, instead of waiting for my lesson with Professor Stein, I boogied down to Patelson's and blew $25.50 on a copy of the *Scaramouche*. I started practicing the Milhaud to the exclusion of everything else, all hours of the night and day. It wasn't that it was a difficult piece, which it's not. But I'd bought a recording — by the Twin Peaks, as it happened — and copying Terese down to the quarter rests was the real challenge.

The Professor canceled my lesson that week due to bronchitis. It always scared me when he got sick because he seemed so ancient. I took him hot soup every day after work and made sure he was swallowing his antibiotics and not sticking them in the flowerpot under the cactus plant. I didn't mention Montagnier. By the time I got to my next lesson, I'd learned the *Scaramouche* by heart.

"You don't look so perky," I said to the Professor when I showed up for my lesson. His big nose was a deeper shade of blue than usual and everything was drooping. Even his tangled eyebrows looked like weeds that hadn't seen rain for much too long.

He gestured from his perch beside the piano. "Come in, Bess, come in," he said with that staccato way he had of speaking when he was impatient. "I have no time to be sick."

"I brought you some medicine," I said, displaying a tiny shopping bag. I'd hesitated outside the Belgian chocolate shop, realizing it was going to cost me the price of five loads of laundry. But it was worth it to see his face light up.

Making it across the Professor's living room was like threading your way through the narrow aisles of a Manhattan supermarket. There were waist-high stacks of music, and nestled in the curve of the Steinway stood a cello case. Its womanly shape was a comforting memory of his wife, dead eleven years. Besides for music and his wife, the Professor's other passion was poker. He had a regular weekly game with a bunch of non-musician cronies from Brooklyn. On the wall along with the photographs of him with Bernstein, Copland, and Horowitz was a framed poker hand he drew at his game on March 11, 1957: the ace, king, queen, jack, and ten of hearts, each one autographed by the other players who were there. Sometimes, when my lesson wasn't going so hot, I would catch him staring dreamily at that spot on the wall and I knew he was reliving the great moment.

"Did you take your Zithromax this morning?" I asked him, handing him the chocolates.

"YesyesYES," he said, waving an arm impatiently and giving me a damp cough just to let me know what he thought of pills. "Don't hover, Bess. You know I hate that."

I sat down on the piano bench and started running through some scales. I could see David Montagnier's music beside the Professor and waited to see if he'd raise the issue. I knew we were kind of teasing one another. After he'd made serious inroads on the chocolates and I'd played a couple of measures of the Prokofiev B-flat Major Sonata, I caved.

"I've been working on something else the past few days," I said. "Tell me what you think." And I proceeded to whip through the Primo part of the Milhaud for him, by memory. It freaked me out a little to play for the Professor because it felt like a performance, but I finished without too many screwups. He gave me a sly little smile. Sometimes he could look awfully young and sassy for an old geezer.

"I believe you've been conferring with a Monsieur Montagnier," the Professor said.

"You want to tell me what you boys have in mind?"

"He approves of the way you play."

"He's been spying on me, right?"

"Eavesdropping."

"Why?"

"Terese is retired. David needs a new partner."

"You've gotta be kidding me." My heart started thumping like a crazy bastard.

"I wouldn't want you to get your hopes up, Bess. He's been listening to a number of people, some of whom have a great deal of concert experience." He lit a cigar and coughed.

"Does he know I can't appear on a stage unless I'm in a coma?"

"You know you only reinforce your fears with that kind of talk. And yes, he's aware of your problem. He's struggled with it himself."

"Bullshit."

The Professor popped a truffle into his mouth. He closed his eyes in ecstasy for a second. Then he shot me a guilty look from under the bushy brows and held out the almost empty box. "You can't afford these," he said, "so you'd better at least have one."

"Nah, ruin the figure," I said. "But you lay off that cigar. It's not healthy."

He glared at me. "On the contrary, it'll cure my bronchitis. And don't you tell me bullshit. David Montagnier has a right to his fears just like any mortal. But I think we're getting ahead of ourselves here. David and I merely discussed your playing through the Milhaud together. What did you think of him?"

"He's not bad-looking at all."

The Professor gave me a little tap on the top of the head. "Phone him. You're ready." He saw me turn the greenish shade of the couch. "It's not a performance, Bess."

"Yuh." I started fiddling with a corkscrew of hair. Each strand is like that ribbon you curl with the flat edge of a pair of scissors. When I start yanking on it, you can be sure I'm on my way to panic meltdown.

I went home and phoned David Montagnier. His voice sounded so neutral that I thought he was the machine and I began leaving a complicated message. I got as far as my phone number when I heard him chuckle.

"How's tomorrow?" he asked.

"Absolutely dandy," I said. I wondered if he had a bucket in his broom closet, just in case.

He lived in a landmark building across the street from Carnegie Hall, with a fancy gold lobby that made you feel like genuflecting. I rode up in the elevator reciting my mantra: *Be still my heart* — left over from another failed experiment to tame my phobia.

He stood in the doorway with his hair all rumpled, wearing a pair of white jeans and a T-shirt. He had a mug of coffee in one hand, and his feet were bare. Damn, how rare are nice-looking male toes, I'd like to know? He ran a hand through his hair and yawned. "I'm so sorry, Bess. I didn't get to bed until four."

"I can come back another time," I said, and felt the color rising into my cheeks just from hearing him say my name with that accent of his. *Uh* oh, I thought. The last time I felt this way, I wound up in a bed I had no business jumping into.

"No, no, it's fine," he said. "Let me get you some coffee."

I shook my head. Any more stimulation of my nervous system and my EKG would sound like Chopin's *Flight of the Bumble*

Bee. He drew me over to his pianos, two concert Steinways side by side in front of a million-dollar view of Central Park. "Jesus F. Christ," I breathed.

"The sad thing is, I hardly ever look out of the window."

"How come the pianos aren't facing each other?" I'd only seen two-piano pairs perform that way.

"There's a choreography to it, Bess, like ballet. You want to rehearse so you can see one another's arms and hands, so that your gestures will be similar in performance when the pianos are separated." He sat me down, went to the other piano, and began running through some warm-ups. "C-sharp," he said. "Come on, I'll race you."

I was still holding my music, which had a damp dent in it from my grip. I set it down, stretched my fingers, and dove in. It was a responsive keyboard with the athletic action I like. We played around like that for ten minutes with David switching from one exercise to the next and me scrambling to keep up. It was fun and loosened me up a little.

"All right," David said. "Ready for the *Scaramouche*?"

"Oh, yeah, sure," I lied.

He came over and put a large sheet of

music on the piano. "What's this?" I asked.

"Your copy of the Milhaud. I always reduce the pages and glue them together."

Duo-pianists don't ordinarily memorize their music, but this was new to me. "You don't use page-turners?"

"Never. They belong in hell with the music critics. They turn too early or too late, they have terrible breath, they moan in your ear. Either we learn by memory or we fix the pages so we can manage ourselves. You set the tempo."

Instead of trusting my memory, I struggled with the unfamiliar score.

"That's fine," David said. "Don't worry about mistakes. I don't care about that."

And then we played. I was hesitant at first, afraid that I was dragging him down.

"Again, Bess," he said. "You're doing well. Stop worrying about your fingers and listen to the music."

The second time through, I started paying attention to our exchange. Then, finally, on the third try, it all came together. The music soared between us, our fingers asking and answering questions in a nearly flawless, intimate conversation.

We stared at each other for a moment, acknowledging that something amazing had just happened. "Again?" he asked.

I nodded.

We played the *Scaramouche* twice more, each time becoming more like one voice. Then David asked if I would like to read through some other more substantial things. We must have worked for more than two hours, mainly on Beethoven, which isn't so difficult to sight-read.

"You must be tired," David said finally. "We'd better stop."

"I'm fine," I assured him, although I could feel my spine fusing into a painful column under my sweater. The thing was, I couldn't stand for it to end.

"Haven't you had enough?" David asked.

I shook my head, and to my amazement, felt tears starting. I looked out the window to hide my face. The next thing I knew, David was standing behind me with his hands on my shoulders.

"You're crying," he said. "Why?"

I shook my head. The word "rapture" was on my self-improvement vocabulary list. I had learned what it was supposed to mean, lying there flat on the same page as "rapacious" and "rapid transit." But I had never imagined that I'd experience it. As if I was about to die, the history of my life

spooled out against the tear-blurred landscape of Central Park. All those childhood
nights with my ear stuck to the radio by
my pillow, clinging desperately to some
dream I couldn't even begin to describe.
Furtive hours with Amadoofus, alternating
Bach with Billy Joel so I wouldn't irritate
my father and risk losing my piano lessons.
The lonely, exhausting, thrilling years at
Juilliard. It all seemed to lead to this sun-
drenched room and this man whose music
was like an embrace. I was crying with joy
and with the fear that this was the first and
last time I would ever feel this way.

I wiped my eyes and stood up, hoping to
get out of there before I made even more
of an ass of myself.

"Will you come again?" David asked.

I liked that he didn't press me to explain
my overwrought state. "Of course," I answered. "I'll come."

He walked me to the elevator. My legs
were wobbly stems that barely held me up.

"I think I'd better put you in a taxi,"
David said.

"No. No. I'm fine." I needed to walk, to
breathe cool air, to remember everything,
every note, every chord.

"I have to be in Paris for a few days," he
said. "I'll phone you when I get back."

He leaned down to give me a kiss on the cheek. He had a clean smell, like laundry drying in the sun. Then I took the elevator and headed for the park. As I walked north, I had the sensation that I was shedding, that there was trash trailing in my wake: dry husks of fear, anger, loneliness — there they go, litter in the breeze, twisting higher and higher above the city trees to blow out to sea and vanish.

The sensation of nakedness made me tremble even more, so I sat down on a bench by the pond and watched a little boy feed the ducks. He kept shouting to his nanny in French. David might have looked like that once upon a time, the dark swatch of hair and tanned skin. The trembling didn't stop. As I gazed around me, it seemed that it wasn't just me. The entire world was vibrating, the leaves, the clouds in the sky, everything was humming. The words of the song were simple enough. They merely confirmed what I'd known for a while.

"Bess is in love," they said. "Bess is in love."

And that's how it all began.

CHAPTER TWO

Whenever anything important happened in my life, the first thing I did was spill it all to Jake Minello and my sister Angelina. Strangely enough though, I didn't feel like telling anybody about this thing with David. I thought about him constantly and in silence for three days, which for me was the equivalent of about thirty years. But by Saturday, it was getting too heavy to hang onto by myself. I hopped on the Long Island Railroad for the hour-long trip past everybody's backyard barbeques and August-fried gardens.

Rocky Beach isn't rocky unless you count the veteran's memorial boulder in front of the bank, and the beach is a mile from town. Jake told me the name came from a Native American word — *roshibak*, or something like that, but he was probably bullshitting me, which was one of Jake's primary forms of entertainment. Anyway, the first thing I always did when I got off the train was to stop by the firehouse. It's not that I was wild to see my father, who'd been working there for twenty-five years.

Our relationship was what I guess you'd call contentious, but the other guys felt like family. I had a Jewish boyfriend once who every time he walked into his apartment touched this thing called a mezuzah, a religious decoration nailed to the door frame. Stopping by the firehouse was my way of tapping the mezuzah. It made me feel more like I was home than when I was home.

"Yo, Bess, whassup?" Corny O'Halloran was six-four and three hundred pounds. Unless he was off somewhere fighting fires, he sat by the door reading James Joyce, drinking tea from a china cup, and dunking a doughnut with his pinky sticking out. Corny thought my father didn't put enough emphasis on education (zero isn't a lot) so when I was little he used to make me repeat the multiplication tables and the state capitals. I love it when they do state capitals on *Jeopardy*. I absolutely rock. Anyhow, if I got everything right, Corny would fish into his shirt pocket and reward me with toffees that were very excellent at yanking out loose teeth. When I got older, I started baby-sitting for his daughter MaryLouise, who had cerebral palsy. It was hard work, and sad. I didn't like getting paid for it but

Corny insisted. What I did was recycle by buying presents for MaryLouise with the money. Corny never found out as far as I know.

"You're always a knockout," Corny said. "But I've gotta say, today you look like you swallowed a beauty pill."

I felt different, that's for sure, and it was on the tip of my tongue about David when my father ambled in from the bunk room, rubbing his face, which meant he'd been sleeping and would be crankier than usual. Suddenly my stomach felt like it was trying to digest a rock, and talking about being in love was the furthest thing from my mind.

"Did you get me the aftershave?" he asked, ruffling my hair, which always made me feel six years old and just about as helpless.

"Well, hello to you too, Dad," I said.

"You know what, Dutch?" Corny said to my father. "You're a pain in the rectillium." He rolled his eyes at me and went off to the kitchen, where life begins and ends in any firehouse. My father's nickname refers to the fact that his mother was Dutch. Looking at his square blond face, you'd never guess there was even a teaspoon of marinara sauce in his blood.

He pointed a finger the size of a cigar at

me. "Hey, I'm working six days a week here," he said. "You got nothing better to do so far as I know." He started leafing through the *Daily News* that was always on the table.

"One, you're not working, you're napping," I said. "And two, last I knew there's a Duane Reade in Elmont." The rock in my stomach melted into lava and started to bubble. I hated to let him see he was getting to me. It gave him too much satisfaction.

"Don't go getting high and mighty on me, girl." He picked up another chair like it was made of toothpicks and set it down so he could put his feet up. He hadn't given me more than a glance.

"Three, I'm not living at home," I said. "I don't have to do your errands anymore."

He finally looked at me out of his beefy face. I had to admit he was physically imposing in the bulky menacing way of your basic albino grizzly bear.

"You watch your mouth," he muttered. "And tell your mother I'll be home about four." He opened the newspaper to Ann Landers and made a show of ignoring me. I stood there for a minute, trying to figure out why his favorite column usually featured complaints about people like him. It was hard to remember that once upon a time we had been capable of having fun together. Then I took the aftershave out of my bag, plunked it down on the table, and left. He didn't thank me.

It was a tribute to how far gone I was that I'd only made it a few steps when I forgot about being pissed at my father and started daydreaming about David Montagnier again. I was taking a bow with him from the stage at Alice Tully Hall in Lincoln Center. We were holding hands and David was giving me a private signal, squeezing my hand in the "shave-and-a-haircut" rhythm which he probably doesn't even know about since he was brought up in France, or so my extensive research told me. But suddenly somebody grabbed me from behind. I figured it was Dad so I swung around, ready for trouble.

"*Uh* oh," my sister said. She had an armload of books. "I guess I know where you just were."

"When they build the asshole museum, he'll be the star attraction."

"You'll be out of here by then." Angie's conversational style took some getting used to. I knew she didn't mean I'd be gone by the time they built the museum, only before Dutch got home at four o'clock. Angie made leaps and didn't bother to fill you in. She paid me back for the effort to keep up by supplying me with vocabulary words. She fell into step with me as the noon whistle blew. It used to be a B-flat but over the years it had slipped down to an A. These days they could tune an orchestra to it.

"I don't know how you stand living with him," I told her.

"Oh, I was found in a basket," she said. Meaning that Dutch considered her an outsider because she didn't look like anyone else in the family. Mumma and I and all the cousins were brown-eyed with brown hair but Angie had silky black hair and gray eyes. Her skin was pale. It was true that my father pretty much left Angie alone, which sometimes hurt her feelings, but she was better off looking breakable. Dutch was the kind of bully who only picked on people he knew could give him a contest, like me. There was nobody else who came in for anywhere near the same kind of shit I had to put up with.

As usual, being around Angelina had already calmed me down. For being only eighteen, she was a very wise person. The need to tell her about David was suddenly physical, like when you have a tickle in your throat and absolutely have to cough it out or you'll choke to death.

"Angie, don't go in yet," I said. "I've got something to tell you." I reached for her books. She never looked as if she was strong enough to lift a paper towel. "I'm in love. I'm crazed. I'm a total goner."

She was silent for a moment. I appreciated her grave expression, her instant understanding that this time I wasn't kidding around. "Are you going to tell me who with?" she asked.

"David Montagnier," I said.

"Not the real one," Angie replied, with such total confidence that I burst out laughing.

"Oh, he's real all right. He has beautiful feet."

"Already?"

"No, I haven't slept with him. We played two-piano stuff in his apartment. Honey, it was way better than sex."

She looked at me in disbelief. Her Bess professing that anything was better than sex?

"Are you two just going to stand out there?" Mumma yelled, leaning out the front door. "Lunch is ready!" She wore her old faded apron, a housedress, and beat-up slippers. I was irritated already. This was

44

not the 'fifties. This was not Iran. She should go back to school already and become a person.

"Coming!" I called back. And she should tell my father to go fuck himself.

"You can't leave me in suspense," Angie said.

"We'll walk to the beach after lunch," I said. "Is Jake coming?"

"He'll be sweaty." Meaning he'd be stopping by after his jog. Jake had free reign in our house. His favorite towel, the big wraparound one, was kept laundered and ready on a peg in the bathroom so he could shower after his runs.

We hurried up the crumbling steps. It was a two-family house that we shared with the Schultzes in a long-term relationship that resembled a good marriage, better than either of the actual unions on either side of the front porch.

Mumma was dragging a big platter of ziti out of the oven. "Jesus, Mumma," I said, "it's only about four hundred degrees in here. You couldn't throw together a little Caesar salad and call it a day?"

We kissed right on the mouth, which is another Stallone thing. We all do that, even Dad when he isn't in a piss-poor mood. Then I held her away to check her out.

Same brown curly hair, brown eyes, and suntanned face. As usual, she seemed blurred, out of focus. Sometimes I thought she'd decided to be a symbolic Italian mother instead of a real person.

"Come sit down, girls," she said. "We'll have a nice ladies' lunch."

We sat at the cramped table in the kitchen. Angie was shooting me wide-eyed looks as I rambled on about running into Pauline Sabatino in Bloomingdale's, which was only the sixth time she'd ever been to Manhattan. We were both thinking about David Montagnier but I was certainly not going to mention him to my mother. She didn't get the music thing, but she knew a star when she saw one and David definitely qualified. First thing, she'd be on the phone to all her relatives in Sheepshead Bay.

"Have you played in any concerts this week?" Mumma asked me. She wasn't really interested, but it was nice of her to make the gesture.

"No, nothing much going on," I told her, and tried to look enthusiastic about the ziti she'd heaped on my plate. It had olives in it, which she knew I loved, but the view from David Montagnier's window was floating in front of my eyes. I blinked to make the picture go away. Angie was gawking at me with a face full of questions.

"You look flushed, Bess," Mumma said. "Have you been wearing sunblock? I could swear you're running a fever."

The front door slammed. I felt my stomach lurch with the thought that my father had come home early, but then a familiar voice called, "Bess? You here?"

I smiled at Angie. "Nope!" I yelled back. So much for the ladies' lunch.

Jake appeared in the doorway, half-naked and dripping wet from a run on the beach. He was medium height with a great body, the sight of which ordinarily produced a little electric buzz in my most important spots. It interested me that I didn't feel it this time. He bent over to give me a kiss, also on the lips but with a little lingering, semifake groan like he couldn't tear himself away. We'd been doing this routine since seventh grade, and except for once, it never went any further. Jake and I did better as friends. I wanted to tell him then and there: *Jake, you'll never believe, something huge has happened.* Mumma handed him a plate, pressed him into my father's seat, and went down to the cellar for more soda.

"You in love or what?" he asked me.

I gaped at him. "What makes you say that?"

"I wasn't born yesterday."

"Shh," I hissed as Mumma emerged with a six-pack of Coke.

Jake reached out and gave me a pinch at waist level. "Putting on a little weight?"

"Fuck you," I said genially. My mother used to nag me about my language but she gave up when she realized she couldn't compete with the guys at the firehouse.

"Do you get any vacation this month?" Mumma asked Jake. He was working full-time in construction and taking courses for his masters in education at the state university. Jake was the kind of person who could teach a mathematical idiot — me — to understand calculus. Patient, clear, and in no rush.

"Yeah, today," he said with a grin, and then looked pointedly at Angie. "So?" he said.

"What?" she said.

"So have you heard anything, dummy?"

Angie shot him a look that said, Shut *up*.

"About what?" I wanted to know.

"The SATs," Jake said.

"Which SATs?" Mumma asked.

A tiny smile fought with the irritation on Angie's face. The pale pink spots that

48

showed up on her cheeks were her definition of a blush.

"You aced 'em," Jake guessed.

"725 in math and 760 in English," she admitted, almost as if she was ashamed of herself.

I got up out of my chair and scooped her into a hug. "You genius!" Out there on Planet Montagnier, I'd forgotten all about my sister's scores.

Angie shoved me back in my chair and said, "It's not a good idea."

I knew what she meant but Mumma needed help. "To tell Dutch," Jake explained.

There was silence while this sank in, and then Mumma said, "I suppose that would be best." My father wanted Angie to go to computer school, where with her brains he thought she'd have the best chance at making big bucks. Angie wanted to study literature. Those test scores were going to rock my father's rowboat till it took on water.

After lunch, Mumma told us she'd clean up if we wanted to go to the beach. "I don't have anything to do anyway," she said with a hint of resentment that annoyed me. I knew there was no point in offering to help her because she'd only refuse.

From long habit, the three of us always walked in the same pattern, me in the middle, Jake to my right, and Angie to my left. We'd been doing that for so many years that if somebody switched positions, we could hardly talk to each other. Heat was shimmering over the sidewalk. Weeds looking for water pushed up through the cracks and fried. My blood was boiling anyhow from not talking about David. I felt bad enough that I'd been so preoccupied I hadn't remembered to ask Angie about her SATs. I figured as soon as we put some space between us and Mumma, I'd be spilling my guts about David Montagnier but for some reason, I couldn't. It was almost a mile to the beach and whoever was brave enough to be out on their tiny patch of lawn waved or said hello. Funny about Rocky Beach. I'd lived there all my life and part of me felt completely at home. But my musical side, well, that was a different story altogether. There was only one person who truly understood what I was all about, which was Mrs. Fasio. And, of course, the entire population of Rocky Beach thought she was a freak. So I waved back and thought, Nice to see you, but you don't know me.

"Angie, look up in the sky tomorrow," I

said. "I'm getting a skywriter to put your scores up there."

"It's nice," Angie said, "but your news is better."

I threw Angie a look that said *not yet,* so she didn't object when I turned to Jake and said, "Maybe I won't be quitting music."

He grabbed a hunk of my hair and tugged. "Whatever you say, Stallone." I knew he didn't buy it, but at least he wasn't nagging me. As I said, he could be patient.

The sand was jammed with weekenders, so we walked down to the jetty, where you could sometimes actually see Brooklyn, if that's what you were inclined to look at. There wasn't anybody else around except for a couple of surfers who were trying to hitch a ride on the dinky little waves. I didn't realize it then, but after seeing beaches all over the world, there's still nothing that can compare to that hundred-mile curl of surf on the south shore of Long Island.

Anyway, we sat on our driftwood log and as usual, Jake started tossing stones into the water. He had some arm. The damn things went halfway to Bermuda.

"My guidance counselor says NYU will

give me a scholarship," Angie said. I held up my hand to slap her five but she just threw me a pitiful look.

The thing about my sister was, she didn't act like a high-school kid. She was a solemn little thing with eyeballs that looked like they could tell you the secrets of the universe. So when she turned and wailed in this MTV-type voice, "I know Dad's not going to let me do it. My life is *so over!*" I had to chew a hole on the inside of my cheek to keep from smiling.

But when I saw her eyes start to fill up, battle mode kicked in. "The sonofabitch *will* let you do it," I said.

"We can work out a plan of attack," Jake said, Mister Practical. "If it doesn't cost him anything, we'll find a way to make him go for it." I put my arm around Angie and gave her a squeeze. She looked fragile, but I could feel her wiry strength.

"The scholarship wouldn't pay for everything," she said.

"Don't worry, Ange," I said. "I've got a little trust fund going for you."

She looked at me like I was nuts.

"No big deal," I said. "I've just been setting aside a little every week. I figured I'd surprise you at graduation." I'd only managed to sock away about fifteen hundred dollars, but it was something.

"I've seen your black sweater, Bess," Angie said. By which she meant I needed a new one, which I couldn't afford.

"Don't be silly," I said. "The money's just sitting there." I figured I could maybe squeeze in a bartending job. It meant getting no sleep but what the hell, I'd do plenty of that when I was dead.

We sat and watched the sea lick the shore. It amazed me that even Angie's crisis hadn't taken my mind off David Montagnier. His music played in my head like a soundtrack and the minute I let my mind drift a little, I was drawn to him again. I could see him standing all in white in the doorway of his apartment with the sun streaming in behind him, lighting him up like an angel.

Jake flung another stone, and with his eye on its trajectory, he said, "So, Bess, are you going to tell me or not?" I knew I wasn't getting off the hook any longer. Besides, I'd always told him everything there was to tell in my life including the episode where I took the rap for Pauline when she started a fire in the girls' locker room. By accident, but she was already on probation and would have gotten chucked out of school. I only got a month's community service and a couple of bruises courtesy of Dutch.

I stood up and started making patterns in the sand with my bare feet. "Okay, it's like this. I've got a bad case. I've never felt this way. It's scary."

Angie shot a quick look at Jake. The stone he was holding dropped out of his fingers.

"Who?" he asked.

"David Montagnier."

"David Montagnier," he echoed. "I don't think so."

I burst into tears. Angie held out her hand and pulled me back down onto the log between her and Jake. I leaned my head against Jake, breathing in his salty smell. Then I choked out the whole story. It felt good to cry. I hadn't even known I needed to.

"You're going to be his new partner," Angie said when I'd finished.

"I don't know that," I said.

"You'll see. Professor Stein's told him all about you."

"Yeah, a twenty-four-year-old prodigy who can't even play in front of two ushers and a cockroach."

"Maybe you'll be able to with Montagnier," Jake said. Something in his voice made me check him out. His smile had a strange twist to it, like he was trying way too hard.

"What?" I said.

"This is going to change your life, Bess," he told me.

"I don't want to be in love with him," I said.

"You can't help who you fall in love with," Jake said in that alien voice.

"He's famous. I'm a nobody from Nassau County. It's totally impossible."

Jake gave my shoulder a gentle shove. "You got a choice, meatball?" This was more like it.

I wiped the tears off my face. "Fucking guy's got me crying already. I don't call that a great sign."

After a few minutes, Angie asked, "Was Cinderella Italian?"

"Why not?" Jake said. "Name ends in a vowel."

That cheered us up. We sat there for a long time with our arms around each other watching the waves sigh up onto the beach. One thing's for sure. Jake was absolutely right — after that, nothing was ever the same again.

CHAPTER THREE

I spent the next week running back and forth between multiple jobs and practice rooms. The usual routine except that I was constantly wondering when and if David Montagnier would call. I'd seen a photo of him at a museum benefit so he was obviously back in town. I neglected customers as I looked for him out the window from my post at the Juilliard Bookstore cash register. And I caused a spectacular collision at Brittany's, a trendy restaurant where the wait staff wore roller skates — some challenge when you were carting a tray full of nachos and some joker wanted to pinch your ass as you rolled by. I was delivering desserts and turned my head to gawk out at Broadway just on the off chance that Montagnier might be passing by. I rolled straight into another waitress. Hot fudge sundaes flew, we did a little roller-derby dance, and down we went. The restaurant gave us a standing ovation. That's what I like about New Yorkers, the warped sense of humor.

Fortunately, I kept the job, which I

needed to pay the rent at my studio apartment on West 78th Street. Plus, that week I deposited another twenty bucks in Angie's savings account and I figured if I only ate a container of yogurt for lunch, I could set aside a little more. The restaurant gave you free saltines, and I knew it wouldn't kill me to lose a couple of pounds. I called in for my messages every time I snagged a free minute, and when I got home at night I stared at the ring button on my phone. I mean, what if I was yawning when it rang and was temporarily deaf? I took extremely short showers and made sure to stick my head out to listen every few seconds. I dried my hair beside the phone. But David Montagnier had obviously forgotten all about me. I kept reconstructing my last conversation with him and thought I remembered some clue that he wanted to work with me again. But French people pout a little when they talk and it's sexy as hell. I'd been too busy watching David's mouth to pay attention to what he was actually saying.

Finally, after not hearing from him by Thursday night, I convinced myself that it was up to me to make the first move. I got all pumped and sat down with a pencil to figure out what I would say into David's machine in case he wasn't there. I was not about to screw up, not when there was no prayer of erasing the message once my voice got stuck to that strip of tape. So after a lot of scribbling and crossing out, here's what I wrote down: *"Hello, this is Bess Stallone.* (I didn't know what to call him for one thing, plus there was the issue of the American DAY-vid versus the French Dah-VEED. I figured I'd just avoid the issue.) *I wasn't sure if you wanted to schedule another practice session but next week turns out to be good for me if you're free.* (And the week after that, and the week after that . . .) *You can reach me at 503-8986. Thanks."*

Sounds easy enough, doesn't it? With a certain understated dignity? So I dialed his number and suddenly the stage fright rose right up out of the floor of my own apartment and grabbed me by the throat. The last time I heard my voice sound like this I'd just inhaled the helium from Pauline's birthday balloons back in eighth grade: "Hi. This is Stress. Bess! Stallone! . . . (long gap with heavy breathing, then:) I wasn't sure if you wanted to do it with me . . . Oh shit, oh fuck. Sorry. Never mind. Sorry."

My hand was so drenched with sweat

that the phone slipped out of my hand, which was probably just as well. I woke up on the floor. I lay there staring at the peeling paint on the ceiling and realized that I'd hung up without leaving my number, but I figured he'd never want to call me after that anyway.

He didn't. Another week went by, during which I fought the need to remain totally trashed in order to forget the phone-machine stunt. When I showed up for my lesson, Professor Stein wanted to know how it went with David Montagnier. I said, "Okay, I guess. How are you feeling?"

"Never mind," he said with a cough. "Did David want to work with you again?"

I started to feel dangerously weepy so I just shook my head and asked the professor to comment on the ornaments I was experimenting with in the Bach D-minor Concerto. Those are the extra finger turns that early composers like to stick onto some of their notes to doll them up. I think of them as hats, like Easter bonnets. Anyway, Professor Stein gave me one of his hawk looks where his eyes narrow and his nose turns almost purple, but he didn't say anything more about David. At the end of the lesson, he went to the window and opened it wide so he could smoke his cigar. It always scared me how he perched on the windowsill like that, but his wife had made him do it so he wouldn't stink up the apartment and now he couldn't break the habit. Summer street sounds blasted in like the brass section of the New York Philharmonic getting cranked up for Copland's Third Symphony.

"I have a gig for you," he said.

A psychotherapist had tried to teach me to short-circuit my knee-jerk response. *Take deep breaths. You can choose not to be terrified.* But there it was, the lurch of nausea in the gut, the clammy hands, the dizziness, the sense of impending disaster. I closed my eyes against the explosion of colors but as always, it didn't help.

"Bess?" The Professor climbed out of the window, sat down beside me on the piano bench, and put his arm around me. I didn't mind the smell of that stogy. In fact, it was kind of comforting. "Bess, it's a competition in Boston with $25,000 in prize money. You can win it easily."

"While I'm lying under the Steinway?" The fireworks had quit popping off but lunch was working an instant replay in the back of my throat.

There was a long silence. Then he said, "I think we have to talk about your future."

60

"I know," I said. "We're wasting our time. I've got to quit."

Professor Stein sucked on his cigar. Then he got up and leaned against the piano so he could look at me. "Darling, I've never seen anyone fight so hard to beat the *lampenfieber.*" The Professor called stage fright by its German name, which, loosely translated, meant being butt-petrified of the lights at the edge of the stage. "I know you're discouraged but I want you to give it one more try. The Ruggiero's ready and so's the Hindemith."

I avoided looking at him — all that hope in his face made me feel too wretched. "I've been checking out the bulletin board for accompanist jobs," I said. "Maybe I could make enough money." That kind of thing didn't freak me out and it would still be a connection.

Professor Stein jabbed his cigar into an ashtray like he was trying to kill something that was living in there. Then he started pacing back and forth between the piles on the floor. He stopped between Beethoven and Grieg. "That talent of yours, hiding behind some second-rate soprano," he said. "It turns my stomach."

"I'd be playing music."

He put his hands on my shoulders, his

old bent and knobby fingers forcing me to look at him. "Humor an old man," he said. "Just this one last time."

What could I say? He had invested almost ten years into me. I owed him. Besides, twenty-five grand would sure as hell look sweet in Angie's bank account.

The morning I was supposed to go to Boston, I got a call from Pauline.

"I'm in a phone booth on 79th and Broadway," she said. "I have to see you. My God, Bess, I *have* to."

"I'm just running to catch a bus to Boston. What's going on?" Pauline had always been a drama queen. Catastrophe could mean anything from a death in the family to losing her *Soap Opera Digest* on the bus.

"Can I go with you? Let me just ride up there with you."

"That bad."

"Oh, shit." Now she was starting to cry. "I don't have any money."

"Don't worry about it, Pauls. I'll buy your ticket."

"But *you* don't have any money," she wailed at me through the phone.

"The music competition's reimbursing me for my ticket," I told her. A lie, but how was she to know?

Sniffles, a wet blow of the nose, and then the time's-up recording cut in.

"Wait right where you are," I said.

Now I was really late, and running in the ninety-degree heat turned my shower-clean self into a sweaty mess. But then I spotted Pauline standing on the corner and didn't care anymore. When you've got a friend who's been around since you were four, who's played in your sandbox and listened to the same endless gripes about your parents and held your hand when your heart was broken and your head when you were throwing up from too many rum-and-Cokes, you just show up.

Pauline had a beautiful athletic body, tall and sleek. Like me, she didn't do so well in school and for a long time she'd just sort of hung around Rocky Beach picking up one crappy job after another. But she was always fantastic with kids and Jake talked her into taking some special ed courses at his college. She loved everything about it, and for the first time she felt like she was good at something besides Rollerblading and jogging. Last semester she was second in her psych class.

Broadway was the usual zany parade, but it was easy to pick Pauline out the way she was standing all forlorn by the phone booth with her arms clutched around her body. She had a big nose and a bony face that had looked strange when she was a kid, like somebody had stuck the wrong head on her shoulders, but now, with her cushiony mouth and green eyes, it all worked to make her striking and sexy.

"Hey," I said.

She spun around and grabbed me in one of her rib-crushers. "I'm *so* sorry, Bess," she said. "You're an *angel.*"

"Are you going to tell me what happened?"

Her voice dipped to a whisper. "On the bus. Are you sure it's okay? It would be so *perfect,* having you all to myself."

"Absolutely. You'll keep my mind off the contest." And it was true. I'd barely thought about the performance since her call, except for an insane hope she was going to tell me that the world was about to end and I wouldn't have time to play before we blew up.

We hopped on the subway, picked up our tickets at the Port Authority and were on the bus to Boston in no time. It was cool and quiet, and I could feel Pauline begin to relax beside me. She took the aisle seat where she could stretch out her long legs.

"Okay, Pauls, spill it," I said when we'd pulled out of the station.

She looked at me with eyeballs the size of medium pizzas. "You remember that time I told Jake his mother was sick?"

We were in the junior high cafeteria having lunch, the three of us. Pauline had suddenly turned pale, set down her burger, and stared at Jake.

"What?" he said.

But Pauline started to shake and couldn't answer.

"Come on, Sabatino," Jake said. "The food's not *that* bad."

"Jake, I think your mom . . ."

Jake was real close with his mother. His father had died when he was little and he was the oldest of the three boys. Now he was getting nervous. He grabbed Pauline's arm. "What about her?" he asked.

"I think she's sick."

"What the hell does that mean?" he asked.

Pauline shook her head and I still remember how the tears splattered out onto her plastic plate. "I don't know," she said.

But we all knew Pauline could get emotional, so we let it pass. Then two weeks later, Jake's mom was diagnosed with ovarian cancer. Pauline had made us swear we'd never mention what happened in the cafeteria, or even bring it up with her, and we hadn't, even though Jake and I sometimes talked about it.

"Sure I remember," I said. "How could I ever forget that? It was weird as hell."

"It just happened again."

I felt the hair stand up on the back of my neck, not that I had any real use for any of that Shirley MacLaine crap, but still, Jake's mother really did get cancer. "Somebody's sick?"

"No. You remember my cousin Andrea from Fort Lee?"

"Yeah." I pictured a shorter version of Pauline, similar face stuck onto a stubby frame.

"She's pregnant. She *was* pregnant. There was a shower last week in Jersey and the whole time I was sitting there *dying* because I knew there was something wrong with the baby."

"What do you mean 'knew'? How 'knew'?"

"The same way it was with Jake's mom. It's like I know you're sitting here with me and if I turn away, I still picture you in my brain. Well, there it was in my head. That baby with its right leg twisted up against its shoulder and its foot all screwed up."

She looked around as if there might be a spy and lowered her voice. "He was born this morning, exactly the way I saw him. My aunt called. Everybody's hysterical." Her fingers tightened around my arm and the tears started again. "Bess, I don't want to know this stuff!"

I put my arms around her, which wasn't exactly easy on a Peter Pan bus, and just held her. I mean, what kind of therapist do you recommend for something like that, an exorcist? After a while, she calmed down and by the time we got to Providence, she was beginning to get into the drama of it all. "It's just the strangest feeling, like not just a suspicion or something but it's in my *core*, this total *conviction*. Do you think I'm some kind of *freak?*"

"I think you're sensitive in a way that other people aren't," I said. That was safe enough. I sure as hell didn't feel qualified to explain something this bizarre.

"Bess, I love you down to the innermost sanctuary of my heart," Pauline whispered. "You're always there for me when my soul cries out for help."

Also when you're knocked up, I could have added. Twice I'd taken her to the clinic back in high school. But God knows she'd have done the same for me. "I'm just glad you caught me," I said. "Two more minutes and I would've been out the door."

"So what do you think I should do?" she asked.

"Well, first of all, I don't really see how you can get rid of it. It seems to be a part of you, like being a jock. And lookit, Pauls, in both cases there wasn't anything you could actually do about the situation. It's not as if you could have changed anything."

"But what if it turns out I can predict the future?"

"So far it seems like it has to do with stuff that's already happening," I said. "You just get an early news flash."

She thought this over. "Okay. Maybe that's not *so* terrible but it would sure be nice if it wasn't always something tragic. I mean, this shit truly bruises my heart."

Pauline had always talked with a mixture of road construction (which, in fact, she'd done for a couple of summers) and romance novel. She read those things the way Jake ate Cheez Doodles. She looked at her watch. "I can't believe I didn't even bring my class notes. I've got a big exam on Monday."

It seemed like the crisis was over. I told

her she could hop the next bus back.

"Oh, no. I'm going to see you through *your* ordeal." She insisted on coming with me to Addams Hall to see if she could talk her way into the audience. There's always a pretty good turnout for the more prestigious competitions and this time there wasn't a seat left in the house.

"Okay, Pauls, you better boogie back to New York. You've got that exam, don't forget."

"Oh my *God*, that exam. But what if you need me?"

"I'll be fine," I said. "But hey, got any vibes about how this is going to turn out?"

She closed her eyes and put her hands on either side of my head. "Yeah. You're going to stay conscious the whole time and you're going to win."

I kissed her good-bye. The truth was, I didn't like having friends and family around when I was performing. It only made me feel worse, knowing that I was putting them through hell while they waited for me to pass out.

There were five competitors, an Asian woman, two Russian guys, a New Yorker from the Upper West Side named Ziggy, and me. Ziggy had been in my Music History class and had one green eye and one brown one, which didn't look in the same direction. He was good. Not great, but good, and for him playing in competitions produced about the same level of stress as doing his laundry. I was slated for second to last. Not as bad as last, but damn close. I sat in the green room, purgatory for me as opposed to the stage, which is hell. I had already passed out in the rest room at the bus station. I'd swallowed a couple of beta blockers and thought I could feel them hanging out in my stomach like the useless little BBs they were. In fact, I thought they were adding to my weird sense of detachment, like I was somebody else and whoever she was, she couldn't play "Twinkle, Twinkle Little Star," much less Hindemith's Third Sonata. I tried to distract myself with a *Gossip* magazine I'd picked up in the station. It registered somewhere in my brain that on page ten there was a photo of David Montagnier with Julia Roberts. They looked real chummy. But at the moment, I was just praying that a meteor would strike Boston and blow it sky-high before I had to perform. Ziggy, well aware of my problem, kept checking me out with first one eye and then the other. I saw the relief as he decided he didn't have to worry about any serious competition on my part.

Despite my efforts at slowing down the rotation of the Earth and therefore the passage of time, my turn came. Somebody walked myself out to the piano. I somehow made it through the first section but then I got stuck in a loop. Panic had erased my memory totally and my fingers just kept repeating the same measures over and over. Then there was the blur of the keyboard, the nauseating motion as it pitched and rolled, and finally the familiar head full of fireworks that ended in a blank.

Ziggy walked off with the twenty-five grand. All I had to show for my final performance was a lump the color and size of an eggplant and the realization that it was over for me. My seatmate on the way back to New York must have thought I was escaping a battering husband because all I did was cry and pop Motrin for the lump. Ten years of struggle and hope and disappointment down the hopper, not to mention having to face that old man with the cigar. I felt like I was standing at the edge of a grave, shoveling dirt on my broken heart. Professor Stein was expecting a report as soon as I got home but I could tell when I heard his voice on the phone that he already knew.

"Thank you for trying, Bess," he said. "You were brave."

"Is there any point in my showing up for my lesson on Wednesday?" I asked.

There was a hesitation. "Yes. Let's talk then." But I could hear the resignation. He was finished.

It was like when my grandmother died, the pain in my chest like a broken rib. I would forget, and then it would clobber me all over again. *It's over for you, Bess. You will never be a concert pianist.* It was the *never* part that killed me. Despite everything, I'd been hanging on to the possibility that one day I'd be rid of the terror and could walk out on a stage free and strong. I was almost surprised that there was no relief, only sorrow and a sickening sense of shame.

It was raining hard when I set off for the Professor's studio on Wednesday afternoon. I didn't take my music with me. It was time the old man focused what limited time he had left on someone who could deliver the goods. He'd done it twenty years ago with Eugene Seidelman and he might still have the satisfaction of creating another star.

It wasn't unusual to find his door ajar

with a shoe holding it open. Sometimes when he's been hitting the cigars pretty hard and there's not much cross breeze, he does that to keep from setting off the smoke alarm. The smell of that funky old stogy was just too much for me. I started crying again out there in the hallway and stood mopping rain and tears off my face. I was damned if I was going to show up all weepy and pitiful. But while I was busy dehydrating myself, I realized that words were floating out along with the cigar smoke. I recognized the voice of David Montagnier. I could almost hear the hiss as my tears evaporated. I shoved my ear next to the opening.

"There's no one to equal Eugene as an interpreter of avant-garde composers," Professor Stein was saying, "but Bess can play anything. The first time I heard her, the hair stood up on the back of my neck. She should have been her generation's answer to Horowitz."

"Tragic for her, perhaps," David Montagnier said, "but it may be good luck for me."

"I tell you, it breaks my heart," the Professor went on. "And it's not that she doesn't have courage, but I've never seen a more extreme case. We've tried everything short of electric shock."

I was surprised that they couldn't hear my heart clattering like a kettledrum on the other side of the door. I realize it was not exactly kosher, my eavesdropping like that, but I was dying to hear how come my catastrophe was David Montagnier's good fortune.

"It's not just her musicality, Harold," David went on. "It's one thing hearing her through a practice studio door but quite another in person. It's palpable, that star quality. She has extraordinary presence."

At that, a surprised snorty noise came out of me, but they still didn't seem to notice.

"What's to become of her, David?"

At first, I thought Montagnier answered, "I wonder," but then I realized it was *I want her.*

"After playing with her only once?" the Professor asked. "You have no idea if she'll be able to perform."

"Look here, Harold, I knew she was the one the first time I listened to her practicing. What made me walk past that studio that particular hour, that day? I haven't been down that hall in years. It could have been an old lady with three heads in there, but I knew this was the person I'd been waiting for. I just knew. She was speaking to me through the door, through her music."

"How are you going to get her out on a stage?" the Professor asked.

"I'm not worried about it," David answered.

This time I covered my mouth. He wasn't worried about it!

"I think either you're deluded or you're a little bit in love with her."

"I assure you, Harold, neither applies. But you'll see, I'll get her past this fainting nonsense."

Putting it mildly, this was a lot to absorb. I was pretty light-headed and had to grip the doorknob to keep from toppling over. Professor Stein's next-door neighbor came out into the hall with her godzilla of a dog on a leash. It shoved into me affectionately and gave me a sloppy kiss on the hand. This seemed like a signal so I knocked and let myself in. Professor Stein was on the windowsill letting in the rain. Montagnier was perched on a pile of Schumann.

"Hi," I said.

They stared at me without speaking. It was a strange moment, really, the three of us stuck there on the edge of something. My eyes went from Professor Stein's weary old face with all its familiar sags and wrinkles to David Montagnier. Once in a great while, I guess life pulls off some unlikely pranks, and this one was a beaut. There he was, David Montagnier, darling of the media and the concert stage, speaker of six languages, romancer of starlets, brilliant musician and intellectual. Who could possibly have been more alien to me? And all I could think of when I looked at him sitting there on a heap of piano music was, *Okay, Bess. You're home.*

CHAPTER FOUR

The following morning when I showed up at David's apartment, he greeted me with a grin like an exploding flashbulb. After the dazzle dots cleared, I realized he was smiling because we were identically dressed in jeans and black T-shirts. God, I'm a sucker for men with long, lean legs.

He gave my shirt a little tug. "A good sign, don't you think, Bess?" and bent to give me kisses on both cheeks. The last time anybody in my neighborhood ever kissed me on both cheeks was when I was twelve and Jake tried to give me symmetrical hickeys.

"What can I get for you? Espresso?" David was asking. The man had an old-world courtesy that reminded me of my grandfather. For forty years, Grandpa was the headwaiter at a restaurant in Little Italy. He wore a flower in his lapel, never raised his voice, and nobody ever gave him lip.

"I'm fine," I said, but I was nervous. "I think I'd like to dive in."

David nodded, pressed his hand against

my spine, and walked me over to what I already considered to be my piano.

We practiced all morning, first the Milhaud, then *La Valse* by Ravel. I'd always dismissed the Ravel as bubblegum music, but once we started digging in, I developed a healthy respect for the demands of the thing. Impressionist music is a challenge for me because it's subtle and I'm not, or wasn't until David got hold of me. But once we started playing, I forgot about everything else, the perfect view out the window, the smell of coffee turning to mud in the kitchen, the E-flat that was slightly off key, even how much I'd wanted to jump the guy at the other piano. Three hours passed in a blur of notes.

Finally, David ran a hand across his face. "Bess, wouldn't you like to take a break?"

Once we stopped, I realized how stiff I was. I never felt it in my shoulders. I always worked hard to make sure I didn't carry tension there because I believed it translated into a brittle tone. But my lower back ached like I'd just had a fusion. "Yuh. Yeah. Yes," I said. David's elegant speech made me self-conscious about my own clunky Long Island lingo.

"Would you enjoy a walk in the park before we get back to work? Or perhaps you'd prefer to be on your own for a while. Shop, perhaps?"

I smiled. Shop, with what? I'd taken personal days for both jobs, which I'd probably lose if I kept this up. "A walk would be great."

"You're not sick of me?"

Oh, sure. Sick of him. Sick *about* him was more like it.

We went into the park, following the same route I had stumbled along the first day I played with David and realized I was in love. The trees were still vibrating.

"How do you feel about those dogs?" he asked.

I looked around for a German shepherd but he was pointing at one of the frankfurter stands that sell hot dogs with a side of salmonella. I smiled. "I like them fine," I said.

We took our hot dogs and Cokes to a bench. It's amazing how many calories you expend at the piano, and we were both starving. When I was working up a new repertoire, I could count on losing five pounds easy.

As we scarfed down our lunch, I noticed how people responded to David. The park was pretty full, with joggers, tourists from nearby hotels, and students relaxing on the grass. Everyone stared at David, I guess out of reflex because he was just so beautiful you couldn't help it. Then in a split second, they'd get it. Most people just smiled and kept a respectful distance. One jogger passed by and said, "Thanks for the music, man." David gave him a sweet little bow. But a pair of middle-aged women changed direction in midstream and started following us, but I mean tailgating in the worst way.

David had been talking about a piano he'd played as a soloist in a royal recital in London. The soft pedal had jammed and Rachmaninoff's thundering Third Sonata came out sounding like a lullaby. In the middle of the first movement, he'd crawled under the instrument in his tuxedo, fixed the problem, dusted himself off and finished the piece.

"Doesn't that bother you?" I asked David, nodding toward the women who had almost rear-ended us when we stopped walking. They just stood there staring at him as if they were part of the conversation.

He barely gave them a glance. "Not really. I'm used to it."

"Who's she?" the shorter one asked David.

"Bug off," I said to her.

David took my arm. "You'll have to excuse us, ladies," he said. "Have a lovely afternoon." We escaped to a spot sheltered by one of Central Park's monstrous gray rocks. Other than a barefoot guy asleep with his hat over his face, we were alone.

"I don't think I'd like that part of being famous," I said. David had stretched one leg out, the other with knee bent where he rested his hand. A few years later when I saw Michelangelo's *David*, I remembered that day and David Montagnier's hand like a perfect piece of sculpture.

"Even when I was small, people stared at me," David was saying. "I don't know why, really. I adjusted, and now I barely notice unless someone is very aggressive and touches me. That's unpleasant."

"You were playing solo in London when the piano broke?" I asked. "Must have been in 'eighty-six."

He thought about it, then smiled. "Yes, you're right. What else do you know about me?"

"Ask me a question, any question," I bragged.

He thought about it for a second. "All right, what was the first competition I won?"

"Stuttgart," I answered. "You played Prokofiev's Seventh. They liked the way you nailed that killer last movement." He laughed. I loved the sound of that, maybe especially because it didn't happen all that often.

"This could be frightening," he said. "Do you know everything?"

"Not enough," I said. "Like how come you never concentrated on a solo career?" There wasn't much about that in the Juilliard library. Not on the Internet, either. I'd checked it out at the World Web Coffee House, where for a cup of joe and twelve bucks you could sit in front of a computer for an hour and find out just about anything. If I didn't have the twelve bucks, it was a dollar for five minutes. I got so I could soak up a lot of information in five minutes.

"I'm surprised you don't know," he said.

"Oh, I read your article about music being a collaborative art form, but I'm not buying it." All that crap about carrying on the two-piano tradition now that the golden age of duo pianists was past and Vronsky and Babin were gone.

He was quiet for a while. Then he looked me square in the face, reached out and cupped my chin. "Because I'm lonely."

I had the feeling I'd just heard something the man had never said aloud.

When I was eleven, we went on a family camping trip in the Catskills. I was sitting on the steps of our cabin one morning when a fawn came out from the trees. We watched each other for a while, and then he came right up to me. I held my breath and very slowly stretched out my hand. The fawn inched closer and touched his nose to my fingers. Then he turned and disappeared into the wild. That brief, featherweight connection between us, a moment's gesture of trust, had brought tears to my eyes. At David's confession, I felt the same sense of privilege.

"Thanks," I said to David, for once keeping my questions to myself.

He stood up and stretched. "Ready to get back to work, Bess?"

No, I thought. I'd rather sit here on the grass until I rot and turn to muck. It's just never going to get any better. "Sure," I said, clambering to my feet and arching my stiff back.

We played for another four hours. It was real concentrated effort, and I was zonked afterward. That day, like the ones that followed, I kept hoping David would ask me out to dinner, or even to stick around for a while after our sessions, but he never did. This went on for three weeks while I stalled my bosses, roller-skated into customers at my night job, and wondered what the fuck I was doing with my life. After all, from this I wasn't making tips and Angie wasn't building up any cash in her trust fund. But David just assumed I'd be there the next day, and I couldn't resist him. I rationalized my weakness by telling myself I was gaining priceless musical experience. The truth was, playing music with David Montagnier was like a drug and I was hooked.

Not that David was hanging around his apartment in the evenings mooning about me. They have a TV in the bar at Brittany's and I caught a glimpse of him coming out of a movie premier with some half-naked babe stuck to his hip like Velcro. Her boobs were cannonballs, compliments of silicone. I spent the rest of my shift forgetting people's orders while I tried to figure out how to drop David the bulletin that mine were the real thing.

Anyway, that last night I had just gotten to sleep about two A.M. when the phone rang. I guess I was dreaming about David because I thought it was him. It took me a second to recognize Pauline's voice.

"Bess. Wake up. Listen to me, honey. There's been an accident."

I switched on the light and tried to shake my brain into consciousness.

"Your dad's been hurt in a fire."

"Wait. Pauls, is this something you know or something you *know?*" In my half-asleep state, I wasn't being very clear, but Pauline got it.

"No, Bess. He's at the hospital with your mom and Angie."

"Jesus," I said. It sank in that she was using the present tense. He wasn't dead, at least not yet. "Where is he?"

"Long Island General." The best hospital in Nassau County. Cops and firefighters get preferential treatment when they're injured on the job.

"How bad is it?"

"They think he might have broken his back. When can you get out here?"

"I'm on my way."

The trains wouldn't be running for another few hours. I only had two twenties in my wallet so I rummaged through my pockets and managed to put together another fifteen for cab fare. Then I dumped some essentials in a suitcase. I must have been somewhat out of my mind because along with the toothpaste and underwear, I slipped in a book of Chopin *Nocturnes* and a candle shaped like a teapot that Angie had given me for Christmas.

I was in some state of weirdness in the backseat of that taxi. The central question in my brain was, What if he dies? There were moments over my life, especially after Dutch had given me a throttling, when I had longed for his death. I would count the bruises on my body and burn with hatred. The purity of that feeling was a comfort and made me feel strong. But now the possibility of it as a reality shook me to my bones, as if my skeleton was trying to rearrange itself under my skin. I made a stab at praying. My father would appreciate that — unlike Mumma, he was a believer. It's just that I figured I'd better hedge my bets. If God was around, I didn't want to piss Him off by ignoring Him.

Scenes from my life smeared across the cab window like the city lights. The past five years, my relationship with Dutch had deteriorated into the bitter words of open warfare or, at best, the silence of an uneasy truce. He had always tried to impose his will on me, from the time I was three and wouldn't eat anything but Cheerios. He had tried bribery, threats, and finally force-feeding. What I did was learn how to vomit at will. Once you learn the knack, it's a lifelong skill. If I could've figured out how to make money from that particular trick, I'd have hired myself out for parties and never bothered with waitressing. Anyhow, I won that battle because my mother got the family doctor into it. I'd lost eight pounds, which is a lot for a pipsqueak.

It went on like that, my dad and me butting heads. The worst were my teenage years. When he thought my clothes were too revealing, he grabbed them from my room and burned them in the barbeque. I retaliated by wearing a tablecloth on my next date. He almost broke my arm over that one. We got into wicked arguments at the dinner table. When I told him I was going to Juilliard, he pounded the table so hard it cracked down the middle. Mumma was always trying to keep us apart. She and Angie were afraid of him, and I was too, but when I get scared I also get pissed. I don't like feeling helpless and when I'm backed into a corner I fight like Mike Tyson, except so far I haven't chewed up anybody's ear.

Anyhow, I hadn't thought about the Cheerios for ages, but once the cab crossed the Queens line, other stuff started surfacing that I would've thought you'd need a team of archeologists to dig up. Once upon a time, back in the paleolithic era when dinosaurs roamed the earth, my father and I had been close. I mean, we had always fought, but there was a tie between us, much more so than between me and my mother. Every Friday before dinner, my dad would walk me down to the beach. He'd served on a ship in the marines, and also his mother had lived by the sea in Europe and taught him to identify different seashells. We used to collect interesting things that washed up in the surf, like polished stones and bottles from foreign vessels and horseshoe crab shells. Once we found a belt buckle that looked like it had come off a pirate ship. We made up stories about all these things. My father had a great imagination and could spin a yarn about anything at all. Hold up a piece of string and he'd have you on the edge of your seat for an hour while he made up some shit about mermaids and sea captains and the ghosts of everybody who'd ever drowned at sea. Some of our beach treasures were beautiful. There was still a piece of driftwood on our front lawn that looked like a sculptor made it. But besides storytelling, we used to talk about a lot of other things on those walks — which bait to use for surf casting, gossip about guys in the firehouse or about my friends at school. I even used to ask him for advice. Sometimes we didn't talk at all but just enjoyed the ocean and one another's company. Maybe it was the sound of the waves and the gulls that smoothed the tension between us, or just that we were out of the house. The minute Dutch stepped inside the front door, a frown line the size of the San Andreas Fault would split the space between his eyebrows. I suppose the companionship of those peaceful times by the shore made it that much more of a betrayal when he turned on me. Anyhow, once I started at Juilliard, we never took one of those walks again.

So there I was zooming down the Cross Island Expressway, flipping like a channel-surfer from one year to the next, bad times and good, with the question humming in my ears like the tires on the road: *Will he die?*

Or maybe he was already gone. I realized I was no longer that angry girl who daydreamed about her father's burial. In my fantasies, he would have died a hero's death so there'd be hundreds of firefighters in uniform. I would hold my mother and sister's hands and weep while wearing a truly great outfit. Those daydreams were safe back when I was sure that Dutch was indestructible. But as we pulled up to the hospital emergency-room entrance I was actually kind of praying: "Don't. Don't do it, Daddy."

Angie was waiting just inside. She was wearing her Mets jacket over her pajamas and as soon as she saw me, she burst into tears. I knew she'd been at it before, too, because her upper lip was swollen like she'd been stung by a bee.

"Okay, baby. It's okay. Where's Dutch?"

"They took him for an MRI," Angie said. "Mumma and Pauline're with him."

"How's Mumma holding up?"

"All right. I guess she's in shock."

"You look like shit yourself. Come on, let me get you a Coke or something. There must be a cafeteria."

We found a room with vending machines and sat down in the pink plastic chairs. I knew I was avoiding the sight of my injured father but it was easy to excuse myself on account of Angie's obvious distress. The girl was just this side of hysterics. I smoothed her hair while she drank her

Coke. "Tell me about the accident," I said.

"It was a five-alarm at one of those beachfront hotels on the boardwalk in Long Beach. They thought everybody was out safe, but Dad saw a hand against a window on an upper floor. He went up the ladder, broke the window, and grabbed an old lady. She was obese and disabled and couldn't hang on. They got the net up just in time because she had some kind of spasm and yanked them both off the ladder. Dad didn't hit right and broke his back. It looks like he might be paralyzed." Here came the tears again. I reached in my pocket for some Kleenex and mopped her up.

"Okay, baby," I said, holding her. Jake is always telling me that Angie is much tougher than she seems, but when we're all in our nineties she'll still be my little sister and it'll still kill me when she cries. "I'd better check out what's going on. You want to stay here and wait for me?"

"No! I'm coming with you!" She had my hand in a death grip. "Bess, what if he can't walk? What if he dies? What will happen to Mumma?"

"Rule number one is no worrying in advance," I told her. "It's a waste of energy,

91

which we're going to need."

They had him lying on a gurney to wait for his MRI. His sunburned face had turned a sickening gray and his powerful body had no more life in it than a sack of sand. My mother sat beside him with her hand clutching the rim of the stretcher. Seeing him like that made me feel alone. Alone and scared. What did I think, that he was going to live forever in a state of superhulkness, fighting fires and being a pain in my ass? First I kissed the top of my mother's head, and then I took my father's hand, real carefully. It had been a long time since we'd made physical contact with any kindness in it.

"Hi, Pop," I said. I hadn't called him that in a lot of years. He turned his face to me. His eyes were swimming. "How're you doing?"

"Pain," he whispered.

"Haven't they given him something?" I asked Mumma.

She shook her head. "One of the doctors said they would."

"And that was how long ago?" I asked.

"An hour, maybe. We're waiting for the technician to do the MRI. He's coming from Lynbrook especially, since Dutch is a fireman. Your father."

"I know who you mean, Mumma. You want to let go of that stretcher? Your hand is going to fall off soon." She unpeeled her fingers.

"Where's Pauline?" I asked.

"She went to get us some clothes," Angie said. "We didn't know it would be so cold."

"Okay, then, Ange, I want you to go down to the nurses' station and ask what's happened to Dad's pain medication. Can you do that?"

Angie nodded. I leaned close to Dutch's face. "We'll get you something to take the edge off, Pops."

"Brew would help," he whispered. "Pint of Guinness."

I put my hand against his cheek. "You couldn't find yourself a skinny old lady to save?"

"How is she?" he asked.

"She's fine," my mother answered. "They're treating her for bruises and heart palpitations."

I'll show her palpitations, I was thinking. We waited a few minutes in silence.

"Where the fuck's Angie?" I muttered finally, just before she walked in.

"They say they can't authorize pain medication until the specialist gets here," she said. "He's at a bar mitzvah or something."

Dad moaned. It was a sound I hope I never hear again, out of anybody. His skin was changing from gray to green. "Turn me," he said. I could tell the pain was so bad it was hard to get the words out. Mumma stood to help him.

"No, don't touch him," I said. Dad's head rolled back and forth. Then he looked right at me and mouthed the words since he couldn't speak any more. *Help me. Please.* Okay, now I was really scared, and like I said, when I'm scared, I get pissed.

I stuck my head out the door and yelled *"Nurse!"* so loud that Angie and my mother jumped. I said to Angie, "Stay right here and don't let anybody touch him, not even Mumma. I'll be right back."

I could have been on my roller skates, I moved that fast down the hall. The first person I saw in hospital greens got an earful. He was leaning against the wall eating a doughnut.

"You! Who are you?" I said, grabbing his name tag. It said *Miles Rorch, Resident.* "You'll do. What the fuck is going on here? You've got a firefighter in terrible pain and you people are jerking off here. I don't care who you dig up, a pediatrician or a goddamn gynecologist, just get my father some medication or I swear to God I'm yanking him out of here and admitting him to North Shore Hospital where he'll get some attention. And they'll hear about it in the newspapers, Miles, you can bet your doughnut on that."

The guy stuffed the remains of his Krispy Kreme into his pocket. "Name?" he asked.

"Stallone."

I could see his eyes open even wider. Sometimes it pays to have the name, but if the guy had gotten the question out of his mouth I might just have decked him. "No, he's not!" I growled.

"Okeydokey," Miles muttered, licking the last crumbs off his fingers. I had the feeling he'd been up for forty-eight hours straight and was looking for a sugar hit. "Where's he at?"

"Waiting for an MRI."

"Meet you there in five," he said, and off he went in a reasonable hurry.

When I got back to my father, he was moaning in a regular rhythm with his eyes closed. I could smell the sooty odor of burning buildings.

Angie explained. "A bunch of the guys from the firehouse were just here. It was nice of them, but it was too hard on Dad, trying to be brave. I asked them to take Mumma for a cup of coffee. She was losing it."

"Excellent." Angie had obviously pulled herself together. It was a relief — one less person to worry about.

In fact, within moments, the chief resident in Neurology appeared and things started moving along efficiently enough to calm me down. They pumped a shot of something into Dutch, got the MRI, and set him up in a private room. I stepped outside and ran straight into Pauline, who had her arms full of sweaters and jackets. As soon as I saw her face, I started to cry. She let everything drop on the floor and put her arms around me. We stood holding each other for a few minutes.

"Thanks, Pauls," I said, and blew my nose. "It means a lot . . ."

"Oh, shut up. What's going on with Dutch?"

I filled her in. Then I asked her if she had any psychic news bulletins about him.

She shuddered. "God forbid."

"Nothing so far? Give me the swear."

She held up her right hand with the thumb crossed in front of her palm like we used to do when we were kids. "What about your stuff?" she asked. "Do you have everything you need?"

"Oh my God. I'm supposed to rehearse with Montagnier." I looked at my watch. "In exactly three hours."

"Jake's coming. We can cover for you."

I shook my head and drew her inside the room where Dutch lay hooked to drips and machines. Mumma's and Angie's frightened eyes fastened on me like I could make it all better. David Montagnier was already a fairy-tale fantasy from a dream I'd had a long time ago. It didn't seem possible that I'd ever step back into it again.

CHAPTER FIVE

Well, we were the cozy little group at 62 Walnut Avenue, accent on the nut. There was Dutch, the wounded warrior, howling like a dog from his wheelchair. It turned out he probably wasn't permanently paralyzed but his spine was going to take many months to heal. With physical therapy, he might walk again but his days as a firefighter were finished. For my father, that was like saying his life was over. What he did was sit in front of the television in his pajamas watching soap operas and yelling, as in *Bess! Where the fuck is my (a) breakfast; (b) lunch; (c) dinner; (d) snack?!* The worst for him and for us was cleaning him up after he'd taken a crap. Until we learned the technique, it took all three of us to shift him so Mumma could wipe him down. The first few times, he cried like a baby. A big man like Dutch, reduced to such a state.

Obviously, there was no way I could leave. I quit all my jobs and phoned David. He told me he had to go to Europe anyway and that he'd be in touch when he got back. After that, I started having nightmares. In dream logic, it seemed the only contact I was allowed to have with music was listening to my Walkman. Desperately, I'd slip in a tape of Beethoven's *Waldstein* Sonata, but after the first few measures, all I got was white sound. Or I'd be up in the cheap seats of a concert hall and instead of musicians, there'd be fish flopping around on the stage. A traffic cop came out and announced that the musicians were never coming again, ever. Nobody else in the audience seemed at all perturbed by this, but I was overwhelmed with grief. I'd wake myself up to escape the nightmares and remember that real life wasn't exactly a comfort.

Three weeks after the accident, my mother told Angie and me to wait up after we got Dutch into bed. We sat at the dining room table while she flipped through a pile of bills. "I'm going to have to get a job," she said.

Well, this was different. Dutch had never let her work. I couldn't even imagine who would hire her. "What about the disability insurance?" I asked.

"It's not nearly enough. His medication alone eats up most of it."

I started to feel a chill creep up my back. I'd been figuring on sticking it out another couple of weeks and then getting back to my life. To music. To David.

"I thought the fire department would take care of him," Angie said.

"They should." Mumma's voice was more exhausted than angry. "Things have changed now with HMOs. Your father had a lot of expensive special tests and procedures and now there's all the therapy. A lot of it's not covered."

"I'm sure the fire department would contribute something if they knew," Angie said.

"You know how he feels about taking charity," Mumma said. I could swear that a third of her hair had turned gray overnight, or maybe I just hadn't been paying attention.

"It's not charity," I said. "For putting his life on the line all these years and doing his job . . ." I looked at Angie for the word.

"Compensation."

"Yeah, compensation. Payback time."

Mumma gave me a tired smile. "You want to try to tell Dutch that?"

We sat in silence for a moment. Mumma kept sifting through the bills as if they might somehow disappear.

"Doesn't it make more sense for us to work and you to stay with him?" Angie asked, watching her college hopes fade into the sunset.

"I'm sorry, girls," Mumma said, turning her face away.

I knew she was right. Dutch needed two people to shift him, and Mumma wasn't strong enough to be much help. Angie was looking at me as if I could pull a rabbit out of a hat, but all I saw was the rabbit hole, and what was disappearing down it was her college education and my music. Obviously, there was no way I could go back to David. It was all over.

Mumma got into a training program at Cartmart, our local Wal-Mart ripoff. It wasn't much but it helped pay the bills. I envied her as every morning she left for someplace that didn't smell of illness. Dutch hated it when she went. "Call in sick," he would tell her. "You're the only one who knows how to handle me."

"That's right, make her feel guilty," I told him.

I know it was hard for her to leave him, but one morning I stood at the window and watched her start off down the sidewalk. I have to say that by the time Mumma reached the corner, she was walking tall. Shoulders square and head high, not at all the person who had been pretty much just one more kitchen appliance.

I kept imagining the headlines: MASSACRE IN ROCKY BEACH. DAUGHTERS GO BERSERK AND SLAY CRIPPLED FATHER. BAFFLED NEIGHBORS STUNNED, "DAUGHTERS WERE SUCH NICE GIRLS."

Pauline dropped in when she could, but she'd been assigned a student-teaching gig way out in Suffolk County and was living with her cousin out there. Jake provided some relief, stopping by every few days even though he was incredibly busy working and going to school at the same time. Everybody else who came to see Dutch talked to him like he'd lost his wits or he was going to die next week, or shouted at him like he was deaf. But Jake was different.

"Feel anything going on in those legs?" Jake would ask him, getting straight to the point.

"Nothing much," Dutch said.

"Well, that sucks," Jake said. "Let's go to work." After coaching high school basketball for years, he was used to injuries and helped us out with physical therapy sessions. Just having Jake around with his no-bullshit attitude was a welcome change.

Once when Jake came in to see him, before the door to his room slammed shut I heard Dutch say, "I lost my balls, Jake. You know what that means to a man like me?"

That brought me up sharp. I didn't make a habit of thinking about sex in the same ballpark with my parents, and would rather think that Angie and I were products of artificial insemination. It had never occurred to me that Dutch and Mumma were losing out on sex even if it had only happened twice over the course of their marriage.

Besides waiting on Dutch and hauling him around, which required the combined strength of Angie and me, the days were an endless cycle of cooking, laundry and errands. Angie and I would bicker over who got to run around the corner to the drugstore. In fact, we were all so exhausted and frustrated that we started to fight about almost everything. It was my job to fold the laundry and somehow I misplaced one of Angie's favorite comfort socks that she wore around the house. I mean, the thing looked like somebody's dead cat, but the loss actually brought her to tears. I can't claim mental health either because when Angie burned the chicken, I went wacko. "I've been looking forward to a chicken wing all day long!" I ranted at her. I'd been imagining how the skin would be crisp and salty and the meat would melt in my mouth. We were all putting on weight and as for me, I was desperate to get laid.

The next time Jake showed up to visit Dutch, I found myself hanging around to stare at that muscular body, which was often wearing only jogging shorts and a T-shirt, even in the cooler weather. After all, there was a precedent. Back in our midteens, we had taken a wild trip into Manhattan to get tattoos. We drank some, and on the way home we took a walk on the beach and one thing led to another. It was Jake's first time, and he wasn't happy with his performance. I needed him as my buddy, not a lover boy, so although it took a couple of weeks for us to get past the awkwardness, pretty soon it was as if nothing had ever happened. We never talked about it.

"What's with you?" my father wanted to know. I stood in the doorway watching Jake massage Dutch's shoulders, which got sore from doing so much of the work for his helpless legs.

"I thought maybe I'd get a few pointers from the expert," I said. Usually I was out of there the second Jake showed up, especially on my night off, which it was. We

104

were always so eager to get a break from Dutch's evil moods.

"You can leave any second," Dutch said, meaning: *Get lost, this is man time.*

"Okay, I'm history," I said. "Jake, you want to stop by the porch on the way out?"

"I don't like interrupting when you practice," he said. I could see the tendons ripple in his forearms as he dug into my father's flesh. If Jake wasn't my co–best friend, I was thinking, I would have been more aware of how great-looking he was, with those sky blue eyes against his tanned face. He'd always had a great smile, a little shy but with more than a touch of mischief thrown in. One of his front teeth had a little chip in it which suddenly seemed very sexy. My plan was seeming more reasonable with every second.

"Come see me," I said, and whirled out of there. I went out to the screened-in back porch to play Amadoofus, the old battered upright that had now been shoved out there to make room for Dutch's hospital bed. Instead of Beethoven, I found myself punching out some jazz tunes. I wished I could pop a pill that would counteract the insanity going on in my body. It wasn't only between my legs. Every part of me felt like an erogenous zone, even stuff that was supposed to be dead, like my toenails. I think my split ends were tingling. I think I was running a fever, I was that hot. What a pathetic situation. Here it was my night off, my big chance to get some relief, and time was running out. I felt like going in there and hauling Jake away by the scruff of his neck.

After what seemed like a year and a half, Jake came out on the porch, leaned over my shoulder, and played a mangled chord. I could smell his aftershave. "What's up, Stallone?" he asked. "You were jumping out of your skin in there."

I stood up like I was jerked to my feet by a string. "Lookit, Jake," I said, "I've got to get laid and it's got to be tonight. Will you do it?"

His mouth dropped open. I could see that chipped tooth.

"I guess that wasn't exactly subtle," I said.

"Not hardly, no." Jake was looking at me like I'd just asked him to perform a magic healing on Dutch, maybe with newt's teeth and pigeon guts.

"I'm going wacko," I explained. I took his hands, which felt so cool in mine. "I can't even distract myself with TV anymore. We were watching water beetles do it

106

on the Nature Channel and I thought I was going to pass out. Even the supermarket's a problem with all those bananas and zucchinis. You're my best friend, Jake. You're supposed to be there when I need you. Will you help me out here, please?"

His face was doing all kinds of unfamiliar things. He'd gone from shock to anger to something I couldn't even figure out.

"What? What?" I asked.

He shook his head. "I don't know, Bess. I'd like to accommodate you, but . . ."

"Would it be so terrible? It's just sex. Can't friends have plain sex without it being a huge deal?" It was tempting to mention that other time, but I restrained myself. Besides, he looked like he might be weakening. "Maybe if we just went over to your place and had a drink we could talk about it?"

He was quiet for a minute. "Okay," he said. "But I'm not promising anything."

In the front seat of Jake's truck, I could tell by the bulge in his running shorts that the idea was beginning to appeal. I watched his hands on the steering wheel, how strong they were, useful hands that did good things for my father, for kids on the high school team, and maybe for me.

The trouble was, they kept turning into David Montagnier's hands. I shoved the image out of my mind and crossed my legs.

"You still volunteering at the nature preserve?" I asked by way of relaxing us both.

He nodded. "Four times a week now. I'm thinking of changing my degree so I can work there permanently."

"What kind of degree?" But don't think I'm getting sidetracked here, buddy, I was thinking.

"Forest management."

I smiled. "Well, that seems appropriate."

He glanced at me. "You are in a very bad way, Stallone."

"Tell me about it."

When we got inside his apartment, which was above his cousin's garage, I put my arms around him. "Do you think the drink is really necessary?" I asked. No way he needed it. He leaned down and kissed me. Now, that was extremely strange, especially since it was a very fine kiss. Sex would be okay, but not kissing. That was just too peculiar between friends. He wanted more of that, but I turned my face aside and gave him a gentle push toward the bedroom, unbuttoning and unzipping as we went. When we lay down naked on

108

the bed, he looked me over from head to foot. "Oh, Bess . . ." he said. It sounded like he was in pain.

"That bad?" I said.

"You're beautiful." He ran his hands along my body.

"I can't hold out for a lot of preliminaries here, Jake. You've got to come inside, right now."

He did, but that was only the first round. He was generous, a lot more expert than I would have thought and of course, he had that amazing body. The first few times, it was like fixing something that was broken. Jake basically repaired my transmission so the car could run again. After that, though, I started thinking about David and it got spooky emotionally. I had the eeriest feeling that David was hanging around beside the bed, watching and not approving, as if he had any right. I fought him by exhausting myself with Jake. Finally, I lay back beside him. "I have to say in all fairness that I wasn't the only horny person in this room," I told him.

"Remember the night we got our tattoos?" he asked. I knew exactly why his mind went there.

"Sure. You still got yours?"

"Yeah."

I shoved him a little so I could see the back of his shoulder where it said "Rocky B" inside a small heart. "I've always wondered, how come there's a heart? You love Rocky Beach so much?"

"Well, maybe not now but that's the trouble with tattoos. Let's see yours."

I lifted my foot in the air so he could see the Chevy logo on my ankle. "I'd still commit a major crime to own a 'fifty-seven Belair convertible," I said.

"It looks good. You look good, Bess."

I didn't say anything.

"So is this going to be a regular thing?"

"Nah, I'll be okay now," I said. "You really did a number on me. Thanks."

He was quiet for a while. I thought maybe he'd fallen asleep.

"Is there something I can do?" I asked finally. "By way of repayment?"

"If we're counting up favors here, you might as well just forget about it," he said. "I'll always owe you big-time."

"Oh, come on, what have I ever done except annoy the hell out of you?"

His voice dropped so I had to lean closer to hear him. "You stayed with me every day at the hospital when my mother was sick. You helped me pick out her stone. You arranged for the wake and the funeral.

You met me at the beach more than once in the middle of the night when I couldn't sleep on account of losing her . . ."

I put my finger on his mouth. "That was different."

"My mother died when you were getting ready for your jury at Juilliard. Don't tell me it wasn't a big deal, Bess."

We lay there in silence for a while.

"So how are we going to deal with this?" he asked finally.

"It'll be fine. Remember that *Seinfeld* episode where Jerry and Elaine did it as friends? And what about *The Big Chill* when the guy fucked his wife's best friend to give her a baby, and with his wife's blessing?"

"Hm."

"You don't sound convinced," I said, and flipped over so I could see his face better. He had that funny unreadable look again. "I hate it when I can't tell what you're thinking," I said.

He grabbed a lock of my hair and gave it a tug. "Don't sweat it, Stallone. You're absolutely right. It'll be fine. Put some clothes on and I'll drive you home."

And he was right. Other than sharing a little smirk the next time he stopped over, it was as if that night never happened.

Things settled back to the dreary routine. Wait on Dutch, listen to Dutch yell, argue with your sister and your mother, dream about a man who's on the other side of the world, try not to think about what might have been. My one great comfort was Amadoofus. Every day I found at least twenty minutes to sit down and play. It was like a visit with an old buddy and it sustained me and kept me at least partly sane. Of course, those sessions also reminded me of what I was missing. Sometimes Angie would grab a moment to stand and listen. In fact that's what she was doing the morning that all hell broke loose.

"It sounds like a heart breaking." Angie was leaning against the door as Amadoofus and I wandered through some Grieg. "I don't know if it's yours or mine," she said. I stopped playing and got up. We just held on to each other for a while. "We're trapped, Bess," she said.

"It's only temporary." But I didn't believe a word of it. Angie smelled like damp leaves. They were starting to fall off the trees, and she'd been out raking our yard, which was roughly the size of your average hanky.

"Even if Dad ever gets better, it'll be too

112

late for us," she said. "There'd never be enough money for me to go to school even if they still honored the scholarship, which they won't. And David Montagnier will find somebody else."

"I'm sure he has already."

"I was scared to ask if you've heard from him."

"Last I knew, he was in Europe."

Dutch shouted for his pain medication.

"You stay here with Amadoofus," Angie said. No eighteen-year-old should wear such a dried-up old lady's face. Dutch yelled again, something about that goddamn piano, and I grabbed Angie's arm.

"Flip you for it," I said, calling tails a fraction after I saw my quarter show heads. "I lose. Go make yourself a cup of tea and I'll deal with the emperor." But then I heard the front door slam. "There's Jake. Get him to take you for a walk on the beach. I mean it. You're out of here."

Dutch had hoisted himself off the couch and into his wheelchair. He was sweating and the veins in his neck were bulging red. "I'm sick and tired of you ignoring me so you can pound on the piano with that moody shit."

"If I don't, I'll pound on you instead," I

said, reaching for a comb to fix his matted hair.

He batted it out of my hand. It went sliding across the floor. "I thought I heard Jake. Where is he?"

"With Angie," I answered as he pushed past me in his chair. "And you're going where?"

"For a fucking stroll in the park." He balled up his fists and slammed them hard against the door frame. "God*damn* it all, Bess." Looking back, I should have realized he was at the end of his rope. There was blood smeared where he'd hit the wood.

"Let me through. I'll be right back with your pills," I said.

We kept them up out of reach on a shelf in the kitchen. Dutch's mood swings had been so crazed we figured we'd better play it safe. I gave him the medication with some tomato juice. He didn't want to get back on the couch, so I left him sitting in front of *Guiding Light*, the only soap opera that was on in the mornings. When I left the room he was growling at the screen. "Come on, Lil, show some spine for once and tell him to screw off."

I closed the porch door behind me and sat down on Amadoofus's old cracked bench. In my mind, David was looking at me across the glossy surface of his piano, hearing every note I played so that his entrance was seamless, so that we were speaking in one voice through the music. My left breast ached like I'd pulled a muscle, but then I realized it was my heart that was hurting. I began playing my part of the *Scaramouche*, not galloping the way it was written, but like a blues riff, real slow and sad. I started getting into it, closing my eyes and hearing David partner the dance inside my head, remembering that during those perfect hours with him I hadn't felt alone.

I don't know how long I played, but it was one of those magical times when Amadoofus transported my fingers to a place where misery couldn't touch me. The jolt back to the real world was sudden and brutal. First came a howl like a battle cry followed by the crash of splintering wood. My eyes snapped open to see my father's hatchet shattering the dried-up timber of the piano casing. I sat paralyzed as Amadoofus shuddered under the blows. With each swing of the axe, Dutch roared like an animal, the force of his powerful arms raising him up out of his wheelchair. There was rage in his voice, but oh yeah, I could hear the joy, too. He swung high above his head and brought the blade down on the upper section of the keyboard. Fragments of yellowed ivory flew in the air. One piece sliced across my cheek, leaving a burning track. The sounding board was exposed like a rib cage in open-heart surgery and when my father struck again, the strings begged for mercy with a discordant twang.

I leapt to my feet and lunged at my father. I jumped on his shoulders and reached for the hatchet.

"Get off! Crazy bitch!"

I was pounding him and trying to grab the axe. He just kept swinging.

"You're finished with it now, girl!" I couldn't believe how much strength he had, stuck in the chair like that. He flicked me off him like I was a bug.

I landed on the floor. "You can never take it away," I said even though he wasn't listening. "It's in my blood." I held up my wrist and pointed to it. "It's in there. You want to get it out, you'll have to kill me."

At that point, I couldn't have cared less if he split my head down the middle as long as he spared Amadoofus. But he raised the axe again and dealt the piano a deathblow. The keyboard came crashing down onto the pile of splinters. I heard myself screaming. It took me a while to stop. My father tossed the hatchet aside and said, "Now maybe we'll get some peace around here." Then he wheeled out. A few seconds later, I heard his bedroom door slam.

Jake and Angie came home to find me lying on the floor with my head on the piano's shattered body.

"What the fuck?" Jake said.

"Dad." Angie knew.

Jake reached out to pick me up but I slapped his hand away and spread myself across the remains of Amadoofus. Pitiful sounds kept rising from the twisted strings, as if he wasn't quite dead yet.

Jake knelt down on the floor. "Come on, Bess. Your face is bleeding."

"Please go away."

After a while, they left. Pretty soon there were shouts from the other end of the house. I'd never heard Jake raise his voice our whole lives. Some commotion, but I couldn't have cared less. I sat up and started picking through the pieces, trying to fit them together. All the king's horses and all the king's fucking men.

They couldn't get me off the back porch. Mumma came home from work and left a plate on the floor beside me like I was the family dog but I couldn't imagine eating. Beethoven was inside my head, the *Adagio* movement from the Seventh Symphony. Jake's lips were moving at me, but nothing was getting through except that majestic dying heartbeat.

I slept beside Amadoofus's corpse. The next morning, my mother came out with a warm washcloth and washed the blood and grime off my face. That felt good. She didn't say a word, just left coffee and toast. I was almost hungry until I thought about Dutch and then the hate twisted my stomach into sickness again.

Angie waited until Mumma left. They must have had their hands full with my father but I couldn't go near him to help. I was imagining a thousand different ways to kill him, mainly using parts of Amadoofus's mangled body. I could strangle him with the strings or choke him with the keys or batter him to death with the sounding board. I knew it was risky to go near Dutch when I was in this state. If I went to jail for murder, what would happen to Angie?

My sister crept over and sat down on the cement floor. She didn't say anything at first, just took my hand and stroked it.

"I love you, Bessie," she said finally.

I didn't answer, but salt stung in the wound on my cheek.

"She didn't stay in their bedroom last night," Angie went on.

I didn't get what she meant at first.

"She slept on the couch," she said.

Then I looked at her.

"I heard her tell him that if he wasn't crippled she'd leave him."

I opened my mouth to talk but all that came out was a croak.

"What? What, Bess?" Angie said, holding my hand to her cheek.

"Just . . . one . . . big . . . happy . . . family."

CHAPTER SIX

I asked Jake to cart Amadoofus away.

"You sure you're ready for that?" he asked me.

"Can you do it soon?"

When he left to get his truck, I picked a souvenir from the rubble and put it in a shoebox — the key for middle C, which had turned even yellower over the years.

Jake showed up an hour later and took Amadoofus away. I didn't ask where they went.

After that, the house seemed to ooze an ugly hopeless smell. The only person holding her head up was Mumma, who was exhausted and pissed off all right, but that wasn't the whole picture. All of a sudden, she'd started bothering with her appearance. Those faded housedresses wound up in the rag pile and she trotted out attractive clothes she used to save for weddings and wakes. Every morning before going off to work she'd read us a list of things to do. It was pretty unnerving, this lifetime nonperson suddenly becoming the queen of efficiency. Already, after only a few weeks on the job, she'd gotten a small promotion, and I could understand why.

Mumma had moved back into the bedroom with Dutch, but things had changed between them. I heard him using words like "please" and "thank you" in his conversations with her, and once when he didn't know I was looking, he reached out and took her hand. But Mumma had put up a wall and seemed to be studying him over it as if he were some kind of species in the zoo. I'd catch her with this look on her face that read How did I ever wind up with him? There was a sharper edge to her, as if the blurred outline was coming into focus. It didn't occur to me that maybe I'd never really bothered to take a close look.

One evening about two weeks after my father killed Amadoofus, Angie and I were sitting in the kitchen playing gin. It was getting dark earlier, and as soon as dinner was over I just marked time until I could go to sleep. That night, Dutch had been cleaned up and was in bed watching *90210*. Angie and I flipped our cards over without talking. There wasn't really anything to say anymore. But then Mumma came and stood in the doorway. She had a strange look on her face. I couldn't tell if somebody had died or just won the lottery.

"Bess, you'd better come," she said.

"What is it?" Angie had just picked up the ace I was looking for and I was in no mood for bad news.

"Someone's here to see you."

Angie and I got up and followed her. I don't know what I expected. Those last weeks had taught me that thinking too much was a dangerous proposition. I'd learned to shut down my brain, move my body around like a machine, and do what was required. I was your basic robot-woman, and as far as I knew robots didn't have a hell of a lot of imagination. In my stupefied state, I was not exactly prepared to see right there before my eyes, standing just inside the front door, Monsieur David Montagnier. He was wearing a tux, with his white bow tie hanging loose, and he was emitting about eight hundred watts in the hallway. I thought I would pass out from love.

"Fuck me," I whispered. This time I couldn't help it.

"Bess," my mother said with that new no-nonsense tone.

"Sorry." It took me a few seconds to remember that once upon a time I had had a life and that there were things you were supposed to do when a person came to call. I went up to David and stuck out my

122

hand. He took it, but drew me closer and kissed me on both cheeks. Somehow I found the wits to make the introductions. Angie looked surprised all right, and a little intimidated, but even with all that she was checking him out. It still makes me smile to think of it. If it had been Ludwig van Beethoven himself in that doorway, Angie would have had that look: *Yes, all right, I'm impressed, but exactly what do you want with my sister?*

David turned to Mumma. "I'm sorry to show up unannounced. There seems to be something wrong with your telephone and I've just gotten off a plane."

"In that?" I asked, indicating the tux. I was hoping he hadn't noticed how evil the house smelled.

"I was performing in London and barely caught my plane. Mrs. Stallone," he said to Mumma. "I'm sorry about your husband. How is he?"

"It's a slow recovery, but thank you for asking," Mumma said. "Wouldn't you like something to eat after such a long flight?" Mumma was poised and gracious. I wasn't used to feeling proud of her.

"Actually, I was wondering if I could speak with Mr. Stallone for a few moments," David said. "I realize it's a lot to ask but I'm not a total stranger, really." He smiled at me. I guess I'd thought that I'd never see that phenomenon beamed in my direction again. I wondered why the entire house didn't fall down from how my heart was careening around like a pachiderm on crack.

"I have to warn you, he hasn't been much for company," Mumma said. If that wasn't the understatement of the millennium. Pauline was allowed to watch the soaps with him so they could gossip about his favorite characters. Except for her and Jake, Dutch would barely speak to anyone. Even Corny from the firehouse gave up when my father told him if he showed up with his bleeding-heart face one more time he'd buy an attack dog.

"Let me just go and check," Mumma said, and went off to drop the news on Dutch. That left the three of us standing there.

"You're thin," David said to me, and turned to Angie. "Is she eating enough?"

"There's a new tailor who's supposed to be reasonable," Angie said.

David looked confused.

"It upsets my sister to see my clothes hanging loose," I explained. "I promised to get them taken in. So exactly what are you doing here?"

David smiled. I knew he liked it that I wasn't big on slinging the bullshit.

"I've been on the phone from Europe with Harold Stein," David said. "He apprised me of your situation."

"He's been checking in," I said guiltily. It had hurt to hear his voice and I think I was sometimes a little short over the phone.

But before I could get any more information out of David, Mumma came back.

"He'll see you," she told David. "He's a little . . . cranky," she said.

"Yuh," I said. "Think Jabba the Hutt."

David disappeared with Mumma. Angie and I stared at one another. I don't know if my eyes were as big as hers, which were approximately the size of Brazil.

"What the fuck is he doing here?" I said.

"That's the handsomest man I've ever seen in my life," Angie said.

Mumma joined us and we all went into the kitchen to wait it out.

"What did Dad say?" I asked Mumma.

"I don't know. They were talking Dutch."

"Wait," I said. "*To* Dutch?"

"No," she said. "Mr. Montagnier, your friend . . ."

She was having trouble with what to call him. I knew how she felt. There was the

French pronunciation, plus that formality of his.

"He thanked your father for seeing him," Mumma went on. "Then he asked him something in a foreign language. It has to be Dutch because your father answered him."

"Dutch speaks Dutch?" This was news.

"Well, you know he was born in Holland. Your grandmother was from there."

"The perfect mother," Angie said. She meant that Dutch never tired of telling us how wonderful his mother was and how beautiful life was back in the old country where people had values. His mother died when he was eight and he came to America with his Italian father he didn't like much.

"I thought he'd forgotten it after all these years," Mumma said. "He's a nice man, your David. I've never seen anyone famous up close. It's strange how he looks almost like his pictures but not really."

"Well, he's not my David," I said.

"I wouldn't be too sure," Angie said. It's always so naked when she says something direct.

"What are they talking about in there?" I said. I shuffled and reshuffled the cards like I was trying out for a job in Vegas.

"Mumma, you'd better learn how to play

gin," Angie said. I was too freaked out to make the leap.

After what seemed like twelve hours — Angie said it was twenty minutes — David showed up in the kitchen doorway. Maybe it was his tux, but the thought went through my head that he was going to bow from the waist and say, "Good evening, I'm David. I'll be your waiter for the evening." I started to giggle. Then I choked. Then Mumma started pounding my back and I had to get a paper towel to wipe my eyes. It was quite the display. After I got myself under control, David sat down at the table. His legs were so long, they got all tangled up with ours. With all the chair scraping, the three of us girls automatically glanced toward Dutch's bedroom. That sound ordinarily guaranteed a temper tantrum. But there was nothing coming from the other end of the house except silence. I wondered if David had killed him as a special present to me, and that's when I knew I was this close to losing it completely.

"What's the story?" I asked David.

"I just made a proposition to your father. Could I possibly have a glass of water?"

Mumma and Angie shot out of their seats while I sat there gawking at him. I was playing a Brahms *Intermezzo* on the kitchen table, which is something I do when I'm truly nervous. I can do it while barely moving my fingers so nobody notices. David took a long drink, leaned on his elbows to look at Mumma. She had that dazed look that I suppose I got when his face was that close.

"You may be aware that I had a long, successful partnership with Terese Dumont," he told her, and waited for Mumma to acknowledge this with a nod. "After she retired, I decided to pursue a solo career," he went on. "I believe I gave it a fair try." True, he'd played with most of the premier orchestras and given solo concerts all over the world. I'd kept clippings of things he'd done since we met.

"I didn't enjoy it," David said. "I was losing my interest in performing and even wondered if I was through with music as a career." A little moan escaped from my mouth as I imagined the pain. This was something I could identify with. "But then I heard about this pianist named Bess Stallone."

"Where did you . . . ?" I started. But David raised two fingers without taking his eyes off Mumma.

"For several weeks, whenever I was in town I eavesdropped on her practice sessions," he went on. "Mrs. Stallone, there are many pianists with technical mastery of the instrument, but Bess is special. She has tremendous emotional power. I know of no one like her."

He got up to pour himself more water. I found out later how airplanes will do that to you, suck every last drop of moisture out of your body until you feel like you've been crawling across Death Valley. At the moment, I was thinking how it hadn't taken him long to feel at home.

"What I've realized over the past few weeks is that I miss the musical partnership. It's what gratifies me as a pianist. If I'm to continue with music, I need Bess."

I saw Mumma shake her head as if she was trying to make his words settle into her brain. I was having the same problem. "But," I said. There were maybe a hundred and twenty *buts* that occurred to me off the top of my head and that was without even trying.

"Please, Bess," David said, "if you'll just let me finish."

"Finish," Angie echoed at me. I'm famous for figuring out the end of a movie by halftime, but I was having serious trouble getting to the resolution here. I clamped my mouth shut, which as we all knew was entirely against my nature.

David leaned against the kitchen counter. "I've been one of the lucky ones," he said. "Success has provided me with a great deal of money, far more than I need. I've been fortunate with investments here and in Europe. What I proposed to Mr. Stallone is a barter arrangement. I'll supply the funds to pay for whatever home care is needed until he recovers. I'll supplement Angelina's scholarship, and I'll pay Bess's living expenses so that she can devote herself to music full-time. In return, I'll have my new partner."

Anybody looking in the window would have thought the three Stallone women had just seen the Virgin Mary hop out of the freezer with a Popsicle in her hand. It was quiet for a long time. Angie was the first to get her brains back.

"And Dutch . . . my father . . . actually agreed?" She must have figured he'd want us around forever, if only for torture purposes.

"After some thought," David said. "He doesn't seem particularly happy with the current situation."

We were all silent. Then Angie spoke up again. At least somebody had her brains switched on. "You're talking about a loan," she said to David.

"No," David said. "You've got what I need and I'm more than willing to pay you for the sacrifice."

"Wait," I said. I was beginning to feel like your basic brisket, shrink-wrapped, price-tagged, and oven-ready. "There's something wrong with this."

"I don't want to leave my job," Mumma blurted.

David, who must have figured we'd all fall down and kiss his beautiful feet, was looking a little disappointed.

"What did our father say?" Angie asked.

"It took some time for him to understand that I'm getting the better deal here. He's a very proud man."

But not of me, obviously, I was thinking. Why would anybody want to pay all that money for old pain-in-the-ass Bess?

"You wouldn't have to quit your job, Mrs. Stallone," David explained. "You can hire whomever you want to care for your husband."

"He won't want anyone else," she said with a sad smile.

"That doesn't mean you have to listen to him, Mumma," Angie told her. Mumma blinked. This type of notion was still real new.

"Beg your pardon," I said, "but unless I'm mistaken, this proposal has something to do with me."

"It has everything to do with you," David admitted.

"Well, thank you. I mean, what if I don't want to be your partner? What if I'd rather stay right here in the bosom of my family?"

David ran his hand across his eyes. Jet lag was kicking in, along with the realization that things weren't going exactly the way he'd figured.

"What if it doesn't work out between us?" I asked David. "We haven't done a single public performance. I've been known to pass out onstage."

"I'm not concerned about that," David said.

"Oh, you're not."

"No."

I didn't know whether to laugh or call the loon patrol.

"It should be equal footing. I mean, isn't that crucial for a duo-piano partnership?"

"You have priceless talent. All I'm offering is money," David said, spoken like one of the truly rich. "If it doesn't work out, you can always come back home."

"We sound so ungrateful," Mumma said. "It's a shock, that's all. But very generous."

132

"I need to think about it," I said.

"Take all the time you want," David said. "Should I phone you in a week or two?"

"Stick around for ten minutes. I don't want this thing hanging." I turned to Mumma and Angie. "What's wrong with this? Help me out here."

"What if Dad never recovers?" Angie protested.

"Don't say that," Mumma said.

"It could happen," I said.

"I'll put some money in a fund that will provide passive income," David said.

"You're really that rich?" Angie asked.

"Yes," David said. "And perhaps Bess will want to contribute once her career takes off."

"I appreciate your confidence, David, I really do," I said. "But this is nuts. You have to face the fact that so many things could screw it up. What if a piano lid falls on my hand? Or on *your* hand? What if you can't stand the sight of me a month from now? I'm a Lawn G'iland babe who's hardly ever been out of New York State with a limited vocabulary and a tattoo who's bound to get on your nerves."

David was smiling. "You have a tattoo?"

"We have nothing in common," I said.

The smile evaporated as his eyes flashed

133

at me. "How can you possibly say that?"

He had me there. We weren't talking about setting up housekeeping. This was about music, our music. I remembered the sounds we had made together in his sunny room. That was real. That was a serious pass at perfection.

I looked at Mumma and Angie. "This has to do with you, too."

"It's your decision, Bess."

It wasn't going to hurt them if I did this. In fact, it would free them. I was scared. It would mean braving the stage again. I studied David as he sat looking down at his hands, waiting. His fingers were trembling. I was moved — was that for me? The thing was, this place that was supposed to be home wasn't home, and the man now bent with exhaustion was.

"Okay," I said.

I could see he was afraid to hope. "Okay, *oui?*" he asked. Sometimes that happened with David when he was really tired or upset. The French slipped out.

"Yes. I'll do it." He took my hand and kissed my fingers. I could see that there were tears in his eyes.

When I walked David out, the Schultz brood was waiting on the porch attached to ours, all lined up by height like they were expecting to be photographed. Old Mr. Schultz had a paper and pencil in his hand ready for an autograph but he chickened out when he saw that I'd noticed. At least the Schultzes were respectful, which is more than I can say for the rest of the neighborhood, which was putting on quite the rowdy display. Everybody was out on their lawns and there were shouts from one end of the block to the other. "Yo! Bess! 'Zat your new boyfriend? Hey, it *is* David! Holy shee-*it!* Yo, *Da-VEED!*" I couldn't really blame them. A big white stretch limo had probably never even driven past, much less stopped on Walnut Avenue. Anyhow, David and I weren't saying much to each other. We were both pretty drained.

"I'll phone you tomorrow," he said.

"Fine."

"Thank you, Bess."

"It's for me to do the thanking," I said.

He kissed me on both cheeks. A chorus of hoots echoed up and down the street.

After he'd driven away, Angie and Mumma met me at the door.

"Well, my goodness," Mumma said, and gave me a hug.

"I was looking for the horses," Angie

murmured, watching the taillights of the limo disappear.

"Oh, they're there," I said. "Under the hood with the pumpkins and the glass slipper."

CHAPTER SEVEN

I was back in the light. Sunshine all over the place. Even the crummy courtyard behind my apartment building with all the garbage cans where the rats disco all night looked gorgeous to me. Why shouldn't they party? After all, life was beautiful.

The first thing I did when I got back to Manhattan was check out the latest research on David Montagnier. Information was power, I figured, so I dropped by the World Web Coffee House and logged on to my favorite sources for the latest news items. There were the usual gushy letters — *Oh, David, you and me were meant to make beautiful music together! Marylou from Des Moines.* (Granted, it was sickening, but I had some nerve dissing Marylou since I was in an identical pathetic state). There was an interview excerpted from a London magazine that made reference to how temperamental David was. Of course, I'd read that he was "moody" and "uncompromising," but none of that kind of crap impressed me. As far as I was concerned, those remarks translated into somebody who cared about his art, which is a difficult concept for some people to grasp. Anyway, the last item was a review of a recent performance from Germany's top music critic:

. . . As always, Montagnier's playing soars. Technically, he's never been better; that sometimes erratic left hand is now as dependable as the right. But at least for this listener something crucial is missing, which has been the case since Terese Dumont's retirement. Could it be heart?

Anything that mentioned Terese Dumont felt like a needle in my brain. I'd already scoured the Web for any signs of the woman. As far as anybody knew, she'd vanished from existence the minute she split from David, as if her partnership with him was what made her real. It was a scary thought.

My favorite Web site — www.lovedavidmont.com — had to have been set up by a bunch of Montagnier groupies who, bless their horny little hearts, also included a bare-chested photo of David playing volleyball on a Caribbean beach. This was more like it. You can be sure I printed that sucker out. I could've drawn you a topographical map of David's pecs by the time I'd pretty much destroyed the photo from handling it, not to mention the drool.

Sometimes doing research on the Internet is like taking a multiple choice exam. I found out that David Montagnier was raised in France, that his mother, Aimee, was very beautiful and a gifted (a) singer: soprano; (b) singer: alto; or (c) violinist. You choose. That his father was (a) a brilliant Italian physicist; (b) an impoverished member of the Greek royal family; (c) a scumbag con artist with a pretty face. Everybody seemed to agree that the father, whoever he was, disappeared before David was born. David and his mother were taken in by the famous Beauchapel salon in Paris. Maurice Beauchapel was somebody I studied at Juilliard, not only because he was a brilliant pianist but because he mentored so many successful musicians. In my unbiased opinion, David outshone them all. Beauchapel had died about ten years ago at the ripe old age of ninety, but nobody agreed on what happened to Aimee. It seemed clear that she'd wound up in some kind of institution, but depending on the source she either died in a TB sanitarium in Switzerland or wasted away in some fancy nuthouse after a nervous breakdown. The whole thing was a spooky replay of the Terese mystery.

Anyway, David didn't give me much time to hang around snooping. The day after I got back to New York, he called to set up a practice session, this time at a studio in Carnegie Hall. Those words were enough to set fireworks off in front of my eyeballs. I had to grab the coatrack on my apartment wall to keep from toppling over. Oh, yeah, this is gonna fly, I told myself. I'll be passing out before I get out the front door. Fortunately, he wanted to meet that actual day, so I didn't have a lot of time to work myself into hysterics. What I did instead was wash my hair three times, just to make sure I got the last sick smell of Walnut Avenue out, shave my legs with extra attention — what did I think, that David Montagnier planned to crawl under the piano and grab my thighs? — and soak my fingers in warm water so they'd limber up. It only takes a couple of days without playing for me to get stiff, and it'd been three weeks since Amadoofus died. It was early November, and why the humidity was close to a hundred percent escaped me unless it was global warming, which is bad news for those of us with a lot of hair. I sat on the bus and imagined I could feel each strand swell as it drank up moisture. This took my mind off where I was going, since every time I imagined the pile of bricks at Fifty-seventh Street and Seventh Avenue, I'd start to get woozy.

I'd been to concerts at Carnegie Hall probably a hundred times, mostly stubbing in after intermission — which gets to be an art in itself. You learn to position yourself outside the doors so you get first stab at sympathetic-looking people who leave after the first half. After a year at this, one elderly couple with Piano Series Number Two would look for me. They just got too tired to make it through a whole performance. On account of them, I heard Kissin play the Tchaikovsky Piano Concerto in B-flat minor. First of all, there's this attitude that Van Cliburn owns that particular extravaganza and anybody else who takes it on is trespassing, and besides, whoever thought it was possible to make that worn-out old thing sound like it was broadcast live from heaven? Well, Kissin nailed it. I was there to hear it and bravo my brains out like the rest of us who will never forget that night.

I've got to admit, it was thrilling to walk in the back entrance on Fifty-sixth Street, give my name to the security guard, and take the elevator to the ninth floor like David had told me. I walked down the hall, checking out the numbers on the studio doors. An old woman in a tutu was doing stretches by the water fountain, and music floated past my ears — Chopin's Scherzo Number Three — nice but a little too heavy-handed, the Ravel Concerto in G, and from down the corridor a more contemporary violin piece, maybe by Webern. No sound-proofing, obviously, but that didn't bother me. I stood there grinning like the village idiot. What a miserable time these past weeks had been — not just the exhaustion, the boredom, the depressing smells of illness and the hopelessness in that house. It was the lack of music. I stood there letting the sounds wash over me and thought, Just let me park here with a bedroll and a change of underwear. I'm never going back to the silence.

I stood outside Room 954 listening to David running through his finger exercises. I let myself in and David stopped playing immediately, came over, and did the usual double-kiss routine. I saw him glance at my hair.

"I'm going to shave it off," I said.

"You will not." He reached out for a touch, but decided against it.

"It's okay," I said. "People always want to. Strangers, even."

But having come that close to something like an intimate gesture, he was suddenly all business. He was even dressed more formally, in slacks and a sports jacket. Just looking at him, I could have laid down on the floor and cried for love, but instead I went and sat at the other piano. There wasn't much else in the room, just one battered sofa and a circular iron stairway leading to a loft. I still don't know what was up there.

The First Rachmaninoff Suite was unfamiliar to me at that point. David explained that it's based on Russian poetry, with each movement another poem. He set my part on the piano and we went right to work. The thing about David was, he could actually show me what he wanted. Professor Stein was the best teacher I'd ever had, but he couldn't demonstrate the really difficult stuff. He just didn't have the technique. With David, a lot of time was saved by those keyboard demos. And after a while, I could do the same for him.

We worked for a couple of hours, and

then David dropped it on me: "Let's take a break," he said. "I want to show you where we're giving our first concert."

"Excuse me?" I said. "Ex-CUSE me?"

He came over and held out his hand. I took it but my knees were already quivering.

"Don't you want to know when?" he asked.

"No!" I shouted. "Tell me tomorrow, next week. Don't tell me now!"

David put a sympathetic arm around my shoulder. I wanted to curl up into his chest and whimper like a dying dog.

"We're going to work there this afternoon and as often as possible," he said. "I want you to get comfortable."

That's like inviting a guy on death row to practice sitting in the electric chair. *You'll get used to it, son. Nothing to it, and then they pull the switch.* But I did the old nod-and-smile as Roman candles started popping off behind my eyes. In the elevator, I had hold of David's arm like it was the only thing between me and certain death.

I'd been to a number of performances at Weill Recital Hall. It's an intimate space, and ornate like a pretty piece of jewelry. The acoustics are really good. I'd listened to a lot of famous people there, so it was a big deal to walk out on that stage.

We stood looking out at the seats while my breakfast said hello from the back of my throat. This was the first time that we would play facing each other instead of side by side. I remember thinking as I looked at David head-on, *Well, this is new, this is actually nice.*

"This place is too small for two-piano concerts," David said, "but I thought you'd feel more at home, like in a living room."

Not like any living room I ever met, I was thinking as I sat down at my piano. I stared at him through the fireworks, trying to stay focused, but then I felt myself start to slide and down I went under the keyboard. Didn't play a note. When I woke up, David had me more or less standing.

"Are you all right, Bess? Did you hurt yourself?"

One thing was lucky. When I fainted, I was usually so limp that I didn't do any real damage. Except for that first childhood episode of the broken nose and the big lump in Boston. "I'm okay," I said, but of course I felt like a horse's ass. Plus I was angry at David for dragging me into this, and at myself for being such a defective jerk and at everybody else including and maybe especially God.

"You see the problem? You get it now?" I asked him, keeping my eyes on the floor so the sunspots would go away.

"I get it." He held me against him until I could gradually raise my head.

"It's hopeless," I said when I could finally look up at him. "*I'm* hopeless."

He didn't answer, but I could feel his strength radiating into me, down my legs, up across my shoulders. "Come on, Bess," he said in that gentle but no-bullshit tone. "You've got your color back. Let's go." He started leading me back to the piano.

"You're shitting me," I said.

"We're not here to play for our own entertainment," he reminded me. "I'm only asking that you try. So no, I'm not shitting you."

I almost laughed, but it's hard to do that when your heartbeat is drowning out your own voice and you can't see anything but big red comets exploding in front of your eyes. David sat me down, pressed his hands against my shoulders, and left me to go to his seat. We played the first couple of measures of the Rachmaninoff before I crash-landed again.

This time he was on the floor with me, cashmere slacks and all, holding me half in his lap. I peered through the sparkles at my legs stretched out like salamis and my toes pointed in opposite directions. I have a confession here, which since I'm trying to be totally honest I might as well spit out. I felt like hell, no question, but it was so amazing to be in David Montagnier's arms even if we *were* halfway under a Steinway Model B. So I just lay there for a minute or two, playing possum and wondering what his cock looked like. I thought I could feel a vague outline under my fourth lumbar vertebrae, and the way things looked, this was about as close as I was ever gonna get to the aforementioned member. I moaned a little just for effect, but at that, David eased us both up off the floor and onto our feet.

"That was better," he said. "You got through six measures. Let's try for ten this time." He left me again to go sit at his piano.

"Are you trying to kill me?" I asked him. "I could get a concussion."

"I'm worried about that," David said. "I was wondering if we should bring a mattress in here in case you fall again."

"In case!" I yelled at him. "In CASE! Of course I'm going to fall again!" I took a deep breath and went on in my best commonsensical tone. "I'm sorry, but if this is your idea of fixing my problem, we might as well bag it right now."

He gazed at me with disappointment and said, "All right, Bess, we'll stop. I don't want to torture you."

I sat there listening to the ball bounce around in my court. If I caved, what would happen to Angie and her education? What about that fabulous red-faced bull moose of a nurse we'd hired to keep Dutch in line?

"Oh, *merde*," I said. "Come on, Dave, let's try it again."

I realized that I'd actually been sitting there, on the stage, conscious, for several minutes while David and I duked it out with our eyeball-to-eyeball confrontation. That seemed like a step in the right direction. Plus, David proceeded to give me one of those true dazzlers, a smile confirming that I was without a doubt the most courageous woman in the universe.

This time, we made it through about twenty seconds' worth of Rachmaninoff, which was not too tacky considering. Then I crashed again, this time face forward, somehow landing on my hand, which cushioned the blow.

I don't know how often I passed out that first day, but enough to feel like I was on a bungee cord. I also wondered how many brain cells I was trashing with this routine. But David picked me up every time, set me back at my piano, and we'd start over or work ahead in the music. I don't think we read through a whole page, but David didn't seem the least bit discouraged. When I was finally so exhausted from fainting that I couldn't see the page anymore, he said in this upbeat voice, "All right, Bess, that was fine. We can start again tomorrow."

"Huh?" I was so spaced out at that point I could barely get my tongue around an actual word.

"We've got the hall at seven o'clock A.M." David said. "Come, I'll get my car to take you home."

I leaned against him all the way down the hall, not caring if everyone thought I was some drunk he'd found sleeping it off in a corner. He stuck his head into the limo once he'd got me installed.

"Thank you, Bess," he said, picking up both hands and kissing them. "You were awesome."

I rolled my eyes at him and was asleep by the time we got to Columbus Circle. The driver had to pry me out of there when we got uptown.

★ ★ ★

It didn't take long for word to get out that David Montagnier had something brewing in his professional life. There was a bulletin in *New York* magazine:

Rumor has it that David Montagnier, after a critically successful stint as a soloist, has zeroed in on a replacement for Terese Dumont. He's not talking, but sources say she's a well-known, brilliant musician. Speculation favors Martha Argerich, given her preference for company onstage.

Scene magazine said that David and his new partner would be giving their first concert in early February. They got that part right anyway. I'd finally let David tell me the date — February fourteenth, which I thought was appropriate. I told him if I made it through in one piece, he'd have to be my valentine for life. He'd chuckled and that had made me ridiculously happy.

David and I both knew that it was only a matter of time before my identity was exposed, and meanwhile, I was still passing out. David had taken extraordinary steps to protect our privacy. The hall was locked tight during each practice session so that the only person to see my tumbling act was the janitor, who'd been sworn to secrecy with bribes of expensive scotch. David experimented with laying a quilted pad under my seat, but decided later that I should be practicing under actual performance conditions. Since I never seemed to get hurt, he took it away again.

During the third week, I made it through four pages of music. It was a major triumph, and David laughed out loud. I'd never got a real booming laugh out of him before and the prospect of hearing it again gave me even more incentive to stay upright. The night we finished the first section of the Rachmaninoff, he broke open a bottle of champagne he'd been toting around just in case and we drank it warm, sitting on the floor with our legs dangling over the edge of the stage.

Because Weill was in use most of the time, we'd been practicing at all kinds of weird hours. The night of the champagne, we were out there onstage from two to four A.M., which I think was totally against union regulations but I didn't ask any questions. In fact, I figured I was doing better because I was just too damn tired to live through the brutal routine of passing out every five minutes. Anyhow, we picked ourselves up to leave — both pretty wobbly after consuming an entire bottle of champagne with empty stomachs and no sleep — and discovered that all the doors were locked. The janitor was supposed to leave the key for one of the exits, but I guess he'd had too much fun guzzling his Glenlochness or whatever the hell it was. David finished messing with the door and turned to me with this gorgeous French shrug that said *No can do.*

"Fuck me," I replied with my customary gift for choosing the perfect phrase for any given situation. "We're stuck in here, aren't we?"

"Fuck you," David said in a friendly kind of way. It sounded so bizarre with his French accent that I started laughing. The champagne helped, of course, and pretty soon we were both hysterical. It had been a long couple of weeks.

I figured, Oh, what the hell, we might as well have some fun. So I went out on the stage and started clowning around. "Ladies and germs," I shouted at the imaginary audience. "I present to you all the way from the continent Mess-your David Montagnier and his fabuloso partner in crime . . ." I made a deep bow. "Who will perform for you from the classical repertory the famous Vaudevillia Sonata Opus Oh-Oh by Fred van Ludwig Jones of Kearny, New Jersey. To your instrument, Mister Montagnier, or we'll have to refund all these tickets and I don't know about you, but I'm broke."

I sat down at my piano and started pounding out that old crowd-pleaser, "Heart and Soul." David got right into the spirit of the thing, improvising all kinds of riffs to accompany me, ranging in style from Baroque to Motown. We were both pretty drunk, so we were laughing our asses off like we were about the funniest pair since Abbott and Costello. We moved on to more elevated stuff like "Sergeant Pepper," "Happy Birthday to You," and finally a colossal keyboard battle between "The Star-Spangled Banner" and the *Marsellaise*. I finally got up from my bench and stalked over to beat him up.

"Shall I defend the honor of our country?" I yelled out at the darkened seats. "Applause! Louder! I can't hear you!" When I put up my fists like I was going to belt David, he swung around so he could pull me onto his lap. Then he kissed me, and kissed me again. Then I kissed him, and there was no more laughing.

"I'm sorry, Bess," he said.

We were barely steamed up but I moved off his lap to sit next to him on the bench. "Well, I'm not," I said.

"It's a very bad idea," he said.

"What else are we supposed to do until that alcoholic janitor shows up?"

He stood, took my hand, and led me across the stage and down the steps to the front-row seats. If I'd thought I was wobbly before, those kisses had turned my legs into overcooked macaroni. He plunked down and pulled me into the seat beside him. "Too much champagne," he said. "I was determined this wasn't going to happen."

"Aha," I said. "So you've been thinking about it, too?"

He wasn't that drunk, because he managed to look embarrassed. "Your hair is so erotic," he said. But his eyes were on my tits.

"Well, then, maybe I should get that brush cut I mentioned. And perhaps a breast reduction?"

He laughed, the deep rumble that seemed to take him by surprise. "Don't you dare," he said.

"Look, anything for the greater glory of

this musical partnership, but I for one really enjoy making out. You are one hot kisser, Dave. For a foreigner."

"Oh, you're a specialist in non-American kisses?"

"Not so's you'd notice," I said modestly. Of course, the crowd raised their hands in the back of my head. Just from high school, three came to mind: the Vietnamese exchange student, an Australian golf pro at the country club where I had a summer job, and the Canadian chef in the cafeteria, except maybe Canada doesn't really count as foreign.

"Seriously, Bess . . ."

I groaned. I hate any sentence that begins like that.

"We can't afford to get distracted," David said. "It's too easy to damage the professional relationship."

"Are you speaking from personal experience?" I figured I'd give it a shot.

"Let's just talk," David said. "We've got plenty of time until he gets here at seven, and I want to know about your life."

"You got a firsthand look at it," I said. "If you're not going to kiss me, the least you can do is spill your guts." I got up and dragged him to a row back under the balcony where it was darker, a better place for confidences.

"If you must know, I was raised by a wood nymph," he said. "She had perfect pitch, of course. Pitch, you know, in the wood."

I gave him a whack. "All right, I'll make it easy for you. Tell me the highlight of the year you turned ten."

He closed his eyes. I could see movement under the lids. "All right. That July I learned to play the parallel passages in the Beethoven *Pathetique*. You know, the second subject in the first movement where it switches back and forth from E-flat minor to D-flat major. That was difficult for me, even though I already had long arms and fingers. I remember being so excited that I waited outside Beauchapel's door all night for him to wake up so I could tell him."

I was thinking that when *I* was ten, I was scoping out the perfect system for playing hooky. It was foolproof, until I got caught. "How about more along the lines of nonmusical memories?" I asked.

"I don't have any others," David said.

"Come on," I said. "You must have had buddies you did stuff with. Trips with your mother."

"I suppose it's possible," David said, "but I don't remember them. I can tell you when I first performed the Brahms F-minor Sonata. And the time I finally played the first Bach Partita through by memory. I was thirteen. Christmastime."

"Jesus, David."

"You're so normal, Bess. It's one of the things I like most about you."

That was clever, a double whammy on his part. First to pronounce me normal — everybody laugh — and second, to toss me bait like that: *one* of the things he liked, knowing I was going to want the whole list. Well, I could corner him later, and meanwhile, I wasn't about to give up. I thought a minute.

"Okay, then," I said, "tell me all about Maurice Beauchapel, and spare no details." If I started out in neutral territory, maybe I could sneak up on Terese Dumont.

"He scared the shit out of me," David said. So much for neutral. David was staring at me like he'd just spit out a frog. *"Dieu!"* he whispered under his breath. He was beginning to fade, so maybe his defenses were down. I zeroed in.

"Scary how?"

David leaned his head back on the seat and closed his eyes. He looked like a little boy who was fighting sleep, eyes half-mast with the thick eyelashes weighing down the lids. "He was so tall and straight. A handsome man but cold. Correct. I was just six when he took us into his salon, my mother and me. Though she was only with us for a year. I don't like talking about it. I should have been with boys my own age. Tell me about hanging out. I don't know what it is to hang out." His voice made another decrescendo, and pretty much died out.

"Nothing to it, just like what we're doing right now. You still haven't told me why you were afraid of him."

"He didn't mean to be severe. I suppose he just didn't know how to act around children. He told me if I didn't practice my scales we'd have to leave, and my mother would become a beggar under the bridges of Paris. I remember that phrase. *Une clocharde sous les ponts de Paris.* I had nightmares about that. But I owe him everything."

"So that was it, just you and your mother and Beauchapel? No brothers or sisters?"

"Music was my family." A sound bite, I thought, produced to ward off probing questions.

"David, it's hard to cuddle up to a book of études."

"To Maurice Beauchapel's credit, he ultimately realized that I needed companionship. He sent me to boarding school when I was twelve, which I know was difficult for him. He was used to supervising all my practice sessions and it meant my studying with another teacher."

"Did you make a lot of friends?"

"I was busy with the piano, night and day."

"I can identify with that," I said, remembering Juilliard. I'd never had much use for anything else myself, a typical piano nerd who was pretty much hopeless at English and science or anything that took me away from the keyboard. David shifted toward me to press his shoulder into the seat. I learned soon enough that David could only fall asleep on his side.

I was imagining a slim solemn boy, straight-backed on the bench, his feet barely touching the pedals, a screen of shiny black hair falling forward over his face as he kept time with the metronome. A boy who was saving up safe memories, perfect moments he shared with his best and only friends — Bach, Mozart, Beethoven and all the others who spoke the language he understood best.

"Did you need the music that much?" I

couldn't help reaching out to touch him, resting my fingers lightly on his hand.

He murmured something I couldn't believe I'd heard so I asked him to repeat it.

"Music flowed in my blood, Bess," he whispered. "Like corpuscles, cells, red, white and the notes, the sounds. I could hear it at night, traveling through my veins. Even as a child, to take it away they would have had to kill me."

I sat and watched him drift into sleep. If nobody'd ever come to unlock that door, it would have been just fine with me.

CHAPTER EIGHT

"Bess, do you have a long dress?" David asked over the phone. In my half-asleep state, the sound of his voice felt like hands moving across my body.

"Yuh," I said. It was eleven A.M. but we'd only finished practicing at four.

"Excellent. I'm picking you up this evening at seven-thirty. We're doing a little concert."

I rubbed my eyes hard, thinking maybe I could poke myself awake from this dream that was turning into a nightmare.

"Bess?"

"You want to fill me in or what?"

"A friend of mine is pastor of a church in Harlem," David said. "His congregation gathers for musical performances Wednesday nights. I volunteered our services."

"I'm not ready yet," I said.

"You are."

I could imagine this conversation deteriorating into an *Am not!/Are so!* battle like I used to have with my sister. "I thought we were a democracy," I protested, and swung my legs over the side of the bed. Cold air blasted my bare feet.

"You were mistaken," David said cheerfully. "I don't want you to overpractice. Go to the pool and do laps."

"Can I use one in Cleveland?"

He laughed. "That's another thing I like about you, Bess. You make me laugh."

So that was two things in my favor. I was normal and I made him laugh. Well, five, really, because he liked my hair and my tits. I felt like I was collecting charms for a bracelet. In the limo, David told me I looked pretty steady. Was I all right?

"Yeah," I said. Considering I'd spent most of the day rocking back and forth on my seat in the bus, which I took all the way downtown and back up again. It was cheaper than a movie and more distracting. David was looking me over. He stuck a ringlet of hair behind my right ear, producing a little electric buzz here and there, mostly there. I figured I couldn't be totally stressed out if I could still get that kind of a jolt.

"I've been wondering," he said. "How did you get through your jury for entering Juilliard?"

"You mean you didn't check that out with Professor Stein? He was there."

He smiled. "Actually, I did."

"Then you know I didn't pass out during my performance," I said. "I did it later on Broadway and Sixty-fifth in front of the deli."

"Ah."

"It wasn't as bad then," I continued. "If I was going to faint, I usually did it afterward."

"That's because you weren't thinking so much about yourself when you were younger. More about the music."

"Yeah, I know. Focus on the music, baby."

Another mantra. I'd heard it at least four thousand times, and finally, finally, it was beginning to happen. David was shoving me into the music as if he had both hands on the small of my back, my own personal guide into the hearts and brains of the composers. It was like I was falling in love with them, too.

"Listen, Bess!" he'd shout at me across the piano, probably when he saw me begin to get scared and woozy. "Listen to the sadness, the loss. Be inside it! Listen!" And he'd pick out a phrase, just two or three chords, even, and make me play them over and over until I truly connected with the emotion in them. Compared to the genius in those passages, my dopey problems became insignificant. In a way, I guess I started realizing I just wasn't important enough to be passing out all the time.

The church was a small frame building north of 125th Street. There were already a couple dozen people, all of them African Americans and everybody dressed to the nines. The women were even wearing hats, which was touching but a little intimidating. We'd have to play well to live up to those hats.

David introduced me to the Reverend Busky Wilcox, a big bear of a guy with a soft voice and a smile to die for. Reverend Wilcox held my frozen fingers in his warm ones and nodded at the two pianos near the pulpit, a small baby grand and an upright. "I'm sorry about that old model-T piano, Miss Stallone. David gave us the nice one, and now we're after him for another."

My eyes were beginning to pepper the insides of the church with those miserable dizzy sparkles. I focused hard on the fact that I was curious how these two became friends. I knew if I asked David, he'd just hand me some bullshit about it being back about the time he learned to play the Beethoven "Spring" Sonata for piano and violin.

"How did you meet?" I asked the reverend. My voice came out sounding like slo-mo, but they didn't seem to notice. I knew I was blinking a lot to clear the spots.

"We used to party together," the reverend said. He and David traded sly little smiles.

"Church suppers?" I asked.

"Let me introduce you to our congregation," Reverend Wilcox said, and I knew that that subject was closed for the duration. He presented us to the audience as "pretty decent ivory ticklers," which got a laugh and made me feel a little more relaxed.

At this point, I thought I was going to be okay, but as soon as we settled at our pianos, me at the baby grand, I felt myself starting to go. I shot David a last HELP! look and down I went. I woke up with David and Reverend Wilcox propping me up on my seat. Out in the pews, there were a lot of bugged-out eyes under those hats.

"What's it going to be, Bess?" David asked me.

I sat for a minute, getting my bearings. The hats were bobbing and murmuring. I gripped David's arm, hauled myself up and took a few deep breaths.

"I apologize," I said to the crowd, which

is weird, I realize, but I could talk to a crowd of ten million without breaking a sweat. You just couldn't ask me to play "Twinkle, Twinkle." "It happens to me sometimes, but don't worry, it's cool." I turned to David. "Want to give it another shot?"

There was a smattering of applause and one hearty "You go, girl!" as David headed back to his piano. Even though I went blank about thirty seconds into the Rachmaninoff and had to start over, we gave them a damn good concert. I was beyond ecstatic. While we were taking our bows, I felt weightless, like I was being lifted up into the church rafters on silver strings. It was way better than any drug high I'd ever experienced. I mouthed to David while I floated up there by the ceiling, "Thank you. Thank you." Because it was all on account of him and I knew it. *I love you,* was what I was feeling, but of course I couldn't tell him that.

Members of the congregation gathered around us to offer thanks. The next thing I knew, Professor Stein was standing there with his blue nose and clothes sprinkled with bagel crumbs and cigar ashes. He took my hand and held it between both of his old crooked ones. He just stared into my face with watery eyes, not finding the words. I, of course, started to cry, and just put my arms around him. His shoulders were bony and I could feel him trembling. *I love you, too, old man,* I wanted to say. *You good old man.*

That was the beginning. David never let more than a week go by without dragging me to some funky joint to perform. We played in a church way out in Brooklyn for three nuns and a drunk who was asleep in the aisle. I wasn't picky, though — I passed out everywhere. We played for Professor Stein's nephew's daughter's weekly assembly in some private school in Riverdale. That was some tough peanut gallery, let me tell you. A bunch of ten-year-old kids who all they wanted to do was throw stuff at each other. Their favorite part was when I fainted, but they also liked the *Scaramouche.* One of them asked what movie it came from.

David even got me on a plane the size of your average housefly to Rochester, New York, where we played in some dead rich guy's mansion, Eastman, I think his name was. I'd only flown once before when Angie and I went to Florida to visit our grandparents in a trailer park near Orlando, but that was a real airplane with real flight attendants, not a toy that you start up by yanking the rubber band around the propeller. The thing was, I wasn't scared even though we were bouncing all over the sky in a blizzard because, apparently, it's always snowing in Rochester.

I noticed that David's face was kind of green. "You're not afraid, are you, Bess?" he said.

"No. This is fun," I said with my face plastered to the window, watching the clouds and snow swirl around us. I felt like I'd flown into the world's most spectacular pillow fight.

"But put you on a stage with a piano . . ."

"I know, I know," I said. We could easily die and I was Miss Cool, but just don't ask me to play a tune in a nursing home for half a dozen old ladies who're too deaf to hear me anyway.

The first time I didn't pass out was at a museum in Utica, New York. It should have made the newspapers, which it didn't, but I'll never forget it. By now, it was January, and let me tell you, I never saw snow like this. Up to your ass and climbing. I was excited because we were going to stay overnight and I figured maybe we could get back into the kissing thing. David had never mentioned the incident at Weill Recital Hall and he'd kept his distance. There was also no more champagne. I don't mean to give the impression that he wasn't affectionate. After our practice sessions, he still massaged my fingers. Then he'd give me the usual peck on both cheeks, and send me home in the limo. I tried wearing sweaters with no bra during rehearsals, but despite his earlier interest in my best features, David didn't so much as give them a glance. If it hadn't been for the night we got locked in the hall, I might even have suspected that he was gay. But I also happened to know he was seeing a very gorgeous model, or at least their picture was in the *Post* every other day. She wasn't just some dumb bimbette either. I'd seen her on interviews and she had a head on her shoulders. I hated her guts, especially when the media asked her about David and she'd give them a little smirk and say, "No comment on that."

I knew David's assistant had reserved side-by-side rooms at the Utica hotel. I'd decided we'd do the concert in the evening, have a late romantic dinner and there, far away from our everyday lives, we'd fulfill our destiny. Yuh.

First of all, it was getting real tough to keep the hordes in the dark about David's and my appearances. The media was making a game out of trying to outsmart us, and was beginning to win a few. Somebody attending a church-basement performance just after Christmas called her brother-in-law, who was a reporter for *Star Interview* magazine. He came running and caught our encores. The guy didn't have a clue about music (he got Beethoven mixed up with Ravel, which is kind of like confusing Marilyn Manson with Barry Manilow), but he found out my name and snapped a photo that showed up on the first page of the arts section. Bess Stallone, sister of you-know-who, the caption said, except they put it right out there.

So even though we were up in the boonies, the word leaked out that we were performing and some local newspaper reporters showed up along with TV people. This was the biggest gig for us so far — a pretty major museum with paintings by people even I had heard of. You'd think I'd have been a total wreck, but all I could think about was those adjoining rooms in the hotel. I had so much sexual energy pounding through me during the concert that my performance was totally electrifying. David kept throwing looks at me like he couldn't believe what was coming out of my piano and I was shooting them right back in a way that I hoped was irresistibly sensual. When it was over and we stood up for applause, I was so turned on that I didn't even remember that this was my last chance to pass out.

I held on to David's hand, bowing and scraping and all the time imagining the candles I'd brought strategically planted around our hotel room so they'd shed a flattering golden glow on my naked skin. Uh huh.

Then this absolutely stunning woman stepped out of the crowd and stood there smiling at David. She didn't say a word, but if you looked like her, you would never have to learn to talk. Sleek black hair pulled back in a knot, olive skin, five foot eleven, legs that started at her neck. I wanted to tug on that expensive cashmere sweater that cost at least ten years' rent and whisper, *No chance you'd go away and never come back?* Then David saw her and his face lit up to match the neon art hanging from the ceiling.

"Francesca!"

"*Caro,*" she answered.

What I wanted to know was, what the

hell was somebody like that doing in Utica, New York? David kissed her on the mouth. On the mouth! Then he asked her a question in Italian which I presumed was, "What the fuck are you doing in this jerkwater town in the middle of January?" and she answered something that had the word Montreal in it. I didn't think Montreal was exactly around the corner, but David just nodded like it made all the sense in the world. He took Francesca's arm and started to walk off with her when he happened to remember that his partner was still standing there like Little Orphan Annie.

"Oh, Bess. Bess Stallone, this is Francesca Mello. Francesca, meet my new partner. My lucky miracle."

I stuck out my hand. "Hi," I said. I hate you, bitch, and the horse you rode in on, I thought, as all those nice sexy juices dried up and blew away.

"You were marvelous," Francesca said with that gorgeous accent that made her lips look like she'd give the world's greatest blow job.

"Thanks," I said, as they started jabbering away in Italian. Finally David turned to me. "Francesca and I are going to grab a bite and catch up. Why don't you come along?"

How many reasons do you want, sweetness? I mean, it didn't take a genius to hear the unspoken request: *I'll give you a dollar if you make yourself scarce.*

"Oh, thanks," I said. "I'm pretty tired. I think I'll just go back to the room and get some sleep." And sob until my eyeballs wash right out of their sockets.

"All right," David said, "but be sure to ask the driver to stop off and pick up something for you to eat." Francesca didn't even try to look disappointed.

As they were making their way through the well-wishers, I suddenly realized I hadn't passed out before, during, or even after the performance. Uh, excuse me, but wasn't this the goal David and I had been chasing all these weeks? And not so much as a job-well-done pat on the butt from Monsieur. For a second I thought of yelling after him: "Yo, Dave-baby! What's wrong with this picture?" But I stifled it and shook hands with the mayor instead. Then I went straight back to my hotel room. I mean ASAP, with no stopping at Taco Bell, since I was still too busy trying to digest the sight of David and his Italian babe strolling off into the sunset to leave room for any damn burrito. I was stuck alone with nothing but a dozen candles to keep me company, and believe me, they're no stand-in for the real thing no matter what you try to do with them.

The next morning, there were flowers outside my door. I don't know where the hell he found them in the middle of the night in a town like Utica, but they were beautiful, and the card said, "Bess, you are the partner of my best dreams. I am so proud of you! Love, D." I knew he meant the fainting, and now I didn't care about anything else except that he had noticed and that he had signed the card with the word "love," even if it meant the kind you feel for your favorite goldfish.

It was the middle of January, which meant there was only a month to go before the big night. Our concert had been billed as "To Be Announced" for so long that a few people on the inside of the Carnegie organization had begun to figure out exactly what was going on. You can't keep something like that a secret. In fact, it was almost ridiculous that we'd pulled it off for such a long time. People started finagling tickets for the Valentine's night concert, so what was supposed to be a small, by-invitation-only audience got totally out of hand. At that point, I wasn't sleeping anyway so it hardly mattered if it was half a hall or the full two hundred and sixty-eight.

I had invited my parents, Angie, Jake, Pauline, and the guys from the firehouse. I hadn't seen my father since Christmas, which had been a pitiful event. Even though according to the doctors Dutch was actually improving, he seemed to be disappearing into a shriveled-up version of himself.

"He looks freeze-dried," I'd said to Angie that first shocking night after six weeks away from Rocky Beach.

"Stir," she said.

I knew she'd left out the "Just add water" part and I appreciated the black humor. But it was unnerving. Plenty of times, I'd wished him dead, especially if I could have had a hand in it, but this guy seemed more like some beaten dog my mother had rescued from the street. Anyway, the bizarre thing was, he wrote me a note saying he was sorry he couldn't come. He'd never given me so much as a birthday card my whole life and suddenly I got this good-luck wish signed "Your father, Dutch." I still have it. It's one of the great curiosities of the western world and ought to go in Ripley's. But anyway, I knew

Mumma would be there with Angie and Jake and also some of the guys. I got them house seats where they wouldn't be in my line of vision.

The big question was what to wear. I wanted to shop with Angie but David wouldn't hear of it. I'd sort of thought a classic black gown would be chic, but that wasn't what he had in mind at all. He trotted me up to Bergdorf's, where I had never set foot in my life and where just to breathe the air costs five bucks a second. Next thing I knew, he had me trying on all these bright colors — aubergine and celadon and persimmon. I mean, back then I wouldn't have known a persimmon if it bit me in the ass. We got a changing room that was twice the size of my apartment and our own personal shopping assistant, who looked like Gwyneth Paltrow. What I really liked about her was that she wasn't frothing at the mouth over David. To tell the truth, I think she was much more interested in me. We went out to show David how fab I looked in foxglove.

"David, *caro*," I said with a thick accent. I liked to give him grief about women like Francesca, since if I wasn't going to get him for myself, I sure as hell was going to take the piss out of the women who did.

"You theenk pear-haps zeez iss a leetle too, you know, *zexy* for *moi?* I mean, how zay will show off zee boobies in a not so nice way?" I gave him a sample bow to demonstrate, and maybe to show off the cleavage. "I still like the black one."

His eyes checked it out but more like he was inspecting a steak for the optimum percentage of fat. "I don't think the color flatters your skin," he said. "Stop being such a pain in the butt and try on that pink one."

"Language, dude," I warned him. "You've been hanging out with the wrong crowd."

He bought me a pale melon satin dress that I have to say did look fairly amazing with my coloring. I tried not to imagine how it would hold up when it crumpled into a ball under my fainting body. Negative thinking. I turned the channel in my brain to a section of the Ravel and let the chords drown out the nasty stuff. The tailor showed up with a man whose very presence made the sales help jerk to attention like he had them all hung on short strings. Turned out he was the Main Man, and if you've ever wondered what a garden looked like walking, this was it. Manicured from head to toe. David knew him well, it seemed, and introduced me.

"How're you doing?" I said.

"Whatever was wrong with my day was just rectified by seeing you in that sumptuous dress," he said, kissing my hand. And all this time, he was looking at me like I was the queen of trailer trash. "Of course, Ms. Stallone will be trimming her hair." He actually reached out like he was about to touch it. I thought David was going to deck him.

"No, she will not," David said in a tone that would refreeze the polar cap and cheer up all those worried environmentalists. The guy flinched like he'd been zapped with a cattle prod.

"Oh, of course, but I just thought perhaps to enhance the dress . . ." he said. "I'm very sorry. Lovely hair, of course."

For a Nassau County mutt, that is. I wondered if this was what it was going to be like, everybody thinking I was David's little ho. But what the hell, wasn't it the music that was the point here, the end of the rainbow I'd been chasing all these years? I could feel myself standing at the very edge of my dream — of playing the world's most beautiful compositions with an outstanding musical partner. I could even now allow myself the fantasy of performing with an orchestra. What bliss *that* would be. Inside my head, I played an old game Angie and I used to entertain ourselves with, presenting one another with impossible choices. *If you were going to die in a month and they gave you the option of a trip around the world or a voyage to the moon, which would you choose? So Bess,* I asked myself as the tailor adjusted the hem in my dress that had the price tag of a midsize SUV, *if you had a choice of sleeping with David or playing the Poulenc Two-Piano Concerto with the Montreal Symphony Orchestra, which would you choose?* I glanced over at David leaning against the wall with his arms folded, watching every move of the tailor while the Main Man bent his ear about how musicians usually have vile taste in clothes and what a delight it was to serve David, who was such an exception to the rule, blah blah-di-blah. David's eyes slid over to meet mine and one lid closed in a wink. *Oh Bess, don't kid yourself, you'd choose this man's bed over top billing with the Philharmonic of the Heavenly Host, God Herself conducting.* What a traitor to my sex.

The next afternoon, there were bits in the *Post* and the *Times* and an item on the *E!* channel. They were all worded pretty much the same, like:

The rumor goes that David Montagnier will introduce his new partner at the concert slated for Valentine's night at the Weill Recital Hall. What the music world wants to know is how will she measure up to Terese Dumont? The young pianist, who was apparently plucked from obscurity, has some tough act to follow.

That's what I like. No pressure. I was a little suspicious that our management (David's manager had become mine, I guess by proxy) had planted this stuff. More tickets, more money. But fortunately there were only a couple of days to go, which I spent not sleeping, eating M&M's, and swimming because David was always nagging me to go. I hated it. Pools smelled bad and made me miss the ocean. But it was true that I felt more relaxed on the rare occasions that I knuckled under and did some laps.

The morning of the big day, which was a Saturday, I woke up at four A.M., swung my legs over the side of the bed, remembered what day it was, and passed out. Well, why not? Might as well get it over with right off the bat. I couldn't even tell you what I did between the time I picked myself up off the floor and seven P.M. I was probably wandering around town like one of those typical Manhattan citizens who yells at the alien invaders who're monitoring our brain waves. But when David arrived to pick me up, I have to say I looked better than I ever have in my entire life, which is not so hard to accomplish if you spend several million dollars on one outfit. David still hadn't let anybody mess with my hair, which I found very touching. He had never come to my apartment before, and it amused me to watch him walking around my one small room picking things up and putting them down again, even testing the faucet in the sink. It pleased me that he took an especially long time staring at the picture of me and Jake that Angie took down by the beach. I was in a bikini and Jake was in his trunks and we both looked extremely buff. Jake called it our *Baywatch* picture. Anyhow, David handed me a box I hadn't even noticed he'd brought with him. I untied the ribbon, took off the top, and saw a perfect orchid nestled inside.

"An orchid. Oh, an orchid." I knew I sounded like a moron, but when I went to the prom at Rocky Beach High all I got was a bigger version of the carnation my date wore in his button-hole. Marlene Webster's date gave her an orchid. So expensive, so exotic. It was the most gorgeous thing I'd ever seen.

"It made me think of you, Bess," David said. "And you ought to have something for luck." He leaned down and kissed me then, a soft one on the lips. Not sexy but not exactly brotherly either.

"I want to keep it here," I said. "Is that all right?" I didn't want to explain that if the evening turned out to be a disaster, at least I'd have something beautiful to come home to.

"Yes. Now come. Phillip's outside waiting for us."

"He's waiting," I echoed, thinking about that stage situated within the hallowed walls of Carnegie Hall, the crowd, the two pianos nestled together. I grabbed David's arm and the world slipped away as I went down.

He caught me before I did damage to the dress but I was pretty shaky. We stood in the doorway for a minute while David kept me upright with an arm around my waist. "All right now?" he asked.

"Um, yuh," I lied. My fingers felt like

hummingbirds. I didn't imagine they'd be too effective at the keyboard.

"Tonight is no different than Utica," he said.

"Oh, fuck you," I said. Even in Utica they'd know better than that.

He just laughed. "All right, then, what can I do to help?"

I leaned against him, which was useful against the wobbly knees. Then I had an inspiration. "Kiss me," I said.

"*Absolument*," he said, and gave me a nice little peck on the cheek.

"Oh, no, Dave, not that kind." I lifted my face and looked into his eyes. He got the point and slowly lowered his mouth onto mine, staying there for a slow, soft merging. My mouth relaxed and opened a little and pretty soon our tongues were touching and exploring and my knees began to do a different kind of quaking. I pulled away.

"Did it help?" David asked.

I just nodded because I didn't want to break the spell. I took his arm and walked down the crumbled stoop to the limo.

You enter Weill on 57th Street a couple of doors down from the main entrance to Carnegie Hall. I glanced at the people waiting outside, remembering how that used to be me. Thanks to David, I was a different person now, musically. I told myself that if this was the end of the road, it had been worth the ride just getting this far.

We'd spent plenty of time backstage so it wouldn't unnerve me on the big night. Weill's got these scary women they like to call ushers but they're probably guards from some maximum-security prison making a few extra bucks. David knew nobody was going to get past them, not even Angie, not even Professor Stein, which suited David just fine. He understood that being with him alone calmed me and made me feel centered in the music. We just sat there in the hanging-out area by the freight elevator, talking about anything but the program — religion, I think. After a while, a technician showed up to tell us that it was time. David lifted me to my feet. I could hear a rumble from the audience. Even without looking, I sensed that the place was packed. Prickles began behind my eyes. I felt woozy. David turned me to him and held my face in his hands.

"Think of Rachmaninoff tonight, Bess," he said. "And Ravel and Mozart and the others. We're going to make wonderful music for them." He gave me another kiss on the mouth, a light one this time. "Are you ready?" he asked me.

"Oh, what the hell," I said, and we walked out onto the stage together.

What we had figured would be a small group bunched up in the first ten rows turned out to be a mob crammed into every square inch, standing room all along the walls and against the back and in the balcony. I didn't look for familiar faces because it would be even harder to focus. The applause was loud and long, which gave me time to adjust to the strange light. With all those bodies in there soaking up the sound and the wattage, the place seemed almost foreign. But so far, there were no fireworks in my head. David's hand was strong around mine, warming my fingers. He looked at me with a smile, waiting until I was ready. Lucky girl, I thought. Think about how lucky you are. When I nodded my head, we separated and went to our pianos. The applause dwindled away into a hush. Thoughts marched weirdly through my head in largo tempo. Professor Stein telling me that concerts are like paintings. You prepare the canvas but you must be ready for surprises. Making art is unpredictable, which is why it's so wonderful. A quote from Van Cliburn, who said that the stage is the loneliest place in the world. But not for me. Not anymore as I looked across and there was David, waiting quietly, no hurry. I knew if I passed out, he'd just pick me up and set me back on the seat. I was okay. I raised my hands, nodded again, and we were off.

What amazed me more than anything was that I actually had fun. I felt like we were all dancing together out there on-stage, me and David and Wolfgang and Ludwig and even the audience. One big celebration of beautiful music. It made me want to weep. It made me want to make love, to anybody, to everybody, and espe-cially to David. If I raised my arms from the keyboard, I believed that I could fly.

When we were done, there was insanity from the audience. People were pounding their feet on the floor and whistling and carrying on, total pandemonium. I stood beside David, bowing and laughing like some nut, and now I could allow myself to look for my group, not that it was hard. Corny, all dressed up, was yelling "Bess! Bravo, Bessie!" and I didn't know then that he would never once miss a concert when I was in New York except when he had his angioplasty. And Max Goldberg, the hook-

and-ladder man with a stammer and a talent for cooking — he was on his feet and cheering with a face the color of his truck. And Jake and Angie, Pauline and Mumma, Angie with her upper lip sticking out halfway to the Bronx from crying. I blew them kisses, and still the noise went on and on. We must have played six encores. The last time we came out onstage, David walked over to my bench and sat down beside me. The audience went silent like somebody threw a cloth over the birdcage. We played a duet, "Sheep May Safely Graze" by Bach. After the last notes had died away, there was no sound for what seemed like a long time. Then again, the explosion of applause and shouts. This is how the famous tradition got started, on that very first night. From then on, we finished every concert that way, side by side at one piano, with that beautiful quiet song from God.

Our manager, Mr. Balaboo, somehow talked his way backstage and he was waiting for us, worrying as usual. Mr. Balaboo's job was to worry and he was very good at it. The moment I became his client, he started fussing over me, whether I ate enough of the right things, whether I was getting enough sleep.

"Bess-dahlink," he said. (I was always Bess-dahlink, like it was my name.) He held my hand in his tiny dried-up fingers. He looked a little like a monkey, small and wiry, with his wavy gray hair sliced down the middle in a perfect part. "That was an extraordinary performance. It must have taken a great deal out of you. How do you feel? Are you all right?"

"I'm so fine, Mr. Balaboo. I've never been so fine in my life."

"I want you to start doing yoga," he said. "I've hired an instructor for you beginning first thing Monday morning. It will help to keep you relaxed."

I was tempted to tell him that all I needed to keep me relaxed at this point was a regular roll in the sack, but I just gave him a careful hug. Even I knew you didn't bear hug somebody like Mr. Balaboo.

"Are you ready?" he asked. "The lounge is packed."

"Come on, Bess," David said. "This part's a performance, too."

The rest of the evening is pretty much a blur, but I still remember a few details. David pressed me through the well-wishers to the bar area of the lounge, where Professor Stein was chatting with some of the world's finest musicians. These people were the famous performers I'd always looked for in the first tier boxes when I talked my way into concerts as a student. They were all there, even Isaac Stern. But the funny thing was, I only had eyes for my old teacher. He was standing there with his purple nose like a beacon and his crooked teeth sticking out, grinning at me. I went straight into his arms and whispered into his ear, "I'll love you forever for sticking with me."

"I'm so glad for you, Bess."

Then he introduced me to the others, who were smiling at our display. First Mr. Stern kissed my hand and I got to tell him how much I appreciated that he hadn't let the wreckers tear down Carnegie Hall. He introduced me to the others, who were very flattering.

Shmuel Litvak, the violinist, said to me, "You must be pretty tough to put up with David."

"Other way around, Mr. Litvak," I said. "I've been a challenge."

"Don't scare her off," David said.

"Well, then, Mr. Angst, this beautiful creature must have reformed you."

Before I could ask Litvak for details, the crowd shoved us apart and I caught a glimpse of my troop standing near the door. Corny, like an overstuffed sofa in his green suit, was gaping at Isaac Stern. Angie probably knew who he was, but none of the others had a clue. Max barely noticed me he was so busy staring at the film stars who were friends of David's. I excused myself and went into the tangle of Angie's, Pauline's and Jake's arms, burying my face in Jake's shoulder, smearing my makeup and crushing my dress. Once I got that out of the way, I kissed my mother.

"Bess, you were wonderful," she said. "I'm so proud of you." She looked like a million bucks. Maybe a billion, in a navy suit. She had a new short haircut, very chic.

"I can't take the credit for what happened tonight," I said to Mumma. "Here's the person who can."

"What did I do?" David asked, squeezing through to do the two-kisses routine on Mumma and Angie. I introduced him to Jake and Pauline.

"What did you think of her?" he said to them, but I noticed he kept glancing at Jake.

"She was like an angel," Pauline said. *Uh oh*, I thought. *Here we go.* "But both of you," she went on, "the music poured straight out of your hearts like liquid gold. It made me weep with rapture."

Angie glanced at my face and stuck out her hand to David. "Thank you," she said simply, and then said it again. I knew she meant thanks for making the impossible happen, for her, for me. But she was odd with him, I noticed. Stiff, and she didn't know what to call him. It was a weird situation, him paying her way at school. He'd recently given her a clothing allowance, too, which she'd refused to use. I had ahold of Jake's arm. It took me a while to realize that his elbow was trembling. I guess I had thought it was me.

"You okay, Jake?" I asked.

"I'm excellent," he said. I supposed a certain shakiness was reasonable under the circumstances, considering his old buddy had just hit the big time. Still, a few quick phone calls were all the contact I'd had with him for weeks.

"We have to make a date," I said. "I don't know what's going on in your life."

"Sure, Stallone," he said. But then David swept me off with apologies and that's the last I saw of any of them.

There was something different in the way David held me as we walked to the limo. His hand was firm against my hip, pulling me close, keeping our strides in step. A few people still hung around, wanting conversation, a handshake, some contact with our success, but David marched me through them all without losing his grip on me for one second. I could feel myself getting even more stirred up than I already was. It turned out that a successful concert was always sexy, at least for me. I guess I just didn't know what to do with all the emotion that came from the fear, the music, the applause — and my body's natural response to most strong feelings has always been, Let me throw off my clothes and fuck. After this first concert, I was absolutely crazy with sexual energy. Either David picked up on my hot vibes or he was in the same state himself. He didn't keep me waiting long. We tumbled into the backseat of the limo (smoked windows, thank you) and grabbed each other and started kissing like we were trying to swallow each other whole. We were supposed to go to a party on Central Park West but pretty soon David asked Phillip to turn around and take us back to the apartment. By the time we pulled up to David's building, we were both halfway naked and the top of my gorgeous satin dress was crumpled around my waist. We rearranged ourselves, said good-night to Phillip (or maybe we didn't), and got in the elevator. Inside there was a little old gent with a cane and a dapper hat. David and I were breathing steam. He held me in front of him to hide the evidence, and his erection was rubbing up against me through my dress. And all the time the dapper gent was passing the time about it being unseasonably mild for February.

"Global warming, perhaps," David said. I vaguely remembered having had the same thought just yesterday.

"I'll say," I agreed. "It's about a hundred and ten where I'm standing."

We finally got to David's apartment but what we didn't make it to was the bedroom. He had the rest of my clothes off the second the door closed behind us. I tried to pull his off too but he wasn't in the mood to wait. So I was completely bare and he was mostly dressed and all it took for both of us was a couple of shoves right there against the door. I'd say that the first round was a record for speed. But we weren't finished by a long shot. We were both so crazed we still hadn't said a word to one another. We sprinted into the bedroom, where it was dark except for the lights from the city glittering outside the windows. David ripped the blankets off in one move and tossed me on the bed. Pianists have enormous upper-body strength, but I was still surprised at how strong he was, like I weighed no more than a puff of air. I spread my legs for him, holding them apart with my hands to open myself to him, wide, wider. He stared at me for a second, whispered something in French, and lowered himself on me. His body was long and lean and almost hairless. He kissed me everywhere, and now it was as if he couldn't stop talking, telling me how beautiful my breasts were, how long he'd waited. Now and then he'd lapse back into French and even my name sounded like music.

I don't know how we had the energy for that night, after the weeks of exhausting buildup to the concert and then the grand event itself. I guess we were just so totally pumped. We kept at it all night long, as if the hunger we'd been storing up all that time could never be satisfied. Instead of sleeping in between, we played the piano for each other. I asked him for the Bach Prelude in C because there was no more perfect piece of music ever written. I told him the way he played it made me feel like I was floating on clear moonlit water.

Sometime around three in the morning, after he'd made me come so many times that I couldn't stop trembling, he got up on one elbow, pushed my damp hair off my face, and said, "Bess, I love you so much I don't even think I'm sane anymore."

I lay back and let the cool air from around the windows slip over my sweat-drenched body. "It's just because of tonight," I said. "The concert."

"No. I've been trying to talk myself out of it for weeks. So many dreams I've had about doing these things with you. You amaze me all the time. There is no one like you." He traced my breasts with his finger, then lower to my belly and lower still, exploring me outside and in. I couldn't believe that I could possibly have anything left, but I could feel myself getting aroused again. Then he kissed me and said, "I want you to love me, Bess." Even with all the evidence I'd been throwing his way, he still didn't know for sure.

"I do," I said. "I do love you." It made me wild to say it after all this time, finally, out loud. I started laughing and then he started laughing. Then there was a whole long stream of French with kisses thrown in for punctuation and we started all over.

CHAPTER NINE

The next morning, which was about an hour later, I woke up first. I lay there thinking, *Who* did you say gave a successful concert at Weill Recital Hall without passing out? *Who* did you say heard David Montagnier declare his love? I had to let it all sink in for a while. Then I got up and stood next to the bed and stared down at David. He was sleeping on his back with one arm across his chest and the other thrown straight out like he was reaching for something. I got about ten minutes' worth of uninterrupted staring during which I memorized all the details, including the two small scars by his left knee and scattered beauty marks just below his navel that looked like the stars in a constellation. As if my eyes were conducting an orchestra, Tchaikovsky's *Serenade for Strings* was pouring through me, leaving waves of skin prickles up and down my arms and under my hair. But then David stretched, clenched his fingers, and opened his eyes.

"I knew you were watching me," he said. He didn't even sound groggy. He just woke up into a fully functioning person, not like me, who needed a portable IV of caffeine to get myself moving from point A to point B.

"Not," I said.

"I was only pretending to be asleep."

"That's why you were snoring loud enough to wake up everybody in Staten Island," I lied, Staten Island being almost in the state of Florida, at least as far as people in Manhattan are concerned. He grabbed for me but I spun away. Not a chance he was going to get a kiss out of me before I'd even brushed my teeth.

"I'm borrowing your toothbrush," I said.

"Fine," he said. "I'm at your service and under your spell."

While I was in there, I poked through his medicine chest. Sometimes you can find out a few things about a person, but his was almost empty. Two containers of Advil for the typically stiff and sore musician. Half a dozen bottles of expensive after-shave and cologne, mostly unopened. I figured they were gifts from admiring lady friends, who were now irrelevant as far as I was concerned. Antibiotics with a year-old expiration date and another prescription I didn't recognize for something called Desyrel, take as directed. It pleased me that there was only one toothbrush, which

I used. I pretty much scoured the inside of my mouth. Then I wrapped a towel around me and went out to find David making coffee in the kitchen. When I got within range, he snatched a corner of the towel and yanked it right off.

"Hey!" I yelled.

"Ah, you look much better now," he said, and kissed my shoulder.

"I won't be naked unless you are, too." He'd thrown on a T-shirt and jeans.

"I'm the host," he said, working his way down my spine with his fingers.

"I thought you were in my service and under my spell," I said, and made a half-hearted attempt to undo his jeans. I have to admit there was something sexy about being bare when he was dressed. We did some serious kissing. But I was weak from lack of sleep, no food, and a whole night of sex. I wrenched myself away and went to track down a shirt.

"Is that Jack in the photograph, with you in your bikini?" David asked. He had made a couple of omelets, which did not live up to my idea of French cuisine. We pigged them down anyway.

"Jake," I corrected him. "Yeah, Angie took that one at Jones Beach." I was flattered that David had paid attention, that he almost got Jake's name right.

"He's also in love with you," David said.

It was hard not to laugh. "Jake's my oldest friend."

"That may be so. But he eats you up with his eyes."

"You're a madman," I said. "Very sweet, but nuts all the same." I didn't want to say Jake couldn't be in love with somebody he'd had a contest with to see who could save the biggest scab. But it pleased me to think that David was so dopey with love that he could imagine such a possibility. The corners of David's mouth suddenly looked like commas so I figured I'd better change the subject.

"What's playing in your head?" I asked him. "Right now."

"Ah." He closed his eyes. "Beethoven Sonata, Number Thirteen, E-flat. The adagio movement. And you?"

"Beethoven. *Moonlight.* Second movement."

His eyes opened wide. "Not truly, Bess."

I crossed my heart. "I swear." It seemed too incredible, out of all the millions of notes written over the centuries, that our inner ears would be tuned to the very same composer. And Beethoven, who for all his tantrums could hand over such perfect moments of sweetness and calm. It made sense, I guess. Both of us were reacting to weeks, months, of trouble and aggravation, which had somehow evolved into this morning of quiet happiness. I went to sit in his lap. He buried his face in my hair.

"My old piano teacher, Mrs. Fasio, used to give me a gold star when she was happy with my work," I told him.

"I'll be your gold star," he said. The hands were wandering.

"My thought exactly," I said.

We holed up in David's apartment for three days, with the phone turned off and the message machine blinking Morse code as in: *How can you possibly not pick up? We are the media calling. We are the world calling.* There was plenty of rolling around in the sack, but we also spent a lot of time at the pianos. It was what made us happy, it was how we talked when there weren't any words and we were sexually used up. Tenderness was Ravel and Mozart, passion was Beethoven and the Russians, and laughter was Mozart again, and there were so many others. Sometimes we played duets, mostly Schubert, so we could sit side by side, our bodies fused. It was all a discovery and it seemed as if

200

we'd never get tired of it.

We didn't say so, but I knew that both of us wanted to ride this beautiful ice floe until it melted away under us. The world wasn't going to leave us alone for long and we knew it. But there would never be another time like this — our sensationally successful debut wrapped in the same few days as the birth of our love affair. When we were hungry, we called downstairs for food delivery. The newspapers appeared outside the door and when certain magazines were due on the stands, David got the porter to pick them up for us. This was more than enough outside world for us.

Two mornings after the concert, David lay in the tub drinking his high-test espresso while I perched on the edge and read him the good news from the *Times* Arts section:

Bess Stallone, David Montagnier's new partner, has the physique of the youthful Sophia Loren and the musical sensibility of the aged Rubinstein. The combination was enough to send New York's luckiest recitalgoers into transports. It can't be easy for any newcomer to balance the brilliant musicianship and crowd-pleasing charisma of Mr.

Montagnier, but this young woman holds her own and more . . .

David started laughing. God, that happy sound I would do almost anything to inspire, except I was never sure exactly what was going to do the trick. The piece went on to rave about specific aspects of the program. It wasn't totally accurate, but hey, I wasn't about to quibble. Then David took his turn, reading to me with damp hands from *The New Yorker*, in "The Talk of the Town":

For those who thought Valentine's Day was simply a strategy to subsidize the greeting-card business, think again. This February fourteenth saw the debut of a brand-new Queen of Hearts when Bess Stallone was unleashed on the music world at Carnegie's Weill Recital Hall. As David Montagnier's new partner, this pianist dazzles the ear and the eye simultaneously, evoking the strapping sexuality and musical genius of the young Jacqueline DuPre.

"Jesus," I commented. "It's hard to tell if it was the music or the tits."

"Clearly a combination of both," David

said, and reached out to haul me into the tub with him. We made quite a splash.

But the next evening, the porter delivered *The Listener* along with our Chinese takeout. We'd gotten so confident that we ate half our dinner before we bothered to see if there was a review. Finally, I got curious, especially since *Ears*, which is what musicians called it, was the oldest and most influential of all the arts publications. There was a nice photo of both of us looking intense at our keyboards and a short article. I started reading while David cracked open a fortune cookie.

David Montagnier has either lost his musical judgment or he's simply head-over-heels in lust. How else to explain his choice of Bess Stallone to replace the resplendent Terese Dumont?

I looked up at David. "Uh oh," I said.

"Give it to me," he said. "We don't need to hear any more of that."

"Oh, come on, David," I protested. "I'm a big girl. I can take it."

He actually made a grab for it, but I snatched it away and went on. Look, they couldn't all be raves:

The most subtle thing about Stallone's performance was her dress, which allowed the first ten rows a tantalizing peek at what purports to be a tattoo on her left ankle. Not one for delicacy, she led Montagnier on a romp through the Ravel, trampling dynamics and nuance along the way. Montagnier backed her up in a slavish demonstration that only made more poignant the unforgettable memory of his and Dumont's sensitive collaboration on this piece nearly a decade ago in Alice Tully Hall . . .

David's face had gone white. "Bess, throw that away."

"No, I've gotta get used to this kind of stuff," I said, and kept plowing through, too dumb to realize I could have read it to myself later on.

The Mozart Sonata for Two Pianos in D major, at least, showed vague signs of human intelligence, and certainly no one can quibble with Ms. Stallone's technical proficiency. Overwhelmingly, however, the impression remains that David Montagnier has traded in Audrey Hepburn for Courtney Love.

I looked up at David. "Ooo, that's pretty good. I guess he didn't like my duds."

I jumped as David came over and snatched the magazine out of my hands. His eyes narrowed in the hunt, as if they were looking down a scope at the crosshairs. "August Nardigger. He used to review art for the *Times*."

"Then he's probably trying to make a name for himself in music by being clever and nasty," I said. "Anyway, he's entitled to his opinion."

"Read under the lines, Bess. This is about social class. Audrey Hepburn, my ass."

I smiled. "First of all, it's 'between the lines,' and second, you can't say 'my ass' with a French accent. It doesn't work." I was trying to be lighthearted about it, but I could see that David was really fuming. I had never seen his face like this, all twisted into a knot.

"I'm going to put in a call to Balaboo," he said, heading for the phone. "Someone needs to tell this snake you don't be so cruel at someone's debut performance." He started to get up to make the call but I got to him in time to grab the phone. I held it in the air behind my shoulder and stared him down.

"Are you sure you want to do that?" I asked him. It seemed a pity that this was how we were going to reenter the world. After a few seconds of eyeball-to-eyeball confrontation, David just sort of deflated. He plunked back in his chair. I sat in his lap and stroked his hair. "Don't tell me you've never gotten a rotten review," I said.

"Of course, but this is different. This is your first . . ."

I kissed him to shut him up, a little one, then a bigger one. "Forget it, David. If I don't let it get to me, why should you?"

"I'm going to remember this Nardigger," he said, melting just a little under the warmth of the kisses.

"We'll take out a contract on him, but can we do it tomorrow? We've got important business." I kissed him some more until the muscles in his face relaxed and pretty soon we were back in the bedroom again. Then he fell asleep but I propped myself up and looked out the window. Snow had begun to fall outside. Snowflakes swirled and billowed into fantastic patterns against the gray light. I could hear heat rising with a cozy hiss from the radiators along the floor. The world was invisible and we were safe inside with the blizzard dancing silently on the other side of the glass. I reached down and laid my fingers across David's wrist where his pulse was beating steady and quiet. I didn't ever want to move from that bed and all I could think was, Okay, God, you might as well kill me right now because it's never gonna get better than this.

CHAPTER TEN

Obviously, we couldn't stay in our cocoon forever. Eventually, Mr. Balaboo showed up in the lobby and explained to the doorman that he wasn't leaving until we let him come up. His scalp was fire-engine red under that perfect part and his pocket handkerchief looked like it had had a nervous breakdown.

"Please sit down, Mr. Balaboo," David said, and poured him half a glass of wine even though it was only eleven in the morning.

He took a tiny sip, and looked at us with a sigh. I had to check to see if his feet were touching the floor. He was so dainty you wanted to stick him on a shelf with your other china figurines. David was always being nagged to change management, but he stayed with Mr. Balaboo because he was a gentleman in a world of sharks. I had to keep restraining myself from kissing him on the head, he was that adorable.

"The calls are coming in so fast I can't keep up," he complained. "You have to make some decisions." Mr. Balaboo kept his eyes off my outfit, which was one of

David's tuxedo shirts and a pair of gym socks. I went to find a robe. Then I stood in the doorway while they talked about dates with premier orchestras — Berlin, Montreal, Philadelphia, Cleveland — and offers of recording contracts.

The blizzard had cleared, leaving a blue sky that was almost painfully bright and turning David and Mr. Balaboo into black cutouts against the window. Antonio Vivaldi was doing his best to drown out the discussion with his winter music inside my head and all the time I was staring at the two silhouettes and thinking, Where the fuck are you, Bess? I mean, give me a break, they're talking Charles Dutoit here, conductor of the Montreal. I knew I would never have been invited to play with them without David, but that was exactly the way I wanted it. At least with David I had half a shot at staying conscious to enjoy the ride. By the time Mr. Balaboo left a couple of hours later, we had a master plan and real soon after that I found out what it was like to become public property.

So this is what our days were like. We practiced together a minimum of four hours a day and then usually had a rehearsal with a visiting orchestra or a chamber group, or sometimes a taping session at a recording studio. David wanted me to move in with him, which I pretty much did, although it bothered me some. I'd been living on my own for a few years, and David felt like micromanaging every detail of my life. He gave half my clothes away to Goodwill and dragged me back to Bergdorf's. It's fine to be able to afford great clothes, but those price tags made me want to vomit. Also that manicured man who had looked at me like I was a Seventh Avenue hooker came sliding over to get my autograph on a store catalog. I almost signed it "Up your ass. Regards, Courtney Love," but of course, David would have chucked me out the window.

So first it was the clothes, then he made me get my first physical exam other than the usual Pap smear, which I had always been religious about, that is, if you can relate religion to a situation where you lie on a table like a dinner plate with your crotch served up as today's special. Anyhow, David's doctor told us I was strong as a horse, which was no big surprise. The only thing was some fluctuation in my blood pressure, which probably contributed to the fainting. He gave me a prescription and told me to use it before my concerts, and I have to say it reduced the sparkles in front of my eyes. Or maybe it was the power of suggestion. Either way, I was happy.

David took charge of my diet, too. He thought I was consuming too much sugar and fat. I explained that Krispy Kremes were part of my body's essential building blocks and that I would start to go downhill fast without them, like with palpitations and unsightly hives and probably even gout. He bought me these dog biscuits from the health food store that I was supposed to eat for energy. I did it, but made him pay by howling like a mooncrazed hound. David hated ugly sounds.

I was pretty good-natured about all this. First of all, I was so grateful to him that I would probably have swallowed cement straight out of the mixer if he told me to. Furthermore, I was crazed with love. However, there was that morning he overstepped. I was minding my business, brushing my teeth beside him at the bathroom sink, and David started in on my brand of toothpaste and how it was too abrasive or some such bullshit. Now, I had been a Colgate girl all my life, and there was simply no way anyone was going to malign my toothpaste. We got into a huge tug-of-war with my Total and next thing we knew, I had emptied almost a whole tube on David, decorating him like a birthday cake with stripes and circles. I have to give him credit for laughing.

Anyhow, the point is, it was a little crowded psychologically, suddenly living hip-to-hip with a personality as gigantic as David's. There was also the issue of money in that basically I was a kept woman. It should have bothered me more, I suppose. I know it tortured Angie to accept money from David, grateful as she was. But in my bones I believed that I was exactly what David needed, and every day there was some new thrill. Take, for instance, the morning we had just finished an exhausting practice session and we looked at one another across the pianos and both said at the very same time, "Bach never played anything the same way twice." What *is* that? I never got used to it, that spooky telecommunication between us, and got delicious prickles down my back every time it happened.

There are lots of debuts you have to get through to make it in the music world, and some of them have nothing to do with tickling the ivories. Every time you talk to a reporter or a benefactor for a concert hall or even a lowly fan, you'd better know how to handle it. I didn't have a clue; I mean, me with the mouth. So what I tried to do was keep it shut and watch a master, i.e., David. We did a couple more concerts, one at Alice Tully and another at the New Jersey Performing Arts Center, a place that shocked the hell out of everybody by being fabulous because it was in — horrors! — Newark. Afterward we'd be mobbed backstage and even out on the street an hour later. Dozens of people would wait, hoping for autographs. I took my cues from David. You did a general kind of smile and only shook a hand if one got stuck right in front of your face. It was always risky — the chance of getting your fingers mangled by some enthusiastic cruncher. You tried to keep on with whatever conversation you were in the middle of, which for me meant nodding a lot, since half the time I didn't even know what people were talking about. I mean, couldn't a person just say, "God, you really touched me," instead of "I found your music simply transmogriphobicalistic?" Usually, I figured it was supposed to be a compliment and said, "Gee, thanks."

After the first few performances, I began to see some of the same people show up. I always kept tickets available for Angie, Mumma, Jake and Pauline, obviously, but they couldn't make it to every concert. And I always saved Corny a ticket. He'd come in that green suit, carrying something delicious from the neighborhood — cannoli, fresh figs, once even a big smelly sausage. He told me he always knew I'd need those multiplication tables he'd made me memorize because one day I'd be making big money. Corny had good musical sense, often picking out the best bits of the performance to comment on. It made my heart ache a little to hear him say, "You did good tonight, Bessie." I mean, it might have been nice to have an actual proud father hanging around.

There was Mrs. Edelmeyer, who thought she was a great concert pianist who had just never been discovered. She pretended she was my best friend, always winking at me and telling her companions things like "Bess and I prefer to play Bach with *emotion*." It was sad, really. David found her beyond annoying, but I couldn't bring myself to blow her off. There was Vernon, a young man with a deformed mouth and liquid brown eyes that looked at me with such total love it always made me melt. He would take my hand — always gently —

bow and make some shy remark about what pleasure I'd given him that evening. After a while I got so I couldn't keep track of which faces belonged to which country. Mrs. Edelmeyer really screwed me up once by showing up backstage in Milan. I didn't know *where* the hell I was.

Then there were the people with money and connections. David would introduce them to me and I would be charming, i.e., if they spilled champagne down my cleavage, I would make every effort not to use the "f" word. These were the types who shelled out enough money to keep the music playing year after year. I'm not above slinging the shit if it means tuning the pianos and paying for plane tickets so a hundred divine fiddlers can get to New York from Vienna.

The bottom line was it became clear to me pretty early on that the most successful performers were the ones who could pull off the self-promotion. You could be the most talented musician on the planet, but if you couldn't smile at the people with clout, you were screwed.

David started taking me out to dinner in fabulous restaurants but we still always ate alone, unless you counted the maître d' and the waiters who were always hanging around looking for tips and soaking up David's glory. I'd watch the staff in sympathy as they scurried around. At least they didn't have to do it on Rollerblades.

I was also now included in some informal jam sessions. Like when the Cleveland was in town, for instance, a half dozen musicians would troop over to David's after their Carnegie Hall gig and mess around. You'd think it would be the last thing anybody would feel like doing, but I guess music is a kind of sickness, like nymphomania. We'd put away a lot of wine and play quartets, mixing it up with a weird collection of instruments, sometimes a French horn standing in for a cello or a clarinet for a violin, whoever was around. It was a tremendous amount of fun, and I could hold my own in those situations since chamber music had always been comfortable for me. But the big test came later that summer when we were invited to a party in Southampton.

For those of you who don't know, for instance if you've been domiciled on a distant galaxy for your entire life, there are two distinct Long Islands. There's the part I come from, which is closer to "The City," i.e., the only city, the Big Apple. (If a New Yorker lives in Great Britain, when he says

"The City," he is not referring to London.) People who live in Manhattan don't differentiate between people from Nassau County, Long Island, and from the neighboring boroughs and suburbs. We are collectively known as "bridge-and-tunnel," which I assure you is not meant as a compliment. Then there's the other Long Island that includes the towns between West Hampton and Amagansett. (Montauk, my favorite, doesn't count because it's too far out and only has Dick Cavett. Or did. I think he sold his house for the price of a small continent.) You walk along Main Street in East Hampton and you might as well be on Madison Avenue. Same face-lifts, same bodies buffed by the personal trainer who gets to use the guesthouse twice a week, jewelry up the wazoo, and underneath the summer dresses, two-hundred-dollar swimsuits with labels that say, "Do not immerse in chlorine," which pretty much rules out the backyard pool.

My experience with the Hamptons crowd was limited to years of waiting on them in restaurants. Some were obnoxious and cheap, some were kind and tipped generously. Whatever, they weren't my people and I was pretty nervous at the idea of mingling with that set out on the East

End. Furthermore, David and I were invited for overnight. I assumed that meant we wouldn't be sleeping in the same bed or even the same room. What if they stuck me with some fancy Park Avenue heiress as a roommate? This prospect prompted me to ask David an important question. He was tossing clothes into his suitcase at the time.

"So, David," I said, sitting on the bed to watch him pack. "Do those socialite women fart like everybody else or do they get their assholes done over? You know, to prevent the unexpected."

He blinked and then started to laugh. "I wouldn't be surprised," he said. "They get everything else surgically modified."

Sometimes I said outrageous things just for the joy of watching David laugh. He was pretty tired of people being awed by him. But this time, he knew there was anxiety behind the raunchy question. He tossed a pair of cotton socks into his bag and sat down beside me. "Are you dreading this?" he asked, slipping his hand under my hair to find the back of my neck.

"Yeah," I said.

"We don't really have to do it."

I shook my head. "I'm gonna have to dive in one of these days. Might as well be near a good beach."

I slept late and thought up enough delaying tactics so we didn't leave until after lunch. It was a perfect Saturday afternoon in mid-June. David suggested that I wear a new pale green linen pantsuit and stood surveying me like I was something he might want to buy in a store window.

"Let me braid your hair," he said.

"Huh?" I said.

He came over and started fussing with it. I could tell he knew what he was doing so I sat down and handed him my comb.

"You're doing a French braid," I said. "Does everybody in France get born knowing how to do that?"

He let his hands drop to my shoulders and I could tell by his voice that he'd gone somewhere else.

"David?" I twisted my head to look at him. He had an expression on his face like he was listening to the Schubert Fantaisie in F minor, so sad and beautiful. I couldn't bear to say anything.

"I used to braid my mother's hair for her before she went to bed. It wasn't often that we'd be alone together. Sometimes playing duets when everyone was out. Those were happy times for me. . . ."

Did you ever hear a heart breaking? I

knew that was what I was listening to so I turned around in the chair and put my arms around his waist.

"What happened to her, David?" I asked him.

He didn't answer for a second. "She died," he said finally. "I had a few precious hours with her long ago, and now she's dead."

I held him without speaking until I felt his body kind of stiffen. "No more gloom," he said. "This is going to be a happy day."

Phillip was downstairs waiting, and I have to say, David was lighthearted after that, making me sing a medley of trashy pop songs. He was a big Madonna fan, so he joined in on "Like a Virgin" and "Material Girl," which sounded really special in a French accent. We had a good laugh when Phillip closed the partition. But maybe the combination of David's talking about his mother and then us singing those old tunes made me think about home. Suddenly I was half choking on nostalgia and guilt.

"David, can I ask you a big favor?"

"Of course."

"Do you think we could stop in Rocky Beach, just for a few minutes?"

He hesitated for a second. "Has something happened?"

"We wouldn't have to stay long, I promise. Only a couple three minutes."

"Okay, a couple three," he said. I'd noticed he was getting kind of peculiar about my sister lately, like when I made my daily call to Angie, he'd stay in the room and pretend not to listen. When I carried on about how smart and beautiful she was, he'd only listen politely without seconding the motion. Last week, I'd reminded her that she was due for her annual visit to the eye doctor to keep track of a muscle weakness she'd had since she was little. When I hung up, he asked me wasn't Angie old enough to take care of her own medical care. I explained that when I turned ninety-three and Angie was eighty-six, I'd be nagging her to scrub her dentures. With siblings, it just came with the territory and since he didn't have any, he was clueless. It seemed strange that David got along famously with my parents — even Dutch, go figure — when it was Angie I wanted him to care about. I knew she planned to be home that afternoon and thought I'd throw a rock and kill a few birds: (a) I'd reduce the guilt factor by visiting the old folks; (b) I'd get David to bond with Angie; and (c) I'd reduce the time I had to spend at the Hamptons thing.

When the neighbors saw us drive up in the limo, an audience started gathering on the lawns, like they'd been waiting around for just this moment. I was beginning to get used to that kind of thing, though, and ignored it. As usual, I asked Phillip to come in and as usual, he declined. The excuse was he wanted to smoke half a carton of Camels, but I know he felt awkward hanging out with us. Anyhow, the screen door was locked so I yelled to Mumma. In a few seconds, she came out on the porch, smoothing her hair and fingering the buttons on her blouse like she wasn't a hundred percent sure they were fastened. Her face was flushed.

I kissed her on the mouth as usual. "Mumma, you look about sixteen," I said, and that was no bullshit. "You been getting collagen implants?"

She blushed some more and gave me a little shove. David bent to kiss her, too, which I could see pleased her, since the neighbors got an eyeful of Marie Stallone being chummy with the great Montagnier.

"How's Dutch?" I asked.

"Better. He's napping but you can talk to him in a little." More messing with the clothes. "Have some iced tea. My goodness, it's summer today all of a sudden."

"Mumma, what's going on? You're acting like you're on something."

"I don't know what you're talking about," she said. "David? I have some delicious chocolate chip cookies."

"Just what the doctor prescribed," David said, and sat down easy as you please. Mumma and I smiled at one another, and I couldn't help but think about the last time David had been in this room, and how he'd made that incredible proposition. If you'd told me he was going to get me to perform in Weill Recital Hall without keeling over, I would have told you that your elevator didn't go to the top floor. And that he would be my true love, lounging at Mumma's beat-up kitchen table in a pair of black linen slacks and a pale blue T-shirt to die for. My David. I had to speak severely to my impeccable sense of decorum not to go jump on his lap that instant.

"I'll just take a plate of cookies out to your driver," Mumma said. "Do you think he'd like some milk to go with them?"

"Jesus, Mumma," I said. "You're acting like you've OD'd on Donna Reed movies," I said.

David got up and took the plate from her. "Let me do that. I'll be right back."

Mumma and I waited until he got out the door. Then I grinned at her. "So what do you think of my new boyfriend?"

"I guess I knew that would happen."

"You could sound a little happier about it." I chewed on a cookie.

"Oh, honey, you know I can't help worrying. You're not exactly from the same . . ."

"Planet?" I finished for her.

"That's right. And he has the reputation . . . well, Mrs. Gambelli says she read he was seeing those twin models at the same time . . ."

"First rule, don't believe everything you read, and for sure, don't believe Mrs. Gambelli. Remember when I got carsick in her smelly old car on the way to church and she told you I was pregnant? Was I? Tell the truth."

"All right. I'm happy if you're happy."

"Well, then you're ecstatic. When's Angie getting here?"

"She's already here. She went to the beach with Jake and Pauline."

There was that quick shifty look to the left that meant she was holding out on me.

"What?" I asked.

"Nothing, I was just thinking about Jake and Pauline. You know she's always had a little crush on him."

"What have *you* been smoking?" I asked her.

Mumma'd been filling up another plate. "I'll just take these cookies in to your father before he sleeps the day away," Mumma said. "Shall I tell him you'll be in to see him?"

"Yeah."

David came back and didn't seem to notice that my head was spinning around like Linda Blair. "Being married to Dutch has finally done her in. She's cracked."

"On the contrary," David said with a grin.

"Meaning?"

"She had sex before we got here."

I threw a cookie at him. "Get outa here!"

"Believe me. I recognize the signs."

I remembered the little button-checking routine at the front door and tried to keep my head from rotating so fast that it flew off my neck and put a hole through the kitchen ceiling. Things were seriously out of whack in the Stallone household. "What signs?"

"She's giving off a scent. I smelled it when I kissed her hello."

"EE-yew!" I said.

"No, it's nice, like cinnamon, and very

familiar to me." He was still smiling.

I thought it over. "Don't tell me like mother, like daughter. That's too sick."

"Bess, darling, there's only one woman I've ever known whose skin smells of cinnamon after making love and that's you."

"Maybe she's been cooking?"

He laughed. "I'll say."

"Hey, that's my pure and virginal mother you're talking about." But I knew for a fact that she never put cinnamon in her chocolate chip cookies, and it got me thinking. "How could they manage, I mean, with Dutch the way he is?"

He did one of those nonchalant European moves that always made me want to grab him. "Maybe they're inventive. Besides, she said your father was better."

"I'd go in there and say hello to Dutch but I'm afraid they may be doing something kinky."

He got up and took my hand. "Come. I'll cover your eyes."

Dutch was lying on the couch with his legs draped over Mumma's lap. They had a football game on TV with no sound. I went over and gave my father a kiss. He did look better, but he sure didn't look like my father. He was much thinner, and his face wasn't that bright red square thing anymore. He was wearing a sweater like Mister Rogers.

"Congratulations," he said to David. "I hear you figured out how to keep Bess from falling on her ass."

So much for Mister Rogers.

David shook hands with him and said something in Dutch. My father shot something back, and they smiled at each other. I was ready to leave already, but then the front door slammed.

"In the living room!" I shouted.

Angie, Pauline, and Jake came in looking windblown. I hugged everybody, remembering what Mumma had said about Pauline's feelings for Jake. She was standing real close to him, but they'd always been affectionate. Then I thought about the night I'd talked Jake into doing it with me. Jake would never tell Pauline. Or would he? What if she did care for him, a guy who had fucked her friend who'd done the thumb-to-thumb needle-prick blood ritual with her in fifth grade? Oh, man. The vibes around here were getting to be more than I could handle. I'd already forgotten my goal to get Angie and David to bond.

"So, Pauls, you got a new haircut," I said, rearranging a strand that was sticking out from the wind.

"Not so new, actually," she said.

Hm, I thought. It had obviously been too long since we'd shared a brew, or even had a good long blab over the phone.

"Hell, cram a few more people in here and we'll have a platoon." Sometimes Dutch liked to pretend he was back in the marines.

"Gracious as always, Dad," I said.

"Thanks."

"Let's retire to the kitchen," I suggested to Angie.

"Leave David here," Dutch said. "And your mother."

"Aye, aye, your dictatorship," I said. "Got anything you want to ask me before I go?" Like how are you? I have to say, if he and Mumma had been steaming up the place, it sure hadn't improved his disposition any.

"Nah, I'll get the scoop from David here." He pronounced it the European way, which amused me in an annoyed kind of way.

Jake, Angie, Pauline and I trooped off into the kitchen. Jake poured himself a glass of juice from the fridge and sat down in front of the cookies. I was checking Pauline out, looking for telltale signs of romance. Jake looked like his usual self, comfortable in a pair of cutoffs and a beat-up polo shirt. He'd obviously been spending a lot of time outdoors because his face was browned from the sun and his hair had its summer streaks. Angie sat like a little nun with her hands folded neatly in her lap, but Pauline . . . there was something different, no getting away from it. For one thing, she wasn't looking me in the eye.

"What's with you, Stallone?" Jake asked me. "I feel like something on a specimen slide."

"Just wondering how school is going," I lied. "It must be tough to switch in midstream."

"It's the right direction for me. Even when the professor sucks, I like the material, and I get to go right out into the preserve and use what I learn."

"Nothing like a paycheck," Angie said.

"Okay, Ange, you lost me there," I said.

"They promoted him," Pauline explained, with a big proud smile. "From volunteer to assistant land steward."

"That was quick. Good going." I held out my hand to slap him five. "What do they have you doing?"

"Same stuff as when I was a kid. Yanking out bittersweet, picking up beer cans,

229

trying to figure out where all those jellyfish are coming from. But I get to work with kids, too. Teaching them about clams and waterbirds."

"He's so good with them," Pauline said.

"Pauline brought one of her classes to see the genius at work last week," Jake explained.

"We learned about the return of the osprey," Pauline said. Then she shot Jake a look like he was personally responsible for the natural order of the universe. And all this time I had thought David was. Holy shit, maybe Mumma was right.

Just then, Mumma and David showed up, which was just as well because I was about to say something tactful like *Are you kidding? This is practically incest already!* Instead, there was a little chitchat and everybody walked us to the limo. When we pulled away, I looked back and saw Pauline slip her hand into Jake's as they started up the sidewalk to the house. She was leaning against him, and I have to say it didn't look like a brother-sister thing to me.

"Wow," I whispered under my breath.

"What is it?" David asked.

"Nothing." You think the puzzle fits together only one way, and suddenly the pieces take on new shapes altogether. I wasn't ready to think about the possibility of Pauline and Jake as a couple, much less discuss it.

"Your sister was wearing the same outfit as last time we saw her," David said.

"I told you Angie's never cared about clothes," I said.

"She's such a pretty girl. She could look so much better."

"You can quit with the clothing allowance, David. She's only going to keep it in a savings account and give it back to you, which she would do tomorrow if she wasn't afraid of hurting your feelings."

"You Stallone girls," he said. "Your family is fascinating."

"If you say so," I said, thinking that's because he didn't have one. "What did you talk to my parents about?"

"They wanted to know what's ahead for you," David said.

"You mean my mother wanted to know."

"No, actually, it was Dutch who asked. He seemed concerned about your flying to Europe."

"It's the one thing he's petrified of. Planes. But he doesn't give a rat's ass what happens to me."

"On the contrary."

"You keep *saying* that. On the contrary

bullshit! You saw how he acted."

"I don't understand what that's about, but he does care."

I saw there was no point in arguing. I leaned my head back against the soft leather upholstery and thanked my lucky stars that I was out of that asylum. When I started to drift off, I remembered the exchange between David and my father when we'd first got there.

"What did you say to him, anyway? When he congratulated you for fixing me."

"I said you were the bravest person I had ever met."

"What did he have to say about that?"

"That you had always been like that and he was sure it came from your mother."

"I don't believe you," I said.

He crossed his heart. Then I took his fingers and kissed them one by one. "Thanks for dealing with him."

"What do I get for it?"

The nice thing about stretch limos is there's lots of room to move around. I crawled into his lap. "Anything your heart desires or that I can think up," I said.

We had a button that raised the partition when we needed privacy. The glass was tinted and soundproof, so we were safe getting naked, or at least in this case, I got naked for fear of messing up my new duds. Fortunately, we weren't pulled over by the constabulary on the L.I.E. — Litter is Everything or Long Island Expressway, depending on how disgusted you are at any given stretch — which is, without a doubt, the ugliest hunk of highway on earth. We would have caused somewhat of a scene, but I felt David deserved a reward for taking Dutch on, and I was beginning to think that if David thought I was so tough, why get freaked out by a bunch of rich dudes in Southampton. Besides, sex was the best way I knew to distract myself, and I was dealing with massive confusion here from our visit to Walnut Avenue. My friends and family were not staying put in their accustomed ruts and I didn't know what to make of it. But when in doubt, shut up and put out, is my motto. That's what I did, and in my opinion, it was one of our better trips of many on America's highways and byways.

CHAPTER ELEVEN

I've seen big houses in my day, but this one rivaled the Mall of America. It made me feel like I'd grown up in one of those Monopoly game houses, little green ones. I mean, why does a married couple with no kids and a cockroach of a dog need a house as big as the *QE2*? But hey, this wasn't my territory so I just took David's arm in a ladylike fashion and walked up the driveway those forty miles to the entrance. *Columns Galore*, that's what they should have called the place. Columns at the doors, columns at the windows, even the little generator shed had columns. I was surprised that the hostess didn't have columns stuck to either side of her dress. Actually, she was very welcoming, just a pleasant lady with lipstick smears where air kisses had front-ended her cheeks by mistake.

She led us through a humongous hallway and out onto a patio overlooking the Atlantic. I say patio, which sounds like a sweet little porch, but this was a stretch of flagstone that would accommodate the Los Angeles Philharmonic. There were a couple hundred people milling around. A thin cloud cover had snuck across the sky, softening the glare, and on account of some wind in the night, the waves were really giving the shore a pounding. Short of fog or light rain, it was my favorite kind of beach day. What I really wanted to do was toss off my clothes and take a dip. But I could see right away that the theme of this party was *Who is Bess Stallone and what's the scoop between her and David Montagnier?* When we walked outside, all those faces swiveled around in unison like they'd been cued. There were a lot of famous people I recognized and a lot more I didn't. I was pretty fascinated by the breasts on the famous director's wife. They sat right under her collarbone and were so big she could easily have rested her head on them and grabbed a quick nap.

"Where's Elvis?" I whispered.

"Any minute," David said. "Ready?"

It was only four o'clock and I knew this thing was slated to go through dinner. A stiff breeze blew our words away from the crowd so I was safe looking up at him with a big fake smile to say, "Why don't we just tell them we're sleeping together and they can all relax?" He laughed, put his hand on that place he liked on my spine, and guided me into the lion's den.

It started out a little rough. I stuck to David like we were glued, but he kept getting drawn into conversations in alien tongues. It seemed like every other woman was an incredibly sexy European film star who said stuff like, "Ah, Dah-veed, kum zhe sooey err-rerz duh too vwahr," etcetera, etcetera. The lipstick smears kept working their way closer and closer to his mouth. Then when David would respond in English, they'd look at me, all fake apologetic, and do some of those little shrugs I could never master no matter how many times I practiced in front of the mirror. Anyway, it got tired real quick and so did I.

Next thing, we got talking with a novelist whose brain was so excellent they should use him to figure out why drivers who dangle their arms out their windows are such road hazards. Also very old people in big white American-made cars. But the guy just assumed I had read all the classics (not), and kept saying things like, "But then, Thomas Mann's use of music symbolism is so patently echoed by Saul Bellow . . ."

I'm making it up, but the bottom line was, I didn't know what the fuck he was talking about. At Juilliard, I read *Catcher in the Rye*, which I liked because I thought Holden Caulfield was a pisser and also because it was short. Everything else, I got the Cliff's Notes and shoveled my way through the exams. David tried to help me out with the guy, but he was drilling me for oil. All he got, however, was mud, as in highly intelligent responses like "huh?" and "wha?"

Naturally, I felt just a tad out of my depth. But then I got a big surprise. On the way back from my third escape to the bathroom, which was the kind of place you'd like to move into with your extended family, I saw Sal Peroni talking to a middle-aged man with a beard and a white hat. At first, I couldn't believe my eyes. Like, what was that lowlife who snagged my virtue on the backseat of his LeBaron doing at this blast? Not that he was a lowlife for doing it, because I was certainly dying to get laid. It's just that it was my first time, and he wasn't exactly sensitive about it. But at this point, I would have been happy to see my friendly neighborhood tire slasher. At least I could understand what the hell he was saying.

I went and tugged on Sal's jacket. He turned around and I could see he was totally pleased. He'd put on a little weight and had lost some hair, but he still looked good in a faintly sleazoid way. He gave me a big squeeze, which was comforting. Enough already with those bony handshakes and nonkisses.

"Bess! Man," he said, giving me the old up-and-down. "You are one gorgeous sight. Congratulations."

I glanced at the older guy who was looking at me with lizard eyeballs. They were pretty much all you could see on account of the hat and the thick white beard.

"Oh, sorry," Sal said. "August Nardigger, this is Bess Stallone."

Since Nardigger didn't extend a hand, I did the nod-and-smile. It didn't register with me right away, I was so busy being knocked out to see Sal.

"What the hell are you doing here?" I asked Sal. Then I remembered myself and said to Nardigger, "We went to school together."

"Among other things," Sal said. So he hadn't forgotten the backseat. "I produce movies now," he went on. Porn, I figured. "I'm bending this gentleman's ear about soundtracks. I want a classical composer for the film I'm working on."

I was almost speechless. Almost. "Sal, you're shitting me." Then, with a nod at

Nardigger again, "Sorry." But Nardigger's expression never seemed to change one way or the other. He just went on looking disgusted, like he'd taken a bite out of a big fat garden slug.

"No classical composer worth a damn is going to write a soundtrack," Nardigger said. It sounded like that slug was now stuck halfway up his nose.

"Didn't Aaron Copland . . . ?" I began.

"Aaron Copland was a whore," Nardigger said.

My eyes must have gone a little buggy.

"The pathetic aspect of it was, he didn't even know it," Nardigger went on. Sweat was making dark splotches in his beard. I figured it was the hat, which wasn't doing such a great job of keeping that head of steam bottled up. He was obviously a composer himself, and couldn't stand how successful Copland had been.

"You're getting pretty worked up there," I said. "Why don't you take off your hat and catch some of this soothing sea breeze?"

Sal gave me a warning elbow as Nardigger barked at me, "I never take off the hat. I'm famous for the hat."

"Maybe so," I said, "but for me, you just got famous for bad manners."

As Nardigger stalked off, it dawned on me, *Nardigger.* August Nardigger of *The Listener* fame. "Oops," I said to Sal.

"The man is ordinarily known to love celebrities."

"You mean he's a star fucker," I said.

"Precisely stated. What say we Eyetalians go for a little stroll on the beach."

Sal was half dragging me down toward the water. I looked around for David. I knew I was supposed to be mingling, but so far it had been like cozying up to a convention of porcupines. We walked along a path to the dunes, slid down onto the beach, and left our shoes in the sand. Then we set off in the direction of Rocky Beach.

"How long you think it'd take us to get to Hard Eddie's?" I asked him. Eddie's was a beach joint where they served fried seafood and beer. I sure could have used a brew about then. And I'd just been feeling so grateful to get out of the old neighborhood. As I mentioned, it had been a confusing day.

"You still think about the old days, a famous star like you?" Sal asked.

"First of all, I'm only a junior star and it's probably only temporary, especially when Nardigger writes his next piece. He didn't like the crack about the hat."

"I always knew you'd make it."

"Oh, bullshit, Sal. You must be a natural in Hollywood, slinging it like that."

"I used to listen to you play. You'd sneak into the auditorium sometimes."

I stopped in my tracks and stared at him. "I never saw you."

"Well, it wasn't cool to like classical music, so I hid. Besides, I was scared I'd spook you."

I watched the waves wash over our tracks and leave foot-shaped pools in the packed sand. "All right, Sal. Since we seem to be holding confession here . . ." I just stared at him. I figured he owed it to me to get there first. He turned away and looked out into the Atlantic.

"Okay, I'm not proud of the way I behaved. But I was just a stupid kid."

"I thought you were a nice guy who I could trust."

"We're talking fifteen years old. They never said they were going to show up. You think it was a bunch of laughs for me, having those guys drooling in the window when I didn't know what the hell I was doing?"

I whacked him hard, but it had been a long time coming. "Screwing when you're fifteen is glory for the guy, so don't hand me your sob story. I was looking to lose it, all right, but I wanted romance. I thought you liked me a lot. I thought you were sensitive. All those poems you wrote in English class. They made me cry sometimes. I don't know how I figured it was going to be so romantic in the back of a Chrysler, but I gotta tell you, Sal, I took a lot of grief for that night. I was tough, but I wasn't *that* tough."

The whole thing had been so dopey, with me drinking Chianti out of a bottle and Sal trying to figure out how to get us both undressed with no room to maneuver. He hadn't been in me for more than two seconds before the clowns showed up at the window, giggling their asses off, but I was technically no longer a virgin. I slung the empty wine bottle at Vinnie Basilio and nailed him on the back of the head. Lucky for me he had a skull like concrete or I could've wound up in the slammer for homicide.

"I liked you a lot. I thought you were the sexiest, most amazing girl I'd ever seen. After that night, I knew there was no chance you'd ever see me again, so I got my punishment, too."

"Sometimes I think I've spent the rest of my life trying to get it right." I regret saying that. First of all, it didn't freak me out the way it would any halfway normal teenage girl. I kept thinking it was funny, me and Sal with our bare asses, not knowing what the hell we were doing, and those goofy boys looking for a thrill. I figured, Now I've got him, I might as well rub it in. But the truth was, we were all dumb kids, even the ones who came for the show. Some of those guys were perfectly decent and we all do stupid stuff, especially if there's booze involved, which for me was usually the case in those days.

Sal was looking like a dog I'd just whacked on the nose with a newspaper. "Come on," I said, pulling him toward the surf. It's hard for me to be near water without getting into it. I rolled my pants up to the knees and started wading back toward the party. Sal stuck to the water's edge where he wouldn't mess up the crease in his perfect white pants.

"Okay, Sal," I told him. "I figure we both showed up here so we could put this one to rest. Shall we call it ancient history?"

"Absolutely." We slapped each other five. "So does this mean you'll go out with me?" he asked.

I laughed, pretending I thought he was

joking. He got the point and didn't push me on it.

By the time we got back within view of the *QE2*, the sun was setting and David was standing on the dunes with a face like Darth Vader on a bad day.

"Uh oh," I said. My new linen pants were still rolled up to my thighs and they were soaking wet anyhow.

"More than just business, you and Montagnier?" Sal asked.

I didn't answer. If *People* magazine wasn't allowed to know, I didn't see why I should tell Sal. We found our shoes and climbed the dunes.

"David, this is Sal Peroni, a buddy of mine from home."

They shook hands, but David's eyes barely brushed Sal. He was concentrating on me. And my pant suit. I would have looked better if I'd jumped all the way in.

"There are a lot of people who want to meet you," David said. Then to Sal, "I'm sure you understand." David was so pissed his hair was frying at the roots. Sal backed off in a hurry with a catch-you-later wave.

"I'm sorry," I said. "Sal and I had some catching up to do. Plus I got tangled up with our pal Nardigger."

"August Nardigger's here?"

"The very same." I wrung some of the water out of my pants and slipped my sandy feet into my shoes. "You can't miss him. He's got a white hat implanted in his scalp."

"He's a snob and a hypocrite." The news about Nardigger didn't much elevate David's mood, but at least it got him off my case. I watched the muscles in his jaw clench. That trick always impressed me. Watch the close-ups of Gregory Peck's face in *The Guns of Navarone*. The trouble was, I got the feeling that David was putting Nardigger in the same category with those bad Nazis who were trying to sink our boys. I took his hand and gave it a squeeze.

"Aw, leave it, David. The guy's a jerk and a loser."

David shook his hand free. It felt more violent than a slap from Dutch, I guess because David's touch had always been so tender.

"He wrote unforgivable things in that column," David said, and off he went to fight for my honor, except I knew he was also still furious at me for taking a leave of absence with Sal. What this did was strand me at the edge of the patio to face the peanut gallery that had been enjoying the little drama between David and me. I gave them a cheery smile and went to fetch myself a vodka tonic.

"More," I kept telling the bartender, until we had a nice ratio of half a gallon of Absolut to one teaspoon of tonic. I gulped down most of it, then plunged into the crowd to do my duty.

I talked to a woman who kept tossing her hair like she was having spasms and whose six-year-old son was a musical genius. It turns out there's a prodigy in almost every family in America. I would be so fortunate to participate in the exciting discovery of another Mozart. Obviously, I have to decline these offers, but in this particular case, I was touched by the mother's wish to support her kid without pressuring him. I knew the drill, and advised her where to go for help. I gave her the standard advice, and at the same time kept picking up pieces of a conversation going on behind my back. Two women, one with a penetrating voice. She was trying to keep it low, but her end of the discussion wafted straight into my left ear:

"They say she's moved in with him . . ."

"August says she's nothing much, but he's such a . . ."

"She plays like a dream, but Mary, have you *talked* to her? I think she's some kind of idiot savant . . ."

Then the other woman must have realized who was standing within earshot. There was a sudden silence, and they moved away in a hurry. I started laughing, which confused Wolfgang's mom. I showed her my empty glass and excused myself to head for the bar. On my way, I got snagged by Charlie Rose.

Now, Charlie Rose is on television late at night and the only people who see him have brains that are too busy thinking deep thoughts to let them sleep. The rest of us, if we're awake on account of drinking too much coffee, are watching the talk shows, the porn channel, or prehistoric reruns of *Star Trek*. I only got into Charlie Rose because David watches him religiously, and I'd gotten hooked on him. So when I saw him at that party, he seemed like someone I knew. He must have been a little surprised when I kissed his cheek with a big, "Charlie! I'm glad to see you! Bess Stallone."

"You're quite the sensation," he said. His face was handsome in a droopy way, like he'd been a large friendly bloodhound in a former life.

"Anybody new can be a sensation," I said. "The trick is to hang in there for the long haul."

"Is it true that you don't get anywhere playing Chopin anymore?"

"Who told you that?" I asked.

"Another concert pianist."

"Well, it's true. The public doesn't like contemporary stuff much, but the critics do, or pretend they do. Let me ask you a question. What's an idiot savant?"

"Somebody who's mentally deficient but has a spectacular talent," Charlie said. "Why do you ask?"

"I just heard somebody call me one."

"Here, at this party?"

"Yeah. They didn't know I was listening."

Charlie looked pretty fascinated. "*Are* you one?"

"I might be," I said. It seemed like a pretty fair description to me, but I'd have to do more research.

Charlie smiled. "I think you should come see me on my show."

"If I can bring my partner."

"I don't want David to monopolize the conversation."

"I'll talk if you ask me about cars. I know a lot about cars."

"My people will call Mr. Balaboo on Monday morning."

We smiled at each other and shook hands.

I set off to find David so I could brag that we were practically booked on *The Charlie Rose Show*. I thought it might help him forgive me, but he was going nose to nose with Nardigger over by the swimming pool — except in this case, it was nose to hat brim.

"The trouble is, most of the time, you don't know what you're talking about," David said. "You should go back to writing about art."

"You simply have an aversion to the truth," Nardigger said. I shoved through the guests to take David's arm, but he didn't notice.

"I find it impossible to understand how you could remain impervious to my partner's musical sensitivity," David said. "It's the quality that drew me to her in the first place." I could hear the tremor in his voice. I'd never heard it before and it made me nervous.

Nardigger just raised his champagne glass with the smug smile of a school bully who's gotten a rise out of his latest victim, all the more satisfying because there was an audience.

"Come on, David," I said. "Let's take a stroll on the beach."

"Not until we hear an apology from this gentleman."

There was a growing circle of people surrounding us now. I could see the hostess's face two rows back, her mouth as round as a Cheerio, except there wasn't anything cheery about it. Her party was going right down the hopper.

"First of all, you're not gonna get an apology," I said. "Mister Nardigger is having too much fun. And second, he's not a gentleman. I'm asking you as a favor to me, David. Let's boogie."

I could feel the tension in his arm, like he was ready to let fly at Nardigger. I was having the same problem, actually, only what I was dying to do was flick off that hat. I figured he had a bald head with a big dent in it where some poor musician had clobbered him, or maybe a huge unsightly wen. I only know what a wen is because my grandmother's friend had one on her chin and it was truly heinous. Anyway, before either of us could lose our self-control, David turned and sailed through the crowd. I tripped along behind with my wet pants clinging to my legs. I was aware of flashbulbs going off.

David picked up our suitcases from the front hall and headed down the driveway. I wondered if we were about to hoof it back to Manhattan, but there was Phillip, waiting in the lineup of limos.

"What's Phillip doing here?"

David hadn't said a word to me, so I wasn't sure he'd answer. "I asked him to wait in case Gwen Champling wanted a lift back to the city." Each syllable got its own personal little icicle.

Well, I thought, I guess *she'll* have to hoof it. I have to say I was completely stunned by the intensity of his anger.

"Who're you mad at, me or Nardigger?" I asked after we got into the car.

"Both."

"Okay, let's start with Nardigger because that's easy. Why should you give a shit about a miserable no-talent who has to take everybody down to get his rocks off?"

"Because he's the epitome of everything that's wrong with this world."

"Wait," I said. That was going a touch far. I mean, war, famine, and starvation? But David was on a roll.

"He's totally self-involved. He sees no one else's point of view. He's power-hungry and cruel. These are the precise qualities that cause human misery on a grand scale."

"You make him sound like Stalin," I said, thinking that such a ridiculous concept would make him see how overblown this whole thing was.

"Exactly!" David opened his eyes extra wide so there was white all around the irises. It made everything he said even more intense.

 I was quiet a second. David was stuck in a groove and it was time to get him out. How, was the question. Since logic wasn't going to work, I decided to try a different tactic. "Have you ever seen his head?" I asked. "I mean, without the hat?"

David looked at me like I was the village idiot or maybe just an idiot savant.

"I'm curious," I said. "What's under there, one of those sweeps that starts at the back of the neck?"

David just leaned against the seat and closed his eyes.

"I got us a gig on *Charlie Rose*," I said, but he was asleep. What I want to know is, how can a person go from extreme rage to dreamland in a nanosecond? The guy was o-u-t, just like that. By the time he woke up, we were almost in Queens and I figured I'd try talking to him like he'd never been pissed at me. But he beat me to it.

"Did you really get us *Charlie Rose*?" he asked.

I smiled. "I think so. Mr. Balaboo should

call tomorrow and find out if he was for real."

He took my hand. "I was jealous, Bess. Of that man you were with on the beach."

"That's why you were mad at me?"

He nodded. "I'm sorry. I can't stand sharing you."

"Well, you sure as hell don't have to share me with Sal Peroni," I said, and gave him a nice long kiss.

"I'm sorry I dragged you away from the party," David said. "We were supposed to stay overnight."

I laughed out loud. "Anytime, babe. Southampton has seen the last of my butt for the next decade." I curled up against him. "You been using lemon soap?" I asked him. The scent was very strong. I could smell it straight through the fabric of his shirt.

"Don't see that man again, Bess."

That was easy. "Okay, David, if you quit worrying about the asshole in the white hat."

He didn't answer. I kept up my end of the bargain, but I wish I could say the same for David.

CHAPTER TWELVE

I tried to reach Pauline to grill her about Jake, but her machine kept answering. Jake's recording said he was on vacation. It took Angie to get it through my dense skull that they were probably traveling together. I also had a little emergency discussion with Mr. Balaboo about David's tantrum on the dunes. It had shaken me up, given the stuff I'd read about David when I was in my research phase — that he was gloomy and even difficult. I'd always dismissed that stuff as bullshit. Mr. Balaboo told me that yes, David had experienced "dark phases" but that there was no artist alive who wasn't a pain in the posterior at one time or another. Did I imagine that I was a piece of cake? That was reassuring. A week passed and by then, David and I had become a media event and I forgot about everything else.

Right off the bat, we got a gig playing that old crowd-pleaser, Saint-Saen's *Carnival of the Animals*. It's been arranged a million ways, for just two pianos, for a bunch of different soloists, with or without orchestra — in fact, I'm surprised the

Rolling Stones haven't done a version. It isn't usually performed with full orchestra but we were invited to play the duo-piano version with the New York Philharmonic under guest conductor Vladimir Chesnikov. This was our first time performing with a world-class orchestra, which was intimidating enough, but in the temperamental-genius department, Chesnikov ranks Numero Uno. So on the morning of our first orchestral rehearsal, I got a little lecture from David.

"It's not just Chesnikov's size, which you'll see is formidable," David said. "He's a maniac for perfection, a real throwback to the old days of the tyrants."

"I heard he gave Gabrelli a nervous breakdown," I said. We'd been practicing day and night and I'd thought I was starving, but suddenly the blueberry muffin didn't look so appetizing. I shoved my plate aside.

"True. Eduardo wasn't prepared, or at least Chesnikov didn't think so. The maestro was so humiliating in dress rehearsal that Eduardo broke down and couldn't perform."

"Didn't Gabrelli sue or something?"

"He tried but nothing came of it. Now, Bess, don't look so sick. You're ready." He gave me a grin full of mischief. "Except for that rubato section."

We'd nearly come to blows over a couple of measures that morning. I wadded my napkin up and tossed it at him. It bounced off his forehead and landed in his coffee cup for two points. First of all, just because I hadn't passed out at any recent performances didn't mean I wasn't petrified. Stepping out onstage was still like hanging by my thumbs over the edge of the Empire State Building. And this was the big time. Not Weill Recital Hall *in* Carnegie Hall but the genuine article itself, Isaac Stern Auditorium. Now, though, every time I started to get that old familiar fireworks thing going behind my eyes, I'd peer through it at David or even think about him and that made all the difference. I threw on a pair of jeans and a cotton sweater. If I was going to get yelled at by the Russian, at least I could be comfortable.

"You're wearing that?" David asked. He was a Ralph Lauren ad in cream linen slacks and a black blazer.

"Yeah."

"Hm," he said, in that way that suggested maybe the French didn't invent cheeseburgers, but at least they knew how to dress.

I threw him "the look," which is what David called the expression I got when no amount of bullying or even a terrific bribe would get me to change my mind. He held his hands up in defeat — a hundred hours of haggling over musical decisions had taught him to pick his spots. I wrapped a couple of muffins in tinfoil for Phillip, the driver, because he was looking too thin, and off we went to face the monster.

Some people love the pitter-patter of rain on the roof or a birdcall in the woods. What does it for me is the sound of an orchestra tuning up. A clarinet snatching a last-minute run-through of a difficult part, a cello practicing a chromatic scale, a violinist demonstrating her pizzicato technique, the rumble of the tympani, and all of it going on simultaneously. Back in the poverty days, I'd crane my neck around a column (they called it "limited vision" at the box office) and look way down at the orchestra. I could imagine being an alien, staring down from my flying saucer and wondering why those Earth creatures were rubbing hairy sticks across wooden boxes or blowing through shiny pieces of metal. It could look strange and maybe pointless, but then, oh, man, some genius like Schumann made dots on paper and organized those funny gestures into sounds that could tear your heart out. Hanging over the edge of the balcony and listening to somebody like Ojawa conduct was about the closest I ever got to religion.

Anyhow, I let David go off to greet Chesnikov while I stood and listened to the tune-up. David's piano was already there, and as I watched, stagehands rolled mine out from the other side. This was before we chose our semipermanent pianos from down the street at Steinway. What they do is keep instruments on hand for particular pianists to use when they're in town. Unless you're like Horowitz and haul your own all over the world with you. But for this first concert, we'd spent two hours at Carnegie Hall the day before trying out various pianos until we found the best pair. It's hard enough to choose one for solo performance — there's something wrong with every instrument. If a piano has extra brilliance, it can lose out on subtleties. If the action's great, maybe the soft pedal's sluggish. A lot depends on the program, like if you're playing strictly romantic pieces. Then it's easier to choose an instrument that matches the music, but most programs are a mix. When you add another pianist to the soup, it really gets complicated. Then you've got the issue of balance to deal with along with everything else.

David came down to the first row of seats where I was trying not to have a meltdown and introduced me to Vladimir Chesnikov. He bowed and kissed my hand. So far so good — at least he didn't bite my fingers off.

"Mademoiselle Stallone," he said, "you excuse me please that my English is not so good. You speak Italian maybe so?"

I shook my head. "Sorry, but it's okay. Just tell David. He'll translate."

He made another bow. "Are we ready to begin?"

"Sure," I said, and we went up onstage. Chesnikov had a conference in German with the concertmaster while David and I did some warm-ups. When Chesnikov hopped up on his podium, everybody started producing "A's" like their lives depended on it.

How to explain what it's like to play music with the full weight of an orchestra behind you? After hours of practicing your little piece in the privacy of your apartment and imagining the instrumental parts, suddenly you're out there with all those amazing musicians, the conductor raises his baton, and next thing you know, you're riding that huge sound like it's a living thing, beautiful and wild and strong. I was so high I almost passed out from the joy of it, forget about being nervous.

The whole first half of the rehearsal went pretty well although the maestro got real peeved when the bassoon came in one measure ahead of us.

"I trust you don't do *everything* too early, Mister Jonas," he said, with this mean little smirk. Of course, the orchestra snickered, figuring they'd better act like they appreciated the joke, but it seemed unnecessarily malicious to me. Jonas was a dorky little guy who was so embarrassed that even his ears turned red. Otherwise, though, things went pretty smoothly for a while, with Chesnikov giving David a few minor suggestions and David translating for me. I was beginning to think that the conductor's legendary tantrums were kind of like those stories we used to scare each other with when we were kids, about the guy with the hook-hand who killed couples parked by the beach at night. Namely, bullshit. I did notice that there wasn't a single other woman in the orchestra.

Finally, we got to the section I especially love. There's a piano entrance that's so soft it's almost a whisper. We're talking swans in the text here so the sound should drift in very quietly. Well, Chesnikov kept giving a downbeat like these swans were more like the Hitler Youth out for their morning marching exercises. Okay, I'm exaggerating, but the thing was, it didn't sound like fucking swans to me. So first I asked David to ask Chesnikov if he could ask if the orchestra could come in a bit more softly. Chesnikov nodded and proceeded to conduct the entrance exactly the same way. I stopped playing, and waved my hand, figuring let me try it this time.

"The entrance, Maestro, could it be more softly, please?"

He glared down at me from his perch. "It *is* soft, mademoiselle."

"But maybe even *more*," I said. I looked at David for help. "How do you say drifting, like swans drifting on the water?"

"*Comme les cynges derivent sur l'eau*," David suggested to Chesnikov. His voice cracked a little and suddenly the orchestra was real quiet. Everyone was staring at Chesnikov and me like we were two trains speeding toward each other on the same track. Even though you know it's going to be really gruesome you can't tear your eyes away.

"Once again, same measure," Chesnikov said, with totally fake patience. The veins in his neck were beginning to turn kind of purple, probably not a great sign, and David was shooting me these shut-*up* looks across the pianos. But when the orchestra came in, it was no different. Too damn military for fucking swans. I stopped playing and put my hands in my lap. Chesnikov lowered his baton, stood very still, then turned to David.

"You must do better to control your woman." Chesnikov spit out "woman" like it meant something close to "vermin." Funny, he used English for *that* crack.

David opened his mouth to say God knows what, but before he had a chance, Chesnikov spun around and started raging on me, poking the air in the direction of my face with his baton.

"I try to excuse you, mademoiselle, because you have no experience. I understand you are not a cultured person and you come from low circumstances. But you behave like an *idiot*." When he said "idiot," he rapped the baton on the lid of the piano with so much force that the sucker jumped out of his hand and slid under the cellos. Not to mention the scar he made in the finish of the Steinway.

Well, this was the second time I'd heard myself referred to as an idiot — and Chesnikov didn't even have the courtesy to add the "savant" part. I suppose I should have been thinking about how maybe this wasn't the perfect way for David and me to make our official debut with an orchestra, but I've just never been able to tolerate a bully. I waited for him to take a breath and then I just started talking normally. I guess curiosity got the better of him, because after a few more screams, he clamped his mouth shut and listened. I pretended he hadn't been acting like a lunatic and talked to him like we'd been having a totally civilized conversation.

"With all respect, Maestro, I'd just as soon David and I don't come off sounding like we're doing halftime at the Superbowl. I mean, our asses are on the line here, too." Then it occurred to me that he probably wouldn't be too familiar with American football. "The entrance would be more correct if it was quieter, that's all I'm saying. No big deal."

"Correct!" That did it. "Correct! COR-R-R-RECT!" Chesnikov turned to David and started yelling in French, but I mean, we're talking major decibels here. I noticed out of the corner of my eye that a pill bottle was making the rounds in the first violin section. The truth is, the amount of beta-blockers sucked down in the orchestra before any performance is directly related to how scary the conductor is, and those fiddlers were popping them like breath mints. Meanwhile, I was trying to figure out what Chesnikov was screaming at David. I figured something like, "Get rid of that crazy bitch or your career is down the hopper."

I was sitting there thinking, *So, Bess, you probably just screwed yourself and maybe yanked David right down with you. Maybe you'd better figure out a way to dig yourself out.* I stood up, went over to Chesnikov, and got hold of his hand, which was kind of like grabbing a guided missile out of the air it was moving around so fast. I could hear the orchestra kind of gasp in unison, like "Oh Christ, what's this nut going to do now, knock the maestro off his stand?" But my touching him was drastic enough to get his attention. He tried to shake my hand off, but I hung on with a pianist's grip.

"Maestro," I said, "Maestro Chesnikov. Please, I'd like to apologize." I figured, Okay, humble pie can't taste much worse than the shit I used to eat when I was a waitress. Chesnikov was gawking at me like

I'd been let out of the zoo just that morning.

"You're totally right. I know squadoosh about most things and I'm very inexperienced. I did grow up in circumstances that would be foreign to you — I don't know if I'd call them low."

His mouth had dropped open a little. I mean, how would you react if an inferior animal, say an orangutan, opened its mouth and started speaking in complete sentences? But at least I'd shocked him into listening.

"I got here because good people helped me and I worked my butt off. I've always admired your work." No kidding, Chesnikov's recording of Beethoven's Fifth Symphony was timeless. "But in my old neighborhood, you speak up if something's bugging you. That's all I was doing. If I was rude, I apologize with all my heart."

Okay, I confess that I had tears in my eyes, but everything I was saying was totally true. I just left out a few things, like how screaming assholes don't impress me because I was raised by the world champion.

Chesnikov surprised me by stepping off the podium and, still holding my hand, leading me into the wings. There were stagehands lined up like spectators at a really bloody boxing match. He shooed them away so we could have some privacy.

"You understand, mademoiselle, that I have the power to ruin you."

I nodded. "I sure hope you won't do that, Maestro."

"You must acknowledge that I am the boss of you here. Of everybody here."

"I understand, sir," I said. "But does that mean I can't question anything we do?"

He took both of my hands and shook them up and down. "One time you can ask, and then we do as I say."

I thought for a couple of seconds. I knew this was as far as he was going to go and also that he thought he was making a major concession — like, Okay, I'll even listen to the little twerp at the piano.

"Okay, that's fine with me."

"Tell me, what is squadoosh?"

That took me back for a minute. Then I remembered and couldn't help a little smile. "Squadoosh is nothing, *nienta, nada.*"

He stared into my face for what seemed like a long time. Then he said, "You're not afraid of me, are you?"

"No," I said.

He did something with his mouth where I couldn't tell if he was pleased or pissed. Then he put his arm around my shoulder and led me back out onto the stage. The racket died in a nanosecond. Instant silence. I went straight for the piano and didn't even look at David. Somebody had retrieved Chesnikov's baton. He tapped it on the stand.

"Mademoiselle Stallone and I have come to an understanding." He made it sound like I'd agreed to be his personal slave for the remainder of his life. But hey, I wasn't about to quibble. "Now, if we are all ready to work," he went on, "we begin again the same famous measure, a little bit soft but squadoosh the rallentando. It's not a funeral." Which meant we were still going to play the damn thing like it was the finish of the New York Marathon, but at least it would be a *soft* marathon.

When we got to the end of our final run-through, the orchestra applauded for ages — which means the strings tapped their bows against their stands and everybody else shuffled their feet. I know it's a strange tradition, but it sure warmed my heart even if I wasn't exactly sure which performance they were so enthused about, David and me at the keyboard or me mouthing off to Chesnikov. I was kind of expecting David to give me a hard time later, but instead he yanked me into a dressing room, locked the door, and kissed me until I thought my mouth would fall off. That is, when he wasn't laughing too hard for kissing. David said the orchestra wanted to award me the Croix de Guerre, which I guess is the French version of the Purple Heart.

That night we got a standing ovation. Chesnikov made a big deal out of kissing my hand and acting like I was his own personal discovery while David was sort of stuck off on his own. Come to think of it, this was probably the beginning of that Bess-worship stuff that started maybe from the time we appeared on *The Charlie Rose Show*. It turns out a lot more mainstream people watch him than I thought, and they seemed to identify with the fact that I sounded more like the guy who fixed their transmission than some fancy piano player. Right after that, *People* magazine did a little piece. Mr. Balaboo said it would promote sales of our first CD. The magazine acted like the article would be about David and me, but it turned out to be eighty-five percent me. Most of the photos were of me, with David kind of hanging out behind like maybe he was my hairdresser. They even took one of me in the kitchen, making it look like I was cooking when I was actually throwing coffee grinds in the garbage, coffee that David had made, obviously. Anyhow, people had started turning me into this folk hero, like I was a classical-piano version of Jennifer Beals in *Flashdance.* So the night of the Chesnikov concert, a lot of ticket holders from the cheap seats had brought flowers and came down during the ovation to toss them on the stage. It was embarrassing, especially since it was obvious they were mostly for me and not for David. I did this thing I'd seen a ballerina do with her partner, which was take the prettiest rose and give it to him, but the whole business was kind of upsetting. The way I saw it, David was responsible for his own success and for mine, too.

Afterward, Pauline and Jake came backstage. It was frustrating because the place was wall-to-wall bodies and all I wanted to do was get them into a corner and find out what was going on. I tried whispering in Pauline's ear when she hugged me, but Mrs. Edelmeyer had brought her bridge partner and wanted to discuss ways to mix legato and staccato in the Bach Partita she was working on. She practically dragged me away from Pauls and started right in explaining to her friend that "Bess and I don't believe in playing Bach metronomically." I gave Pauline and Jake a helpless look and that was the last I saw of them. Vernon showed up, of course, except all I got to see were his eyes over somebody else's shoulder. It was completely nuts in there.

David and I got into this habit after our concerts of driving around in the limo to discuss the performance. We sure couldn't do it backstage in the conductor's suite, and there was usually a party or a jam session afterward. So we'd escape with Phillip for half an hour or so and drive around the park or even just sit in traffic until we'd picked our performance apart note by note. That night, I was more worried about David's feelings being hurt than anything else.

"I'm uncomfortable with all those groupies from the balcony and Chesnikov making such a big deal," I said.

David busted open a bottle of champagne, which he could do without so much as a dribble onto the leather upholstery. He handed me a glass. "Why uncomfortable?"

"Because I'm just a little snot from Rocky Beach. You're the star."

"You have to understand, Bess. The public has a very short attention span. You're a novelty now, but over time, they'll get used to you and it'll be your work that counts."

I didn't want to say anything about the media madness that had been humming around David for at least ten years.

"They all *should* be excited," he went on. "You're the most inspiring performer to show up in a long time." He raised his glass. "To the little snot from Rocky Beach." Then he laughed. "My God, you really made Chesnikov go ballistics."

We clinked glasses, and we were off on our nitpicky routine with me complaining how we were too rigid about making a diminuendo on every single falling cadence and him arguing that otherwise we would have overwhelmed the orchestra in those spots and me answering back that there's no way we could ever overpower that orchestra, and on and on. It was fun and constructive and put all the bullshit in perspective because wasn't this really supposed to be all about the music?

After that we went to a Park Avenue party that would have been painful except a bunch of people from the orchestra were there and we got a little jam session going — David and me on piano doing a funky duet kind of thing (you should hear my walking bass line), a viola, an oboe, and a trombone. We played Sondheim and Brubeck and McCartney, and we all got drunk. Then David and I went home and made love a few times, still riding the adrenaline.

I woke up feeling like I'd been hit by a cement mixer. Happy enough from all that music and sex, but wrung out. I staggered out of bed to look for David. He was sitting at the kitchen table with a pile of newspapers. When he raised his eyes, I thought somebody had died.

"What happened?"

"The reviews."

"We got panned?"

He shook his head. "Smith gave us a rave. So did Barstable and Larson and Newburger."

"That just leaves . . ." I went over and picked up *The Listener*.

"Nardigger."

I read it in silence, except for some snorts, sniffs, and curses. I've repressed most of it, but unfortunately I still haven't been able to forget the part where he said:

David Montagnier continues his sad decline, making a career out of pandering to the public in a way we haven't seen since the late lamented Liberace.

I pictured August Nardigger at his laptop with his white hat covering up his giant carbuncle, chuckling away as he did his best to ruin our careers. David was looking so mournful it seemed like a good idea to make physical contact. I drew up a chair so that our thighs would touch. "So what's the deal with this asshole anyhow?" I asked. "Why's he got it in for you?"

"Maybe he's got a point," David said.

"You've got to be kidding me. Look at this. Here." I read to him from the other reviews, winding up with Smith, for thirty-five years the most respected critic of the *Times*.

David Montagnier, always a first-rate technician, shows not only renewed energy but a depth of interpretive sensitivity that surfaces in only our finest musicians. As a soloist or as a duo pianist, Montagnier has always pleased the ear. Now he is simply sublime.

"What's wrong with that?" I asked.

"Nardigger may be cruel but he's not

stupid." David got up and went to stare out the window. "I feel sometimes that I'm not the artist I was," he said. "It happens to so many musicians, taking the easy route. And now we're about to go off to London to play the *Carnival* again, and the *Scaramouche*, for God's sake."

"And the Blemberg, don't forget, which you sure as hell can't say is pandering to public taste unless the public likes listening to a bunch of alley cats screeching on the back fence. Not that I have anything against alley cats." David and I had fought over that one. There are other contemporary composers who write interesting stuff that doesn't make you feel like somebody's splitting your brain with a hacksaw. He'd won, but only in exchange for a beautiful Sonata for Two Pianos by Yang Su. I thought it was like water flowing over rocks but David maintained it was more like water flowing through the dishwasher. The point was, we played plenty of controversial music, so it was clear that Nardigger was either misinformed or full of shit and it was hard to understand why David would let the guy get to him like this. I had never seen him so disturbed. Not just pissed or upset or aggravated, all of which he'd been at one time or another. But so shaken. I put my arms around him from behind and pressed my cheek against his back. I thought so much love would have to sink into him from my body to his. I didn't realize then that Nardigger's words had seeped into a dark place in David's mind where they were festering like evil little worms.

David spun around so fast he almost knocked me over.

"We're getting out of here." And off he went half running into the bedroom with me loping after him.

"Where? What?" Last I knew, we were only supposed to be thinking about what to pack for London. The U.K. makes you go through all kinds of complicated paperwork to perform there and nothing was for sure yet.

"Put some things together for the weekend. We're going to my place upstate."

"Upstate? What place? *David?*" I felt like I'd wandered into the wrong apartment. Who was this guy and what the hell was he talking about? He looked like my David. He was gorgeous all right, but he was tossing stuff around like we only had ten minutes to get out before Godzilla consumed Manhattan.

"Bess, if I'm not mistaken, you have an important date coming up." He shot me a little grin that went a long way toward reassuring me.

I thought a minute. "Oh, yeah. My birthday." Big deal. We'd just played at Carnegie Hall and he was talking about birthdays. "How did you know?"

"I have my sources," he said. He was slinging jeans and flannel shirts into his bag.

"Where is this place and how come I never knew about it?"

"It's in the Berkshires about twenty miles from Tanglewood."

"Okay, that's part one. And?"

"Aren't you going to pack? You'll need warm clothes. The nights can be cool even in July."

I went and sat down in his suitcase. Not on it, in it. It was the only way I could get his attention. "Talk to me," I said.

"I have that house and two more apartments — one in Paris and one in the Virgin Islands. I wasn't trying to hide anything. The subject just never came up."

"Hey, look, David, I shared one bathroom with three other people for most of my life. You're talking a lot of real estate here. Plus, I don't know, it seems important where you choose to hang your hat. What do you do about music in these places?"

"Oh, they all have pianos. Now are you going to come with me or not?"

I climbed out of his suitcase. "What the hell," I said.

"Okay. Be ready in ten minutes."

At the time, I swallowed David's explanation that Phillip had a family obligation and couldn't drive us. Instead, David had rented a four-wheeler and drove it himself. I got a huge kick out of David's driving. I don't know why I expected him to be somewhat lame behind the wheel. In fact, he was really good at it but *fast*. I hadn't been on the Autobahn yet so I didn't understand that in Europe, if you're going seventy, it's like you're barely out of first gear. We got a ticket from a trooper on the Taconic, which David seemed to think was par for the course. God knows how many points he had on his license.

Anyhow, it only took us about three hours even with the ticket to get to the mountain house. I called it that because to me, a Long Island person, where standing on a road bump gives you altitude sickness, the Berkshires seemed positively Alpine. To get there, we had to drive into the woods along a dirt road. When you got to a lake, the road ran alongside it for a while and then stopped at David's. He not only owned the house but also the woods for miles around, even the lake. I didn't know you *could* own a lake.

"You see why we didn't bring the limo?" David asked, slinging our bags out onto the porch.

"Yeah, but I still want to know what's up with Phillip." I'd thought the guy told me everything important that happened in his life. Like a couple months ago his bedroom wallpaper slid off. I kid you not. Phillip woke up in the morning and it was lying in these sad piles on the floor. I couldn't figure out why he didn't tell me something was up with his favorite niece, which was the bullshit David was handing me.

But David took me inside and I couldn't believe how beautiful it was. He had a caretaker who'd aired it out so it wasn't musty like a place that's been empty for too long. There was a light piney kind of scent in the air, maybe from the thick wood planks on the floor and the paneled walls. Huge windows made you feel like you were living in a tree house. And the lake glistened out back like a silver platter.

Where the house sat, the water made a kind of protected cove. You could sit on the back porch and watch the deer who came to drink on the opposite shore.

"How can you stay away from here?" I asked him. He stood behind me with his chin resting on my head.

"I knew you'd like it," he said. Something in his voice made me think other people hadn't, like maybe Terese, but I didn't want to spoil the mood by asking. I swiveled around in his arms.

"You're full of surprises. You got any other little secrets that just haven't come up?"

There was just the weeniest hesitation in his face, enough to get my antennae buzzing. "David?"

But he led me over to the piano, a rare Model C Steinway that they don't even make anymore. "I got it at an estate sale," he said. "You want to give it a try?"

I sat down and ran through some Brahms intermezzi while David went to mess around in the kitchen. As far as I was concerned, we could stay in this place for the duration, like a thousand years or so.

The caretaker had stocked the fridge, so we ate a cold picnic out on the back porch and watched the light die over the lake. I was never happier than when I was near the water — the ocean, a lake, a river, it didn't matter. I felt clean and peaceful just looking at it. I guess that's why I was drawn to music that reminded me of water. In fact, David got so sick of me nagging him about how we should play with a more "liquid tone" that he threatened to submerge me and my piano in a big tank and make me perform in scuba gear.

But that night I didn't think about rehearsing or performing or the new demands that I knew would be exhausting. We drank wine and watched the deer across the little cove, dipping their heads to drink and sending ripples to us like it was their side of the conversation. We sat for a long time in the dark. Silence is something you forget when you're surrounded by the city symphony. Even in the middle of Central Park, you're aware of the beat — the sirens, a boom box, a helicopter overhead. I had forgotten about silence. I inhaled it with deep breaths like the sweet clean air.

By nine o'clock, my eyes wouldn't stay open. David, on the other hand, seemed wired, which at the time I assumed was his response to the place, that it energized him.

"I've gotta hit the sack," I said. "Point me in the right direction."

I remember David throwing a quilt over me and I was out. I don't think I dreamed. I don't think I moved a muscle until the next thing I knew, David was stroking my cheek and whispering in my ear.

"Bess . . . Bess." The way he said my name was full of excitement. "Bess. Wake up."

"Is it morning?" I asked.

"Yes. Two o'clock."

"Two?" Boy, was I confused.

"Come with me."

I let him pull me to the edge of the bed. While I sat there nodding off, he put my socks and shoes on and wrapped me in a warm jacket.

"Are we leaving? Are there bears?" I was so groggy I hardly knew if I was awake or dreaming.

He led me out onto the porch, holding me tight beside him. We stood there for a moment, looking out over the water. Lights floated across the surface as far as the eye could see.

"Did the stars fall in the lake?" I asked, still more than half asleep. I felt like I was gazing down into the sky.

"Come," David said. He led me to the

water. There was a raft waiting there and on it was a piano and a chaise longue piled with blankets. We stepped across and David settled me in the chair, tucking the blankets all around me. Then he pushed us away from the shore with a pole and we were floating with all those stars. When we drifted close I could see that each star was a tiny boat with a candle on it. I turned to David, who was watching my face in the shimmering light.

"Happy birthday, darling," he said. He kissed me on both cheeks and went to the piano. He played the things he knew I loved, starting with the Bach Prelude in C major that I'd told him the night we got locked in Weill Hall reminded me of light and water. The man truly paid attention. Then the sweetest of Chopin's Nocturnes, the *Berceuse* and the Third Sonata in B minor, Debussey's *Claire de Lune* and *Sunken Cathedral*, the first movement of Beethoven's *Moonlight*, Scriabin's Étude in C-sharp minor, and on and on as I lay there drifting in light and music, floating in the summer sky. I cried. Of course I cried. I still cry when I think of it. I'll never forget it. Never my whole life long.

CHAPTER THIRTEEN

You would think, knowing me, that I would have tortured David with questions about the logistics. But the funny thing was, I didn't. I remember he pulled us back to shore by a rope that must have been attached to a tree. Then we went to bed and made love, and there was this feeling it was for the last time and that maybe the world was going to end. I remember hearing vehicular sounds in the night, like something heavier than cars, and I'm sure that Phillip had a hand in it. I slept very late, and when I woke up, the lake was naked, no float, no candles, only little wrinkles from the breeze. But I didn't want to know the details. It was magic, that's all, and I wanted it to stay that way.

When we got back to New York, the first thing David did was call Mr. Balaboo to get him to buy a computer, to be delivered immediately. Now, David was about as talented at computers as I was at floral arrangement. He knew there was something called the Internet. Beyond that, you were barking up the wrong brain.

I was trying to figure out what clothes to take to London. From what I understood, the temperature on any given day ranged somewhere between 20 and 80 degrees Fahrenheit. I slung another fold-up umbrella into my suitcase and said, "Are you getting electronic on me?"

"Everybody ought to have a computer," he said. "Take both of those sweaters."

"Won't it be like asking a guppy to fly the space shuttle?"

He rolled his eyes at me and made like he was swimming. But within an hour, we had a fabulous laptop with a modem and a printer, the whole works. Forget everybody ought to have a computer. Everybody ought to have a Mr. Balaboo.

I remember that David laughed that day. My cell phone went off and I reached down my V neck, pulled out the phone, and answered it. As soon as I hung up, David said, "Where exactly do you keep that phone?"

"Between my tits, sometimes if I'm in a rush," I said. "It's like with egg cartons and paper towels." He was looking more and more confused. "You know, in your grocery bags, the eggs between the towels, so the eggs don't get broken?"

For some reason, David found that extremely funny. Maybe I remember his laugh because they got pretty rare after that. It turned out that what he had in mind was for me to search the Internet and track down every review August Nardigger ever wrote. I told him I thought he'd wasted his money, that Nardigger's old reviews wouldn't be on the Web, that there might be some in *The Listener* archives. But he wasn't kidding around. Once I had the thing installed at a desk in the bedroom, he pulled up a chair and started ordering me around the World Wide Web. David was right, actually. There were a number of reviews that went back a few years, and they were all nasty. It was the same old stuff, basically — David was a pretty boy who cashed in on his good looks and could never be taken seriously as a pianist. With each item, David became more and more agitated until he started hopping up after each one and pacing around the room.

"Didn't I tell you Nardigger wants to destroy me?" he asked. He kept grabbing clothes from the pile on the bed and putting them down again. I could tell he wasn't even aware he was doing it. "See if you can find the one he wrote about the Berlin concert in September 'ninety-one."

"No, this is stupid," I said. "You're getting your Jockeys in a twist over nothing."

He wagged a finger at me. "Know your enemy, Bess."

I laughed. I mean, I really thought he was joking. Nardigger, that twit, with who-knows-what unsightly avocado-size wart hiding under his hat. The enemy?

David glared at me for a few seconds, a white-faced furious look that made me feel like I'd just been hit with a blast of polar air. It gave me goose bumps.

"I'm going out," he said.

"Phil's coming in an hour to take us to the airport," I said.

He didn't answer, just swept past me. I heard the door slam. There was the odor of lemons, so strong that I checked to see if we had left a slice or peel lying around the bedroom somewhere.

David was only gone for twenty minutes or so. He came straight into the bedroom, handed me a bunch of baby roses, and told me he was sorry.

"I was a horse's asshole," he said. "Forgive me."

Well, who can hold a grudge after such a graceful apology? I let him kiss me and then I asked him if he smelled lemons.

"Do you, Bess? You smell lemons here?" The way his face looked, it was like I'd mentioned some deadly gas leak that was going to wipe us out any second.

"Lemons, not cyanide," I said.

He wrapped his arms around me. "I'll never hurt you again," he said. "I promise."

A lot of commotion over a new laptop, I was thinking, and maybe tension over this trip together. It's one thing to fly to Utica, New York, and something else to cross the Atlantic. Of course, I didn't realize at the time that the lemon aroma was coming from David's skin, and that when I smelled it, we were not going to have the kind of day you can stamp on your calendar with a big fat smiley face.

This being my first trip abroad, in fact my first trip out of the northeast except for the one vacation at the trailer park in Orlando, I was counting on some pep talk, some encouragement, some shared excitement. But all the way over to London on the plane, David studied the handbook that came with his computer. He didn't seem pissed anymore, but I actually counted the words he said to me and they came to a grand total of twelve. That's "Do you want to get out?" times two.

So about London. It's a joke how it's just like in the movies — double-decker buses,

flowers hanging off the outsides of build-
ings, and cops with those helmets made for
coneheads. I guess the thing that surprised
me most was the way the Brits put their
kids on leashes just like their dogs. Not
that we had much time for sight-seeing.
About two seconds after we got to our
hotel, there was a call asking us to perform
in Rome in three days.

We stayed in Claridge's, the kind of
place where you get arrested if they catch
you with a hole in your socks. It was *hushed*
in there, too, which only made me want to
yell something rowdy about the queen, another thing that could get you arrested. We
got this suite that had a bedroom, a living
room with a fireplace, a bathroom where
you needed a map to find the sink, and a
wraparound terrace. Everything in there
was plaid — the furniture, the carpet, the
walls, the curtains, the bedspread, even the
picture frames. A wee bit overboard, in my
opinion, except I liked that they had a bar
stocked with single-malt scotch — in
keeping with the theme, I guess. I'd never
tried the stuff before, and it turns out to be
right up there with Bud as my beverage of
choice. Another thing about the bathroom,
the showerhead in there was as big around
as a dinner plate, and I'm not exagger-

ating. You felt like you were in a rain forest, not to mention you needed a ladder to climb into the tub. There were also all these mysterious buttons next to the light switch that were for summoning servants, just in case you needed an emergency housemaid to iron your knickers.

The concert was at the Royal Festival Hall. With a name like that, you'd be thinking gold leaf and statues, but it was just an ugly concrete building. I figured the British audience would be too well bred to scream their brains out, but I was wrong. They went wacko and we had to play five encores. Afterward, there was a party at some lord's house.

"What do I call the hostess?" I asked David.

"Lady Barton," he said.

"I might giggle."

"Fine. You giggle," he said, and then gave me a huge fifteen-second kiss. I felt as though he was gradually thawing out after that frozen look he'd given me over the Nardigger business. Maybe it helped being a few thousand miles away.

"Are you nervous to be meeting all these lords and ladies?" he asked.

"Nah, only curious."

"You were uncomfortable at the Hamptons thing. What's the difference?"

"I won't ever be again," I said.

"Why?"

"Because I realized, Okay, maybe that person speaks better English than I do, and she's gorgeous and brilliant, but I think to myself, *Yeah, but can she play Prokofiev's Third?*"

He lifted my hand to his mouth and kissed my fingers one by one. "Don't you think it's odd, Bess, that our backgrounds couldn't be more different and yet we're on equal feet? I feel we're twins."

"Shit, I hope not!" I didn't correct him on the equal feet, which I liked a lot better than equal footing.

"Twin souls," he said.

"Okay," I agreed. "Our souls occupy the same psychic peapod."

We pulled up in front of this place that I thought was Buckingham Palace but which only turned out to be the city residence of Lord and Lady Barton. Their main domicile was in Something-on-Rye, which I assumed was not a slice of Pepperidge Farm. I took the elbow of my twin pea and we had ourselves a perfectly charmed-I'm-sure time with the royal types, although it wasn't exactly happy hour at Hard Eddie's.

That night, we were a little the worse for

wear from all that curtseying and bowing, so we went straight to our roomy plaid bed without any fooling around. That first night in what I called the Braveheart Suite, we pretty much collapsed.

That is, until three in the morning when all that booze kicked in and I had to pee desperately. I was still half-drunk and jet-lagged besides, so I kind of stumbled around in the dark looking for the light. The button didn't seem to work, but I managed to find the john. I flushed, and headed back out to grope my way to the bedroom and what I found instead was the starched chest of a very tall man. He must have been wearing black because he was totally invisible. I, on the other hand, was bare-assed naked. I yelped loud enough to wake the queen mother. A voice rose up out of the black figure, and I must say, it didn't seem the least bit perturbed. This is what it said:

"Madame, you rang?"

I swear. Oh my God, it was the fucking *butler!* Instead of the light switch, I must have pressed the button that said "Valet." And they don't even lock the doors, because as everyone knows, a butler is beyond theft and so discreet that no matter what he finds when he opens that door, he'll never tell even if they torture him.

Well, obviously, I started laughing and couldn't stop. And apologizing and snorting and making who the hell knows what kind of rude American noises. What he said, as he let himself out, was, "Not to worry, madame." If you timed him, I'm sure it took at least five seconds to say those four words, not like me, where even my longest sentences average about half a sneeze. Then of course I went in and bounced on David and made him wake up so I could tell him what happened.

The London papers were pretty kind to me. I figured they wouldn't approve since there's supposed to be such a rigid class system over there. Lady Stallone I'm not, but maybe it doesn't count if you're from the colonies. Anyhow, I got very respectful reviews, even from the superbrainy types. David wasn't so lucky. Not that they slammed him or anything, but there were references to his lacking energy and dragging the tempo. The *Times* even suggested he needed to brush up his technique. I felt a little queasy from jet lag and couldn't sleep, so I got to the papers first. I wondered if I could get away with stuffing them into the trash, but obviously that was pointless. I waited in dread for David to wake up and watched him read the reviews over his espresso and scones, watched his shoulders droop, watched his fist clench and loosen. He looked up at me with eyes that seemed to belong to somebody else.

"It's Nardigger," he said. "He's gotten to them."

"What? No, David. No, that wouldn't happen."

"You're naïve, Bess. In this business, they're all in league with one another."

I went over and draped myself around his neck. "It's just a little phase. Please don't worry so much."

"What do you mean, a phase? Do you notice a decline in my performance?"

"No, no, I mean the critics. You've just hit a bumpy patch with them. Not even bumpy, just the tiniest little blip. Look, David, Raven says great things about you. Wouldn't any pianist be ecstatic to get this review from such a respected critic?" I grabbed Raven's review and pointed at the good parts. *"David Montagnier's customary perfect taste and fine ear for dynamics.* What's wrong with that?"

"Keep reading."

I didn't have to. I remembered.

Despite his many virtues, Montagnier

still struggles with consistency in the fluid passages, a tendency perhaps most noticeable in the Saint-Saens. But it's a minor irritant in an otherwise sensitive and stirring performance.

"He said it was minor," I murmured. I heard how lame I sounded.

"Do you think I'm inconsistent, Bess?"

"Absolutely not. That's bullshit."

"I don't believe you." He buried his face in his hands. "Maybe Nardigger's right. I'm losing it."

"David, don't say that. Don't do that to yourself." I made him push his chair back so I could sit on his lap. I hugged him and kissed his face. He let me maul him for a minute, and then he gave me a pathetic smile that was supposed to fool me.

"I think I'll go over to the hall and practice for a while."

"I'll come with you."

"No," he said, gently removing me from his lap. "You don't need to work on your consistency."

I let him go and then I shredded the reviews into confetti and dumped them in the plaid wastebasket.

When David came back, he announced

that we were going to take a break from making love. That was the way he said it, like screwing was a chore you look forward to interrupting.

I had been having a perfectly fabulous time watching ballroom dancing on English television. My stomach still didn't feel so hot, so I had my tea and biscuits beside me on a silver tray that weighed as much as me. "Any chance we can talk about this?" I said.

But David had already gone into the bedroom to start packing for Rome. "It's interfering with my concentration," he called out.

"Well, fuck me," I said to myself, only maybe it was more like a wish. When I thought it over, I realized we hadn't made love since the night of lights on the lake. I decided that given David's state of mind over the reviews, I wasn't going to give him any grief right then. But no way was I going to let him get away with it for long.

The funny thing was, David suddenly seemed more relaxed than he had in days. He held my hand on the plane to Rome, and gave me a nudge so I'd look at the old lady across the aisle. She was wearing earphones and bopping around in her seat like it was all she could do to keep from getting up to dance. Mostly the people you get in first class look pretty boring, all those financial types on business trips. But this old bird was wearing running shoes and jeans and had done a great job making herself up. I mean, really skillful with the foundation and eye shadow. Anyway, David found her fascinating, too, and he kept whispering theories about who she was. It made me happy to see him so cheerful, especially since I realized now, maybe with the perspective of distance, that he'd been acting weird ever since the Hamptons party. That look on his face when he was standing on the dunes, the dark strange expression that was so not the David I knew. It was like he'd lost his sense of humor. So I curled into him and enjoyed the comfort of having him back.

Well, maybe it was because I'm Italian, but I went wild over Rome. What a town, even though it was hotter than hell and smelled like you had your nose stuck up an exhaust pipe. I loved the washed-out, beaten-up earth-tone colors of the build-ings, the chaos in the streets, the shouting, the laughing, the music in the language, the sexy clothes on both men and women. And you cannot, I repeat, cannot, get any-thing bad to eat there. We even stumbled on this place the locals called the Dirty Man, where they made these incredibly delicious sandwiches called *panini*. It's a madhouse in there. In fact, you can hardly fight your way in because of all the motorbikes parked outside in the narrow street. I don't want to know how it got its name, and furthermore, I don't care. But there are dozens of places like that.

The first day, we had a good time exploring, and as I said, David was relaxed and affectionate. Hiking over to the Vatican from our hotel, he gave me a long and really interesting lecture about how neuroleptic research shows that playing the piano is the most complex activity the human brain can undertake. Obviously, I needed a fair amount of tutoring before I could get that concept into my neuroleptic head, but it fascinated me to think about the process of making music as a kind of science. For me, it had been, Okay, you stick your fingers on the keyboard and then you tell them what to do. What's complex about that? So I was pretty gripped. It made me feel a little smarter.

So that was nice, more like the first weeks of our relationship, and the Vatican was ridiculous. We climbed all the way up into the dome of St. Peter's. A far cry from

St. Agnes' in Rocky Beach, where during mass they had to put the communion stuff on Mrs. Monaghan's card table. Our statues that were supposed to pass for saints looked like the sculptor hung out in the police station and used a lineup of local car thieves for inspiration. So Michelangelo was quite the step up.

The second night we played in the *Sala di Concerti*. It's funny, you'd think that Rome would be a big musical center, but it really isn't. David said he'd arranged the gig so I could see the city and get a little break, but the important Italian event was scheduled for Milan.

We were in Rome for almost ten days. I should have been bummed that we weren't making love, but the thing was I still didn't feel so hot so I didn't even mind. I kept expecting my stomach to settle down, but I was always queasy. David made me eat, and actually, that did make me feel better for a little while. Plus walking around once I could get myself to put one foot in front of the other. David enjoyed showing me the sights. He'd spent a lot of time in Rome with his mother when he was a child, and it was a happy place for him. He hired a car, and let me tell you, you people who think it's nuts driving in Manhattan?

A day in Rome, on foot or behind the wheel, is a day inside a video game, either the one called "Get the Driver" or the other called "Get the Pedestrian." And *everybody* yells. I really got into the spirit of the thing. Whenever anybody tried real hard to run me over, which was every other block or so, I'd start waving my arms around and yelling fake Italian at the top of my lungs. It was exhilarating and besides, it made David laugh, which was rare during those days.

Our performance was only okay. I sensed that David was off his game. He got a little tangled up in the Rachmaninoff, which was bizarre since he knew it so well. Nobody noticed except for me — and David, of course, and the reviews were ecstatic. Since they were all in Italian, David had to translate. When he finished reading them to me, he tossed them in the garbage like they were nasty.

"What?" I said.

"They don't know what they're saying. 'Montagnier played with his customary precision'? I played like an amateur."

"You did not," I started in. "The Ravel was perfectly . . ."

He turned on me, actually raising his voice. "Don't do that! Not you, Bess. I'm going out."

And he did, leaving me in the hotel room with my heartache and heaving stomach. After a couple of hours, he came back, this time bearing panini in their paper wraps. He looked like such a sad puppy I could hardly be angry.

"I thought you'd appreciate these more than flowers." There was a plate under a plant by the window. He washed it off and set up a little picnic for us. We had wine and fruit from the basket the hotel had sent up when we checked in.

"I shouldn't have spoken to you that way, Bess. I'm sorry." He leaned over and gave me a kiss. Not a sexy one, but sweet just the same. "I count on you to be honest. It's what I value most about you. Please don't bullshit me."

I had to smile even though I wished there were other things he found more valuable, like my tits, except they weren't feeling so perky these days either. They hurt even when I walked, so I had to fasten my bra on a tighter snap to counteract any jiggle.

"How sad that it's my character that counts," I said. I was still smiling, but fishing, too.

"I know this is hard on you, about the sex," David said. "It's not easy for me, either. Please don't think I'm not attracted to you, Bess. I want you as much as I ever did."

That made me weepy, but I dipped my head so he wouldn't see. "What'll happen when you get really horny, David?"

"The energy will go into our music, that's all. It'll start to pay off soon."

I was waiting for him to ask what *I* would do, and frankly, I didn't know what I would tell him. I didn't want anyone else. I was certainly not much interested in sex anyway when I was carting my stomach around in my throat. Still, the time would surely come when I'd be crawling up walls. I looked at David sitting across from me with his legs propped up on the hotel ottoman. He had a dripping gooey panini in one hand and a glass of wine in the other. His face was burned from our walks in the Italian sun and there was something adolescent about his expression. He seemed fragile and hopeful all at once and it was all I could do to keep from throwing my arms around him. I just smiled some more and told him that I was positive that everything was going to work out just fine.

David left Rome a day early to do some "family business," he called it. Something to do with real estate in the south of

France. I didn't even give him an argument about going along. I still felt completely wiped out, and figured I'd take the day to sleep. Then, by the time I met up with him in Milan, I'd be ready to rock and roll again. And that's exactly what I did. Sixteen straight hours of sleep. I don't think I've ever done that again in my whole life.

For somebody who's got this totally complex neuroleptic process going on in her brain, I could be outstandingly dense. It took me until we got to Milan before I realized that it wasn't jet lag that was making me feel so lousy. I remember the exact moment I figured it out — in a break during rehearsal at the concert hall. I went to the john, half nodded off on the toilet seat, and when I was fixing my hair — I can't usually comb it because it's too thick, I just pull my fingers through it — I stared at my face in the mirror. I looked like somebody else.

"You're pregnant, Stallone," I said to myself. And it all fell into place: tits the size of volleyballs, nonstop nausea, so zonked all the time I could barely keep my eyes open. My period was so unpredictable I never bothered to keep track of it, but the last time I could remember having it was before the Hamptons party. I'd used an IUD for years and figured it was foolproof. Guess again. I went into a stall and did a little exploration. No string. The damn thing must have fallen out and I didn't even notice it. I never heard of that happening, but there was no doubt in my mind. I was knocked up, and it had to have been that perfect night of my birthday, and now I had the perfect souvenir to commemorate it. So I stood there grinning at myself. One of the concert hall administrators came in to pee and caught me. She must have thought I was simpleminded, but it was all I could do to keep from telling her. I wanted to find the nearest phone and call Angie. As for David, I didn't have a clue what to do. A few weeks ago, it would have been simpler. We were sleeping together, and I had a lot more confidence that we were in a seminormal romantic relationship. We were still in something, but I couldn't tell you exactly what it was. By the time the administrator had flushed the toilet, I'd decided to sit on the news for a while before telling David. It never occurred to me to terminate the pregnancy, and not because I was brought up a Catholic. I wanted this baby.

It turned out that next to David's presence, pregnancy was the best possible cure for stage fright. It still hadn't been easy for me to step out onstage, but at that point I didn't give one shit about the performance. All I cared about was sleep. I longed to get through the music and take me and the baby back to the hotel to bed. I must have looked like some kind of druggie up there. But as soon as I heard what our notes sounded like in that incredible hall in Milan, I woke up in a hurry. That place has maybe *the* most fabulous acoustics in the world. It's a concrete monstrosity like the London hall, someplace you'd take your airplane to get fixed, but whoa, what happens to your notes — they just soar in there.

Afterward, the crowd pelted us with roses, which was a new one for me. They just couldn't get enough of the three of us (I'd already started thinking of the baby as a member of the group), and when we sat down together to play our duet — the Bach — I thought they were going to have to call in the riot police.

Ordinarily, after a reception like that, I would have been so sexed up I would have jumped David no matter what. But with the baby and all, I just lay there in my separate bed — David had started reserving two queens as opposed to one king — and thought about the little person growing inside. One thing for sure, it would be able to carry a tune.

The reviews were almost as hysterical as the crowd. David read them to me with satisfaction.

"You see, Bess? It's working. We were losing our concentration, that's all."

"I hope you're not thinking of making this a permanent deal," I said. Now that we were pregnant, I needed to think more clearly about the future and what kind of family this baby was going to have.

"For the time being," David said. "You can be patient, can't you?"

I just looked at him.

"Humor me, my darling." He stood beside my chair and held my head against him. "It's our time to become the best we can be."

"All right," I said. "I'll see how long I can hang in there."

He leaned over and kissed me, then started pacing. He was more excited than I'd seen him in a long time, almost agitated. "Mr. Balaboo called," he said. "If we can stay in Europe another month, he can line up four more concerts."

"When did he call? I didn't hear you on the phone."

David smiled. "I don't know how you slept through it. The phone's right next to your ear."

Don't you know why? I wanted to say. Can't you tell just by looking at me? I was bursting to tell him, but something held me back. And I didn't tell him, not for a long time.

CHAPTER FOURTEEN

We had quite the tour, kind of like the Beatles' first trip to America. First of all, duo pianists are totally respected in Europe. The attitude in America is that the repertoire is limited, that you can't really tell how each artist is performing, and it's just kind of a novelty act. Europeans think a duo demands more from the pianists than solo work. You're not only performing extremely demanding music, but you're coordinating it with someone else in what has to be a seamless whole. It turned out that we were just about the hottest U.S. import since blue jeans. We'd never played better. Of course, I felt as if I had support from the little helper curled up inside me. But what a bizarro situation — David absolutely manic, which is I guess how he reacted to celibacy, and me with this huge secret I didn't know what to do with. I look back and wonder why I waited so long to tell him. I guess I was just too afraid of how he'd react.

While we were away, Mr. Balaboo had been busy making P.R. heaven out of our triumphs in Europe. Everybody wanted us, from the White House to Jay Leno. On the plane home, David plotted our gigs for the next couple of months while I thought about where to find a great obstetrician. Side by side, in row four of first class, the two of us who'd been such passionate lovers only weeks before, and now look.

I wondered where Phillip would be dropping me off from the airport. For all I knew, if David wanted me out of his bed I wouldn't be welcome in his apartment either. But no, there was no mention of a change there. Maybe David wanted me nearby so we could practice at three A.M. if the mood struck. Before we got out of the limo, David pulled me next to him and held me for a long time.

"Thank you, Bess. You've given me more than I could ever have imagined possible. I love you so much." His arms felt like steel rods. And there was that sharp scent of lemon again. I wanted to kiss him but I didn't trust myself because the old sex drive was saying, Yo, Bess! *Hell*-o. Besides which, he was not just the man who had made music possible for me. He'd also given me a child. Talk about love. He didn't know the half of it.

The next day, I went to see Angie. We

met in Soho at Jerry's, which is to a coffee shop what the Sistine Chapel is to subway graffiti. We settled in a booth across from one another. Angie looked beautiful, rounder, with more color in her face.

"I guess I don't have to ask if you're feeling good," I said.

She smiled. "I'm happy, Bessie. School's going well and now . . . actually, I've met someone." She broke off.

"Tell me."

"His name's Ben and we just barely started seeing one another. But I don't want to jinx it."

"Okay, honey, then what about Mumma and Dutch?" Our father had apparently gotten it into his head to start hounding his congressman and the local newspapers about rights for the disabled.

"He thinks he's Christopher Reeve," Angie said.

"Is anything happening with his legs?"

"As long as she gets to go to work, she's happy. She got another promotion."

I took the leap. Angie meant that things were status quo with Dutch's condition. She knew what my next question would be and saved me the trouble of asking. I shook my head. "Who ever would have thought Mumma'd turn out to be a career woman? Our Lady of the Apron and Ziti."

Angie smiled. "Did you know that Pauline moved in with Jake?"

"No. That's very cool."

"It's very dumb," Angie said.

"Why? Pauline's nuts about him."

"True." She looked at me with both eyebrows raised, little bridges arching over stuff I didn't feel like discussing. As far as I knew, nobody was aware of the fact that I'd slept with Jake not so very long ago. Now *that* was dumb. Angie was still staring at me. "So? Are you ready to tell me what's going on?" she asked.

"A lot."

"I read about you everywhere."

"Yeah, next thing I'll be a centerfold."

"How's David?"

"Strange. But that's not the real news."

I stared into her face, willing her to figure it out. It didn't take long.

"You're pregnant."

I shoved around to her side of the booth, threw my arms around her, and started crying. The relief of sharing it, especially with my sister, was overwhelming.

"How far along?" she asked.

"I'm not sure exactly. I think it was my birthday. That was the last time we were together."

"Why? He won't hurt the baby."

"David doesn't know."

I could feel her body tense, but I wasn't ready to explain. First of all, the tears were streaming and I was having a hard time not taking great big sobbing gulps. It was quite the scene, but we were in Soho, after all, where people were expected to be a little over the top. At least I wasn't a crying person with a big silver peg sticking out of my nose.

"When are you planning to?" she asked. She waited a couple of seconds. "Or maybe you aren't going to keep it."

"Of course I'm keeping it! I'm keeping it!"

"Well, why haven't you told him?"

"Because I'm afraid he won't be happy and I can't stand it."

I loved Angie even more because she didn't say, *Oh, sure he'll be happy.* She wouldn't come out with one of those dopey remarks even if it was in front of her nose on a cue card. We sat in silence for a few moments, me with my head on her shoulder. Then I moved back to my side and I told her everything.

"So what next?" she asked at the end of my tale.

"Know a good obstetrician? I think I'd

better get checked out."

"And you've got to tell David."

"Yeah."

The doctor Angie found for me confirmed that I was about ten weeks pregnant. I made a pact with myself that I'd tell David when I hit the magic twelve-week mark at the end of the first trimester. In the meantime, I was feeling better and we were really busy, not only performing, but also finishing up a CD. I still got tired, which made it possible to sleep in the same bed with David. Possible, I said, not fun. I often woke up in the middle of the night and lay there staring at his beautiful face, wanting to hold him and make love to him and wishing that he would want me so much he wouldn't be able to help himself. But even asleep, he looked tense. There was a deep line between his brows and his eyelids were always restless like he was having bad dreams.

I was beginning to have trouble zipping my jeans, but I still didn't tell him. I would decide on a day, and then something would happen to make me put it off. Like the night we had a jam session after a concert out in Newark. A bunch of guys from the Philadelphia came back to the apartment, mainly strings, and David seemed more relaxed than he'd been since Europe. I had decided I'd drop the news when everybody left. But then somewhere along the line the conversation turned to practicing and memory. One of the violinists said he practiced on planes, without his instrument. He'd just think back over the music and all the choices he'd made over the years about interpretation and it was as good as a regular session.

"I do that," I said.

"You do?" David seemed surprised.

"Yeah, I can get through an hour-long work that way note by note. It's a help when you don't have access to a piano."

"I've never been able to do that," David said in a real quiet voice.

"No big deal," I said, but I could see that to David it was some kind of failure. He got up and went into the bedroom, at which point I knew two things — the party was over, and I wasn't going to tell him about the baby.

The next day, I called Mr. Balaboo and asked him to meet me for a drink at the West Bank Café, which is all the way over on Ninth Avenue where I knew David wouldn't catch us. If you told Mr. Balaboo seven o'clock, you could count on him being there at six fifty-eight. When I got there, he was perched on a stool at the bar with his little feet dangling. If it weren't for his gray hair with that middle part, he could have passed for a kid waiting for a milk shake. He took my hand in his dainty monkey paw and kept hold of it, pulling me near for cheek kisses.

"Bess-dahlink," he said.

I ordered a club soda and lime. No booze for my baby at her tender age — I'd already made up my mind that she was a girl. "I'm worried about David," I said.

He nodded.

"What does that mean?" I asked.

"As am I," he said. Then he was quiet again.

"Lookit, Mr. Balaboo, we're not plotting to overthrow the government here. You think being concerned is disloyal?"

"All right," he said. He took a sip of his vodka, which he always insisted on drinking from a champagne glass. "This isn't the first time David has had difficulties."

"What kind of difficulties?"

"Mental-health issues."

"You want to hand me the straight story here, please?"

"He's had some bouts with depression.

Actually, it's more like manic depression."

My turn to be silent.

"He's never told you?"

I shook my head.

"He went on medication for a while several years ago, and then again after Terese left. It was somewhat disastrous."

I looked around as it occurred to me that this was the kind of conversation every *E!* network or New York magazine reporter had wet dreams over. I picked up our drinks and moved us to a table in the corner.

"Disastrous how?" I asked him when we were settled.

"Side effects. He became very agitated. His hands shook so much he couldn't perform."

I figured I might as well give it a shot. "Exactly why *did* Terese leave? And where is she?"

Another long silence, then, "Terese was too fragile for the music world."

"So she had a breakdown?"

"You could call it that."

"Is she in an institution?"

Silence, then, "Bess, I feel uncomfortable discussing this. You should ask David."

It's funny how things that don't seem to

register at the time suddenly rise to the surface. "That little side trip David took in Europe, before we got to Milan? Did that have something to do with Terese?"

"Bess-dahlink . . ."

"Oh, fuck it. Forget Terese. What can we do for David?"

"I wish I knew."

"I can't bear to look in his eyes," I said. "There's too much suffering in there."

"He's not playing well. He's lost his confidence."

"I haven't noticed that," I said. What I guess I meant was, I didn't want to hear that because truthfully, somewhere deep down, I *had* noticed. "Does he have a psychiatrist?" I asked.

"He's seen a few but he's not inclined to think positively toward them. Perhaps . . . these things tend to pass off on their own. If we give him some time."

"He's wound up awfully tight," I said. "This morning he was talking to himself in the shower."

"I thought, with you . . . He's never been so happy. You must know that."

"Yeah, well, the honeymoon seems to be over." But there was comfort in hearing the truth, even if it was real bad news.

"Perhaps you can persuade him to get

help," Mr. Balaboo said. "I've had no luck at all."

"Okay," I said. "I'll give it a shot."

Then and there I made a resolution to have it out with David that night. It seemed the wisest thing to do, put all the cards out on the table — the baby card and the mental one, too — and that way at least we'd be honest again, the way we were in the beginning — or at least the way *I* was.

When I got home, David was sitting at the laptop, scrolling through Nardigger's reviews, not just about himself, but for other musicians as well. He didn't even say hello.

"He uses the same phrases over and over, Bess. Listen to this, about Evgeny Kissin: 'How regrettable that such monumental talent be squandered in an adolescent display of flashy pyrotechnics.' And two months later, this is Nardigger on Martha Argerich: 'While Argerich's monumental talent is undeniable, how regrettable that her displays of flashy pyrotechnics be untempered with mature interpretation.' "

I dumped my jacket on the back of a chair and went to pour myself a glass of water. I wished it could be booze. I called in to him, "The critics are always on Kissin's case, not just Nardigger. They can't stand how he makes the public so delirious."

I went into the bedroom with my water and stood beside David. He hardly knew I was there. "When Kissin's seventy years old, they'll start giving him decent reviews."

"I've printed out a whole series of Nardigger's pieces, starting in 1990. I'm going to send them to *The Listener* so they can see just what kind of viper they've got working for them."

I put my hand on his shoulder. "I'm not so sure you should do that."

He looked up from the screen. There were splotches of color on his cheeks and his eyes were open too wide. "You used to be supportive, Bess." Then he jumped up so fast he almost knocked me over. I instinctively put my arms over my stomach. "Don't you think it's about time the musicians repossessed some power from these jealous no-talents?" he said, flipping through piles of printouts. "They can still wreck a career with one bad review."

I took his hand and led him to the living room couch. The only light was from the city outside the windows. I hoped the darkness would calm him down a little.

"We need to talk," I said.

David's body was coiled in the corner of the couch, ready to spring. "All right. Fine." But he glanced at his watch, not that he could even see the dial.

"I've just been talking with Mr. Balaboo," I said.

"What's wrong? Didn't the Charleston concert come through?"

"We're worried about you."

He was silent, but his eyes glittered at me in the half-light.

"You're not well," I said. "This thing with Nardigger . . . it's . . ."

He didn't let me finish, just hopped up again and started walking back and forth in front of the window. "You think it's unhealthy to fight back? That's the trouble with artists. We're taught to be passive, let the lawyers take care of us, and the agents and the managers, and never do anything for ourselves. That's healthy? No, Bess. For the first time, I'm standing up for myself and for the rest of us who've been at the mercy of the Nardiggers of this world."

"Please sit down, David," I said, "and don't get up until I've finished. I can't talk to you while you're bouncing around like this."

He sat, but he kept checking his watch. "Do you have an appointment?" I asked him.

He shook his head. "No, I'm sorry, Bess. I don't mean to be rude, it's just that there's so much to do."

"I want you to see someone about medication," I said.

He stared at me.

"It's one or the other. Either you're way too excited or you're in a black mood," I went on.

"Taking care of Nardigger will help that."

I shook my head. "Just see someone. Mr. Balaboo gave me a name."

But David leapt up again and turned on me in a fury. "You Americans, forever going to psychiatrists and popping pills. It's not the answer to everything. I tried medication and it made me into a lunatic. . . ."

I stayed put, hoping that if I was calm I could get him to quiet down. "That was years ago. There are a lot more options now, tons more choices. They'll just make you normal again."

That did it. "Normal! What's *normal?* Because I give a damn about injustice I'm a crazy man? I'm a creative personality, that's all. Look at Schumann. If he was alive today, they'd label him bipolar and pump him with Prozac until he couldn't write another note."

"Oh, David." Then I really did start to cry.

He stopped shouting and came to stand in front of me. "It's been a stressful period, I admit that. Maybe I'm a little irrational sometimes, but Bess, we're at a crucial point in our careers. We could become respected fixtures in the musical world, or we could disappear forever. We have to prove that we've got staying power. I feel responsible for that. I'm willing to work hard for that."

"David, I'm pregnant." It just fell out of me. It was the last thing I meant to say and probably the worst possible time to say it. I just couldn't hold it in anymore. I covered my face with my hands to keep from seeing what his eyes did with the news. Finally, after a long silence, I forced myself to look up at him. Even in the dark, I could see that his cheeks were wet. He dropped to his knees in front of me.

"Oh, Bess," he said.

He wrapped his arms around me and laid his cheek against my belly. "Oh, Bess," he said again. I can't tell you what it meant to feel him hold me that way again. All those lonely weeks seemed to melt away and I didn't want to move a muscle. Just let us stay like this for hours and days and months until the baby comes, and I knew I sounded like Pauline but I sent a silent thank-you to my little girl for bringing the man I loved back to me at last.

CHAPTER FIFTEEN

The next day, David seemed almost to forget that we had a baby coming. Every now and then, I would catch him looking at my belly with this puzzled look on his face. But we were so crazed in those days, recording in the studio, rehearsing and performing. It was easier to just keep my head down and shut up. I was preoccupied anyway with complete adoration of my baby. Angie asked me if I was going to have an amniocentesis, but it wasn't an issue for me. Even if this child had the chromosomes of a warthog, I wanted her. I was in love with her. I never felt lonely. I didn't even miss sex anymore. And if David was continuing his obsessive campaign to mess up Nardigger, he waged it when I wasn't around.

Then we were invited to perform at the Kennedy Center in Washington. I suppose it should have been the highlight of my career. First of all, I'd never been in Washington, D.C., in my life. There'd been a tour in high school which I told my parents I signed up for. While my class headed south on the Jersey Turnpike, I was in a

Ford pickup on my way to Albany, never mind why. So here was my chance to check out the sights, take a tour of the White House, see the Lincoln Memorial. Instead, all I wanted to do was shop for maternity clothes, which is what I did as soon as we were finished rehearsing. How strange that just a few weeks before, I was pestering David to hang out with me whenever we had a free second, hoping I could light a fire under him. He did ask me where I was going. When I told him shopping, he looked a little surprised, that's all.

What I remember most about that concert was red. Red all around, like the whole place was the inside of a gigantic raw heart. Mine and David's and the baby's and everybody's who was in pain and feeling too much. I even wore a red dress. We performed mostly the same program that we did in London with the addition of a reverie composed especially for us by the American contemporary Lorna Wiggins. It all went along just fine until the Bartók Sonata for Two Pianos and Percussion, which we'd played, oh, maybe a few thousand times, give or take. We'd got to the crescendo at measure 209 when David lost it. He just suddenly seemed to be playing some other music entirely. He stared at me like he'd just had the shock of his life. If you suddenly got pushed onto the subway tracks, that's how you'd look, with a face screaming *Help me!*

I didn't know what to do. I slowed down, which confused the instruments even more. There was a crazy jumble of sounds. I finally put my hands in my lap, at which point David got up, closed the lid to his keyboard, and left the stage.

I remember stumbling backstage, and somebody telling me that I had to go out there and entertain all those people who'd paid good money to come hear us, that there were senators and all kinds of important people there. I think I told that person that even if the Holy Ghost Himself was in the front row, I was out of there, excuse me very much.

Holding my belly all the way, I got back to the hotel suite by telling the cabdriver there was a twenty in it for him if he made it in seven minutes. David was tossing his stuff in his suitcase. I grabbed him and held on tight. He fought me for a minute but then he just went limp in my arms and cried and cried. My beautiful man with all that genius and talent in such despair, and he couldn't even tell me why. All he kept saying was, "It's all coming apart. It's coming apart."

I made him sit on the couch and take a sip of vodka, which calmed him a little. Then I turned off the phone, which had already started ringing nonstop, wrapped a blanket around him, and held on. He was cold, icy.

"What can I do, David?" I asked him.

He just shook his head.

"Do you understand how much I love you?"

He nodded.

"We can fix this," I said.

He didn't answer. I looked into his eyes and felt like I was falling down a well into a scary place.

"I'd like to call a doctor," I said.

He shook his head.

"Please, David." I forced myself not to get worked up, but I was pretty scared.

"No. Just stay here."

So I lay there on the couch with him until eventually we both fell asleep.

When I woke up about two A.M., he was on the cell phone pacing back and forth. "Then get me a charter," he said. "We can be in Milan in a few hours. You'll book us something for next week. They'll be happy, you know they will. They loved us in Milan."

I was wearing a mashed version of my

red gown. I wrapped the blanket around me and went over to him. "What's going on?"

David put his hand over the mouthpiece. "I'm trying to explain to Balaboo that we have to go back to Europe right away. It's the only way to erase what happened on-stage tonight."

"I don't get it," I said.

"Here, you tell him," David said. "Tell him to hire us a private jet."

"Mr. Balaboo?" I said.

"He's off the charts, Bess," Mr. Balaboo's voice said. "He needs a hospital."

"What's this about planes?"

"He says everything was wonderful in Milan and that you have to go back to-night. See if you can keep him quiet until I can get the doctor there. It took me a while to get a referral from his old psychiatrist in New York, but we should make it within the hour."

"Please." I hung up. Thank God. Mr. Balaboo was staying right in the same hotel, which made me feel a little less pan-icked.

"What?" David said.

"He's seeing what he can do. It's not that easy at two A.M., but you know Balaboo. He's resourceful." I felt awful sort of lying to him, but I had no idea what to do. I just wanted him to calm down. "Sit with me on the couch for a minute while we wait, okay?"

He sat. I could see he was exhausting himself, as if he was trying to jump out of his own skin. I was afraid to talk, afraid that whatever I said would only agitate him more, so I sat beside him and massaged his fingers the way he had done for me so many times. He actually began to doze off again, and while he slept I looked at his face and remembered back to when we first met, how he'd taken me for tea at that little place on the West Side near Juilliard, how he showed up in Rocky Beach in his tuxedo, how he set about turning me into a musician with the confidence to perform in the world's most prestigious concert halls. How he had made me feel worthy of being loved and how he had given me the life that was now growing inside. There had been so many miracles. Couldn't we just have one more?

David wouldn't let Mr. Balaboo and the doctor take him away, but he agreed to stay in the hotel with me, until he felt better, he said. So we did. He watched TV most of the time and when we talked, it was only about what we were going to eat (not much — he had no appetite) or the weather or the actors in the TV show. I learned very quickly that most subjects got him stirred up, including music, people in our lives, the past, the future, and hardest of all, the baby. He seemed to have forgotten that I was pregnant, and when I brought it up, he became almost wild.

"How could that happen? We didn't plan it. How could anybody bring a child into this world, Bess? Besides, we aren't even sleeping together." And finally, "Are you sure it's mine?" After that one, I had to excuse myself to go into the john. I cried into the bath towel so he wouldn't hear me.

He was supposed to be taking medication, but I could never be sure he was really swallowing. He'd put the pills in his mouth and take a sip of water, but I had the feeling he was faking. I felt completely out of my depth. But he wouldn't hear of going to a hospital and he couldn't stand for me to be out of his sight. The things that kept me going were, (a) I would have done anything, anything, for him, and if that included living in this hotel for the rest of our lives, well, we'd adjust. And (b) the knowledge that I had a little dependent inside me kept me focused. I didn't have the luxury of falling apart.

We were in that hotel suite with the gray carpet and raspberry curtains for three and a half weeks. Mr. Balaboo was a brick through it all, flying back and forth between New York and D.C. and giving me breaks to get outside for walks. One of the hardest things was not being near a piano, so Mr. Balaboo arranged to let me practice on the cocktail lounge baby grand, not a bad little Baldwin. We got to know the room service people intimately. I remembered the first time I ever stayed in a hotel, with my mother and sister when we went to a family wedding in Massachusetts. Next to sex, I thought it was about the most perfect experience life had to offer. A bed that somebody else made, a sink that somebody else cleaned, and sweet-smelling soap all wrapped up like a Christmas present. Well, let me tell you, after twenty-five days at the Washington Dorset, I got plenty sick of it.

The last night, instead of sleeping in his own bed, David crept into mine and put his arms around me. I automatically curled into him, just like the old days, and soon we were making love again. It wasn't the same, partly because we were silent and we'd always been pretty talkative, telling each other what felt good and what we wanted. But that night I was afraid to say anything that might put him off or get him upset. Besides, David seemed to be in a dreamy state, like maybe he wasn't even totally awake. We both came at the same time like we were riding a gentle wave. He whispered that he loved me and then we fell asleep. It seemed like a gift.

But now I come to the really hard time. It's the part of my life that lives in a dark room where I try to keep the door shut tight. Every time I open it a crack, Mussorgsky's *Night on Bald Mountain* shrieks out, music brought to you straight from hell. But so many idiotic stupid hurtful things have been said. It's important to me that the truth be told and I'm the only one who can tell it — never mind the media gossips who seem to think they were standing in my panty hose through the whole thing.

CHAPTER SIXTEEN

The cramps woke me first thing in the morning. I snuck out of bed so I wouldn't wake David and headed for the bathroom. As soon as I stood up, about a gallon of water poured out of me. I got a bath towel, stuffed it between my legs, and called Mr. Balaboo. I'm not sure Mr. Balaboo ever really sleeps. He answered the phone at six A.M. like it was four in the afternoon.

"What's happened?"

"I need a doctor," I said.

"He's worse?"

"It's for me. I'm pregnant and there's something wrong."

There was silence. Then, in the kindest voice, "Bess-dahlink. How far along?"

"I'm in the second trimester. I think my water broke."

"Call an ambulance and get them to take you to St. Francis' Hospital."

"I don't want anyone to know." The cramps were getting worse. I could feel myself leaking something that was warm and thick.

"Use the name Roberta Schuman. I'll

332

alert the hotel manager, and then I'll meet you in the emergency room. Don't let them touch you until I get there."

The last few times he'd come to Washington, Mr. Balaboo had stayed with a friend in Georgetown. The hotel life was getting to him, too. Poor Mr. Balaboo. First David, then me. I left a note on my pillow for David, threw a couple of things into a shopping bag, and waited in the living room of our suite for the ambulance. I could hear it coming, the high whine that sounded like a child crying. I made the medical team be quiet on account of David. I could see that they recognized me, but they didn't make a fuss and got me out of there in no time.

Mr. Balaboo was waiting at Emergency with a sleepy-looking woman who turned out to be Dr. Berke, the head of OB-GYN at St. Francis'. She reminded me of Eleanor Roosevelt, which was reassuring.

Look, the details aren't important. They tried hard to save my pregnancy. Everyone was incredibly kind. It didn't become news until much later that I had ever been pregnant. The press knew something had happened, but since they couldn't get the true scoop, they used their imagination: I'd OD'd on painkillers, I'd had a lump-

ectomy, I had a severe anxiety attack —
one paper even said David had beaten me
up, but I sued the bastards and made them
pay for that fairy tale.

But I lost the baby. It was a girl. She
would be four years old this month. I still
think about her a lot. For a while, I didn't
imagine I'd ever get over it. But of course
you do, more or less, even if you don't
forget your whole life long.

They kept me in the hospital for a week,
mainly because Mr. Balaboo thought I
needed a rest. I would wake up every day,
look out at the gray sky, and wish I could
go back to sleep so I wouldn't have to feel
anything. Mr. Balaboo brought me CDs
for my Discman, which was a help as long
as I didn't listen to Chopin or Bach. Something about those two twisted my insides.
And then one morning he showed up with
the best present — David. I had just finished not eating my breakfast and was
lying there trying to decide if I would (a)
stare out the window, or (b) stare at the
TV with no sound on. Out of the corner of
my eye, I saw the door open and there he
was, shiny and clean-shaven and dressed in
a V-necked sweater and jeans. Whoever
made up that saying "a sight for sore eyes"

knew what they were talking about. Mr. Balaboo gave me a little wave from behind David's shoulder.

"I'll be out here," he said, and closed the door.

David came over to the bed and sat down next to me. He reached out and stroked my hair. "My poor Bess," he said.

"I lost our baby," I said.

"Is there any pain?"

I couldn't answer that one, just put my hand on my heart to tell him, *Yes, here.*

He took my hand. "They're going to let you out tomorrow," he said. "Would you like to go back to New York?"

"David, do you think we did it? By making love. Do you think we killed our baby?"

"The doctor says no."

"You asked, too?"

He nodded. "She told me that people ordinarily have intercourse straight through. I don't want you to think about that anymore. I want you to think of the future now."

Tall order, I was thinking. But there he was, looking like his old self, his body relaxed and his face calm.

"You seem well," I said.

"I'm sorry for what I put you through," he said.

"You couldn't help it, David."

I saw his eyes go dark for a second, like he was revisiting that terrible place, but then he blinked and it was gone. "Let's go home," he said. "We'll get back to the music if you're up to it. Can you do that, Bess?"

"If you're there, I can do anything," I said.

He leaned over and kissed me. I felt like he'd just reached into my chest, taken my broken heart in his hands, and put it back together again.

I was better when we first got back to New York — except for a daily crying jag, which usually hit me when I first woke up and remembered that I was no longer pregnant. David and I were sleeping in his bed, but although he was affectionate, there was no sex. I didn't care. I was having enough trouble getting a grip without unleashing that part of me. Besides, my hormones were all screwed up from the miscarriage. I wasn't even interested.

Mr. Balaboo wouldn't let David schedule any concerts, which I thought was wise given his recent meltdown. What we did was work every day on new music.

It was therapeutic for both of us. David started feeling confident again. Without consulting Mr. Balaboo, he volunteered us for a benefit concert at Alice Tully Hall.

I was nervous about it, and so was Mr. Balaboo.

"After you fall from the log, you must get right back on," David told me from across the pianos.

"I think you mean horse," I said.

"Of course you can forget how to ride if you don't practice."

"Okay, David," I said, "we'll do the concert. Just don't let yourself get worked up."

"I'll be perfectly fine," he promised. "If I give you any trouble, put a little Valium in my toothpaste."

His sense of humor had begun to return. Well, not exactly *his* sense of humor, but somebody's. I took it as a good sign. But the stronger David got, the shakier I became. I had lost a lot of weight and I was sad all the time. Not just about the baby, but about David and how things had changed between us. It was not my idea of a complete relationship, sleeping in the same room and never fucking even if I didn't feel like it. Just the fact that I didn't feel like it was depressing in itself.

At least the concert went off all right except I thought David was too hyper afterward. He was talking to the backstage fans in choppy little sentences and his eyes looked haunted. My old friend Mrs. Edelmeyer kept shooting him funny looks. After all, she'd been watching him for years and was as much a Montagnier expert as anyone.

"How's David?" she asked me, taking liberties as usual.

"Fine, why?"

"He's acting peculiar," she said. "You sure he's all right? We have to keep an eye on him since the Washington fiasco."

Enough already, I thought. "Will we see you at the piano series next fall?" I asked sweetly. She wasn't *that* thick, just wished me well and moved along. But her observation had made me nervous. I saw David talking to Patty Kopec, a friend of Itzhak Perlman's. Patty's head cranked around to me with a look that said, *Whassup with him?* I wanted to tell her how David had gone someplace else now and I couldn't get him back. How I missed him and our baby.

I knew what the rest of the evening would be like. I'd haul David away from the crowd so he didn't get too agitated. Then we'd go straight back to the apartment, wash up, climb into our opposite sides of the bed, and shout good night across the vast desert of white linen. I just couldn't face it. When Jake, Pauline and Angie showed up, I asked them if I could please take them for a drink someplace.

They gave each other a group *Uh oh* look.

"Just for a nightcap," I said. "I need a break from the scene."

Yeah, I know, everybody is hearing drumrolls. The famous episode. Look, at least I didn't trash a hotel room like Johnny Depp — but he probably didn't do it anyway. If there's one lesson to be learned, it's that you can't believe what you read.

We went over to Eighth Avenue to a little bar I like called Monkeyshines. Corny name, but maybe that's why the snooty types stay away. On the way, Jake talked about the wildlife preserve. He'd obviously found his life's work, being near the water and feeling like he was making a difference.

"I feel guilty about spending so much time out at Ben's," Angie said. "The apartment goes empty for days, whenever I don't have class. He's throwing money away."

"Ben's paying for two places?" Pauline asked. Even after all these years, she still hadn't gotten the hang of Angie's conversation.

"David's got it to throw away," I said. But I didn't want to talk about him. I felt uncomfortable having left him, even though Mr. Balaboo said he'd make sure David didn't hop on any planes for Italy or anything.

The bar was overflowing with people, which suited me just fine. They looked like locals — artists, unemployed actors, off-duty cops, a real assortment. We found a table for two in a back corner and jammed ourselves in tight. I ordered us a round. Then I ordered another. I socked the stuff back in a big hurry and waved to the waiter.

"You sure you want another, Stallone?" Jake asked me.

"Oh, yeah," I said.

"Bess, you're upset," Pauline said.

"You got that right," I said.

"Let's take her home," Angie told Jake.

"I don't think so," I said. My vodka arrived and down it went, smooth as an oil slick. I tapped the guy at the next table. "I haven't felt this good in months," I explained to him.

"Aren't you Bess Stallone?" he asked. He had a ring through his eyebrow.

"That looks great. I want one of those." I turned to Jake. "Got your Swiss Army knife?" He always had one in his pocket. "Let's give me one like this gentleman here." I took the hoop out of my ear, gold with a diamond in it. David had bought the pair for me in Rome. "Use this."

But my neighbor had passed the word around and the next thing I knew, a piano was produced from behind a crowd that had been using it to lean on.

"Come on, Bess, play something!"

"Sure!" I shouted. "Great thinking! Where's that vodka?"

So the next thing, I was sitting at that old upright piano banging away all the old favorites — Billy Joel, Madonna, the Beatles, the Stones. "Reminds me of Amadoofus!" I yelled to my group.

"How about some Beethoven?" somebody called out.

"In a minute," I said. It was hotter than hell in there, especially in my long gown from the performance. Plus I was plenty drunk by then. "Gotta lighten the load," I said, and started to strip. The crowd was screaming, "Go, Bess!" I got down to my underwear and when I was comfortable began playing a semi–rock 'n' roll version of the *Pathetique* Sonata. It works pretty well with a boogie beat, or at least it seemed that way in my trashed state. Roll over, Beethoven. And over and over.

Anyhow, I knew Jake was trying to get at me through the crowd. He made it finally, but not until a lot of flashbulbs went off.

Well, you've probably seen the photos. They were everywhere including on the Internet, with cool captions like *Bare Bess Flies Solo*, and *How to Misbehave without Dave*. I deserved them all. Furthermore, I never found that earring.

When I woke up with the beat from Ravel's *Bolero* splitting my head, David was standing over me shaking the *Daily News* in my face.

"Get up," he said. I hardly recognized that cold voice.

"No," I said. "I don't feel so hot."

He reached down and yanked the covers off me. "Put on a robe," he said.

I felt like he'd dumped ice water on me. I did as he said and followed him into the kitchen.

"How could you do this, Bess?" he said. "All these months building a career for us,

342

and you've gone and spoiled it in one idiotic night."

"I was just letting off steam. It was so damn hot in there." I peered at the photo. There were some advantages to my recent lack of appetite — at least my tits weren't hogging the picture like a pair of albino watermelons.

"Listen," David ordered me. " 'Bess Stallone, half of the famous piano duo with David Montagnier, treated a West Side bar to a rollicking ragtime rendition of Beethoven's "Moonlight Sonata." ' "

"It was the *Pathetique*," I said.

"How do you expect that we'll ever be taken seriously now?" I saw that he couldn't have cared less if I'd peeled off the last layer and danced naked on top of the piano. It was the music he was freaked about.

"It's hard enough in this country," he said, "trying to convince the musical establishment that a two-piano team has something important to offer. You've turned us into a joke."

He ripped the photo into shreds and spun around to face the window like I was too repulsive to even look at.

"I'm sorry, David," I said. "I was feeling bad. I just needed something . . . something fun. I needed to laugh."

He turned and spit his words at me like they were poisonous darts flying out of his mouth. "You with your needs. Music requires sacrifice. Did you expect an ordinary life? We tried that and look where it got us. We got so obsessed with one another that we completely lost our focus."

"It was never ordinary," I said.

But he didn't hear me. He just kept shooting holes in me. "It's not possible to get away with it, Bess. The world notices. And then you went and got pregnant, for Christ's sake! And here I was thinking now that you've miscarried, we'd have a chance to recover the ground we lost."

"You were happy I lost our baby?"

"I was ecstatic," he said.

I was on him, fists pounding at his chest. He grabbed my hands, his face like chalk, his eyes sick and dark. "We were so close to perfect," he said. "We were better than Vronsky and Babin, better than any of them. We could have made a contribution." He held my hands up in front of my face. "These fingers are God's instruments! You dragged them through shit!" He squeezed them hard, twisting.

"You're hurting me. David, stop."

But he only tightened his grip. I closed

my eyes and took deep breaths. Suddenly David started to shake. He dropped my hands and held his own up beside his face as if he didn't trust what they would do. I've never seen anyone tremble all over like that, so that it was visible to the naked eye.

"David." I didn't dare touch him.

He didn't say another word, just gave me one more look with some tortured stranger's eyes and left the apartment. I never saw him again.

CHAPTER SEVENTEEN

It took me a while to pull myself together. I don't know how long I sat on the floor where my legs had crumpled under me. Then my hands started to throb real bad. I didn't want to look, but I made myself and saw that they were already starting to swell. I got up, filled the kitchen sink with water, dumped in all the ice cubes from the freezer, and started soaking my fingers. I must have been thinking something, but I don't know what it was. I don't even know if I was feeling anything, except maybe shock. It was hard to stand there by the sink with my knees all wobbly. I finally had to drag a chair over because my legs just wouldn't hold me up.

Gradually, my head began to clear. It was just a really bad fight, I told myself. We'd get past it after a while. We'd lost a child. We'd lost our relationship, or maybe misplaced it. We were each trying to find our way through our own personal crises. On top of that, the concert life takes a tremendous toll on performers. Look at that two-piano pair from Belgium — nobody knew to this day what became of them.

They simply disappeared off the face of the earth. Look at Moskvy and Nordstrom, Terese, wherever she was, and poor David Helfgott. What made us think we'd get off scot-free?

By then my hands had turned into blue lumps. I took them out of the water, wrapped them in towels, and stood staring out the window. The smell of lemon hung in the air. I thought about David's face and what I saw in it before he left — the rage, yeah, but also the terror and despair. I phoned Mr. Balaboo, which was quite a trick. I had to use my pinky.

Then we waited. Hours dragged by without a word from David. It got dark, and a cold November rain started falling. We paged Phillip, but he hadn't heard anything. Nobody had. At midnight, Mr. Balaboo called the police. Ordinarily, they make you wait longer before they consider somebody missing, but given David's prominence and what Mr. Balaboo called his "fragility," the cops went into action. We insisted on complete secrecy, and got it, at least for those two terrible days.

They checked out the hospitals, the hotels, the bus terminals, the airports, and train stations. Finally, first thing the following morning, they tracked him to a twenty-four-hour rental-car office in upper Manhattan. He'd taken out a four-wheel drive after midnight and asked for a map of New Jersey and points south. I didn't believe a word of it.

"He went north," I said. "Get Phillip."

"You can't go anywhere, Bess-dahlink," Mr. Balaboo said. For the first time in history, the part in his hair was uneven. It looked like jagged lightning across the top of his head. "You should be in the hospital."

I'd refused to go for X rays. I couldn't leave the place that tied me to David, even if the thread was stretched to the snapping point. "I'll pack my hands in ice and wrap them in plastic bags. We've got a cooler. Come on."

I was wild to get out of there and follow David north to the mountain house. I knew he was there. The police got in touch with their buddies upstate. One cop car followed along behind us at a discreet distance.

Mr. Balaboo kept trying to get me to wear my seat belt, but then I couldn't rock back and forth. I felt if I didn't move, I'd go out of my mind. The one thing I did do was keep on popping the Advil Mr. Balaboo said I had to swallow to reduce the swelling. As it was, my fingers felt like they'd just been unloaded from the banana boat.

It was noon by the time we got to the road that led back to David's house. I could see tire tracks in the mud.

"It could just be the police," Mr. Balaboo said. "They must have gone up there right away."

I didn't say anything, just kept rocking as Phillip took us up the long drive. It had been raining there, too, and ice caked the edge of the track. There were patches of snow back in the woods. A couple of police cars were parked in front of the house but no sign of an SUV. I couldn't get out of the car. I started crying.

"I'll go on in, shall I, honey?" Mr. Balaboo said. "You just stay here and rest a while."

"Oh, God," I said. I swear the only thing that kept me from going nuts was the back of Phillip's head. I stared at it and for some reason it comforted me.

They were in there for what seemed like a long time. When Mr. Balaboo came out, he was holding an envelope, just a plain number 10. He got in the car and handed it to me. It had my name on it in pencil in David's handwriting.

"Is he in there?" I asked.

"No. This was on the piano."

"You'll have to open it for me," I said.

Mr. Balaboo slit it carefully along one side and handed me a piece of paper from a pad David always kept by the piano. He'd used it to jot ideas about the music when we were working.

The writing was so faint I could hardly read it. The press never knew about this letter. But there was one, and here is what it said:

Dearest Bess,
You made me completely happy. I'm just too tired. Forgive.

D.

"Oh, no. Oh, no. Oh, no. Oh, no. Oh, no. Oh, please. Oh, no. Oh, please."

Mr. Balaboo sent Phillip inside to get me a double shot of something. Whatever it was, I guess it kept me sane. Only just.

They started dragging the lake, but they didn't find him. In the afternoon they located the SUV farther north, at the boat landing on Black Bear Lake. It didn't take them long after that. I imagined him on the surface like the candles he had sent drifting into the dark for my birthday. I imagined his face luminous in the night, floating, then dipping under and the light going out.

I don't remember a whole lot about the next few days. Phillip and Mr. Balaboo drove me back to the city and put me in the hospital. Phillip became my bodyguard. He was fierce about keeping the media and almost everybody else away from me. Angie and Jake came. Pauline and Mumma with — believe it or not — Dutch, in one of those handicapped vans. My father didn't say much, just hung out in the corner of the room, reading the cards on my flowers and looking uncomfortable. Professor Stein brought me chocolates and sat by my bed and let me cry. He also showed me an article that said Mr. Balaboo told some nosy reporter who was looking for dirt on David to "fuck off." I didn't believe it but Professor Stein swore it was true.

When I got out, I went straight to my old apartment on the West Side. I just couldn't face those two pianos at David's. I was so grateful that I'd kept my little hole all those months, and even more grateful that I'd never had the phone service switched off. There were three messages: (1) a solicitation for the Friends of Carnegie Hall; (2) Angie saying Oops, she'd dialed the old number by mistake; and (3) David playing the Bach Prelude in C major that he knew I loved more than anything. He didn't say a word. I knew he had sat at the piano in the woods and told me everything he felt in his heart the best way he knew how. I saved that tape, of course, but no one else will ever hear it.

CHAPTER EIGHTEEN

My baby was gone, David was gone, and now the music, too. They had taken it with them, leaving silence inside my head for the first time in my life. I was nothing, a blank, a zero with eyes. I sat inside my apartment with the lights out and the shades drawn and stared at the television with the volume off. But only cooking shows — everything else freaked me out.

The dead zombie part was the easiest to bear. But then the pain would hit like a car crash. I held a pillow to my chest to keep from splitting open. I was losing pieces of myself, like a spider who was having its legs plucked off one by one.

I did some pretty crazy shit during those first weeks. For instance: My hands were slowly healing. You would think I'd have been relieved, but I couldn't stand that the bruises were disappearing. They were where David had touched me last, and sick as it sounds, I never wanted them to go away. So one day when I didn't think I could take the misery one more second, I grabbed the Manhattan yellow pages and slammed them down on my left hand. It felt like fire was shooting up my arm. I sat there crying with relief that some other agony was giving grief a contest.

I was lucky that Jake showed up just then. I didn't answer the door, but Angie had given him a key and he let himself in.

"What the fuck, Stallone?" he said, taking in the book and my ugly hand.

"I'm sorry," I said. "Sorry."

"Jesus, Bess, your fingers. Couldn't you think of something else to trash?"

He went to the freezer for ice but there wasn't any. So then Jake just picked me up and carried me out. On the way to the emergency room, he called Mr. Balaboo on his cell phone. I wasn't even curious how Jake had his number, but I found out later that there was a kind of network in operation. Mr. Balaboo showed up with the doctor who'd been treating my hands. The upshot was that they wanted to put me in the hospital, i.e., mental ward. I knew I'd better come up with some instant stability or I was doomed.

"I lost it, I admit it," I said. "It won't happen again."

"How do we know that?" Mr. Balaboo asked.

"Because I'm promising."

"You're promising you won't pull this exact trick and I believe you," Jake said, "but what else have you got up your sleeve?" He knew me so well.

"What do I have to do to stay out of here?" I asked.

The doctor was one of those glamorous orthopedic types who treats the New York teams. He gave me his stern look, which I guess was supposed to intimidate me but it only made me want to pop him in the nose. Since I didn't wither properly, he addressed the rest of his comments to Mr. Balaboo as if I wasn't in the room.

"Does she have anyone who can stay with her?"

"We can hire someone," he said.

I shook my head at Jake. No way. So he jumped in and saved my ass. "Sure," Jake said. "Her sister can. And I can. And her mother. We'll rotate. It'll work out."

I started crying again, but nobody seemed to think that that called for an immediate injection of Thorazine. Not that I would have minded.

They sent me home. Jake stayed overnight on the tiny couch with his feet hanging off the end. Pauline was a peach for loaning him out and volunteered to take a turn. I just didn't think I could cope with the tragic attitude.

So for the next three weeks, Angie and Jake and Mumma hung out with me in that dark hole. Mumma was the hardest, but I do remember something she said that stuck with me, in the dark when we were falling asleep, which was maybe when it was easier to confide things.

"I think I know the way you felt about David," she said. "The love of your life, that kind of thing."

"Yeah," I said, wondering where this was going.

"Your father took my breath away."

I didn't know what to say. The way she said it was like it was in the past, but I didn't really want to know. I guess we both fell asleep. Mumma wanted so desperately to make it all better that she kept making suggestions. But I didn't want to go to a concert or a movie or back to Rocky Beach to see Dutch or the guys at the firehouse. I didn't want anyone coming to visit. She even offered to take me to mass at St. Patrick's. It tired me to have her around even though she meant well, but it just wasn't fair to ask for more time from Angie and Jake.

They were perfect. Angie was a gentle, loving shadow, holding my hand, slipping me a plate of food without fuss, and climbing into bed with me when she heard me wake up crying in the night. She never initiated a conversation, never turned on the TV, just waited for signals from me. She washed my hair, she rubbed my back, she taped my hands, she lived up to her name and then some.

Jake was more difficult, but looking back I realize he was nudging me out of my miserable rut. He didn't ever ask if I wanted to do something. He just announced.

"Put on your jacket, Stallone. We're going to see the sky." Having no choice made it easy. I obeyed. We would go to the park and watch the jet trails. I remember once the sun was going down and there were pink streaks in the sky. Pink against blue. Jake saw the way I was staring.

"What?" he asked.

"Blue for boy, pink for girl," I said.

"You had a double whammy, Stallone. Everything's going to remind you."

"Forever?"

"No," he said. "For a while."

I remembered how devastated he was when he lost his mother. "Your mom was one cool dude, Jake," I said.

"You got that right."

"You still miss her?"

"Oh, yeah."

"Does it still feel like you're going totally crazy?"

"No," he said. "That passes."

"What am I supposed to do to help it along?"

"You're doing it. One foot in front of the other."

The pink had deepened into soft purple. "Thanks," I said, and leaned my head against his shoulder.

"No sweat. Come on. We're going for pizza."

"In a restaurant?" I asked, panicked.

"You can do it."

So I did it.

My baby-sitters had stayed with me for a month when it was decided that I wasn't going to do any more finger crushing. Although I hadn't gained any of the twenty-five pounds back, at least I'd stopped losing weight. I was slowly weaned, with members of the trio gradually leaving me alone for longer stretches. The big event was getting through a night on my own. The phone rang a lot. Once I had Angie on the line when Mumma called. Then the second I hung up from them, Jake called. It made me laugh, which I think was the first time since David died.

"Is that a laugh?" Jake asked.

"I guess so," I said.

After we hung up, I figured he'd phone the other two right away to tell them.

Mr. Balaboo and Professor Stein came to me after four months to ask if I would like to start playing again. The great Dr. Glamour-puss said it was okay, they explained. In fact, that it would be good therapy.

"No," I said.

"Your fingers need the exercise," Professor Stein said. I let him smoke his cigars in the apartment and the place was filled with a blue fog.

"There have been many inquiries," Mr. Balaboo said. "People want to hear you."

"You guys been rehearsing this or what?"

Mr. Balaboo looked a little sheepish but not Professor Stein. "Just exactly where do you see music fitting into your life, Bess?" he asked.

"It doesn't."

"Well, that's a tragic waste," he said.

"The world will get along just fine without Bess Stallone's stirring rendition of the *Waldstein* Sonata," I said.

"Get along, yes," Mr. Balaboo said. "The world can get along without a lot of things — starlight, Picasso, perhaps even chocolate . . ."

I didn't answer.

"Forget it," Professor Stein said to Mr. Balaboo.

"For now," Mr. Balaboo said.

I broke out a bottle of wine and that cheered them up. Mr. Balaboo smoked a cigar and I even took a puff. Lung cancer didn't scare me. Living did.

My first day out on my own, I walked down to Tower Records to pick up a CD I'd ordered. It was David's first and had only been released in Europe, so it took a while to locate it. Otherwise, I had them all. I'd somehow lost track of the fact that Christmas was two weeks away. There were so many people on the streets and so much noise. Inside the store, they were playing holiday selections by somebody singing half a tone flat. It was like she was dragging her fingernails across my skull. When I got out of there, I was totally wiped out. A cab pulled up to the corner, so I slid in.

The second I sat down, we got rear-ended. Not a huge jolt, but enough to send me banging into the seat partition. The driver spewed some choice words in Spanish and got out to check the damage. I got out, too, and stood on the corner trying to get my knees to stop quaking. There was an African-American man waiting for the light, holding the hand of a little girl who was maybe his granddaughter.

"You okay?" he asked.

"A little shook up, but okay," I said. I'm Cinder-fucking-ella, I wanted to tell him, and my prince wasn't supposed to die.

He gave me a sympathetic smile and then winked to tell me he didn't quite believe me. It was the wink that did it. Kindness — it was a killer. I turned away to hide my crumbling face and started up Broadway. I couldn't wait to get back inside my cocoon.

CHAPTER NINETEEN

My fingers got better way ahead of the rest of me, maybe because a suicide shoves the grieving process into a whole other dimension. It's bad enough to lose somebody to an early death, but when they murder themselves . . . man, the questions never end. I kept imagining David in those last hours, on the drive upstate, in the house in the woods, as he sat by the piano playing to my answering machine. What was he thinking? Was he crying? What exactly was he feeling that he could wade into that lake, sink under the surface, and welcome the water into his lungs? I wondered if he choked, if he changed his mind when it was too late. The whole thing was unimaginable, and yet it had happened. I listened to his telephone tape, the Bach, over and over, hoping for clues. I read his letter, held it up to the light even, as if there were answers hiding between the lines. I got so pissed at him, and then felt guilty for my anger. He had the right. Anybody has the right. But that was in general, in theory. Not my David. How could he leave me that way? He knew I couldn't possibly function without him.

Then there was the "if only" syndrome. I was totally convinced that I could have saved him if only I had been quicker to follow him. If only I hadn't provoked him. If only I'd held him and never let him out of my arms, out of my sight. If only I'd been worthy enough, lovable enough so that his feelings for me were stronger than his need to escape the pain. This line of thought got really grim at night. I kept dreaming I was drowning, and I'd wake up all tangled in my sheets from trying to kick my way to the surface.

Stir into all this the fact that I was still sad about the baby. I kept thinking if I hadn't lost her, there would be something of David left in the world. Our child would have carried his light like a little lantern into the next generation, and now that light was snuffed out forever.

Six months had gone by since David's death. My hands looked almost normal, although two knuckles were swollen and I couldn't wear the ring David had bought me in a little funky shop in Baltimore. The trouble was, I was still fighting to get out of bed every morning. It seemed so pointless. But I'd made a deal with Jake and Angie that we'd E-mail each other first thing in the morning and before bed at night. And let me tell you, if I forgot, one of them was on my doorstep in a heart-beat.

On a depressingly springlike May morning when the sky was the palest blue and the birds wouldn't shut up, I sat down at David's laptop to do my check-in. I'd inherited his computer along with a ton of money and the mountain house. There wasn't a will, exactly. Mr. Balaboo said that a month before David died, he set up a trust. Although the media couldn't get at the terms, I was told that as a beneficiary, I could read it. I really didn't give a rat's ass. All I knew was that he'd left me more than I could ever spend and that he'd even provided for Angie. Looking back, I wonder if it was such a hot idea for me to have all that money. It only made it easier for me to sit on my butt and feel sorry for myself instead of lacing on my Rollerblades, memorizing the daily specials, and hustling tips for the rent. Anyway, that particular morning, I noticed that Jake had left me a bombshell along with his daily greeting. Here's what it said:

"Wake up, Stallone. The sun's shining and you could use a walk in the park. Here's a new item for your address book:

"Terese Dumont, Via Dandolo 72, Isola Como, Italy (Tel: 011-394-588-1413). I think you should go see her. Get yourself a ticket."

My fingers were shaking so much it took me a couple of tries to get Jake's telephone number right.

"Is this for real?" I asked.

"Morning. Sure, it's for real."

"Nobody's ever been able to find her."

"It didn't take that long."

"How'd you do it?"

"Ever hear of detectives?"

"It must have cost a fortune."

"You can pay me back. Call your travel agent."

"Why should I?"

"You're stuck, Stallone. Maybe it'll help and maybe it won't, but you're a useless lump the way things are."

"Why, thank you," I said.

"Anytime. Let me know."

It took me two days to get up the courage to phone Terese. It wasn't a great connection, and I don't know if the long silence after I gave her my name was because of that or because she was shocked or angry or something else. But she said to come if I wanted to. I started packing as soon as I hung up.

To get to Terese, I had to fly to Milan. That wasn't easy because it resurrected so many memories, good and bad, of the trip with David. I picked up a rental car and drove north to the lakes. You'd think I would have been nervous about doing this on my own, but by then I was obsessed about meeting with Terese, and I would have gone by skateboard if that was the only way to get there. It was the first time I'd really cared about anything since David died, and I felt almost as if I was expecting to see him waiting for me at the other end of the road. And let me tell you, some road. First you drive north up into the mountains into almost bloody Switzerland, and then you go most of the way around the far side of an extremely long lake so you can get to a ferry that takes you to a tiny little island. You leave your car at the dock. They don't let you drive on that island. And I have to say, it's one of the most gorgeous places I've ever seen and if you were planning to be a fairy princess as your vocation, this is exactly where you'd set up shop.

I was the only ferryboat passenger who wasn't a local. Everybody was inspecting me, but especially the captain, who looked too old to be breathing regularly, much less operating a rickety, slippery raft. When we were secured to the dock, I asked how to find the Via Dandolo.

"Signorina Stallone?" he asked.

So I was expected. At my nod, he waved at the highest point of the village. "Up, up," he said, showing me the two teeth that were still left in his mouth. I had the feeling that if I hadn't passed inspection, those pegs would have sunk into my ankle.

The island was basically a mountaintop sticking out of the lake, so the town was built onto a steep slope. The houses were pale yellow stone with the battered, washed-out beauty only centuries of weather can produce. It was some climb to the Via Dandolo. I stopped once to ask a woman who was pegging laundry if I was going the right way. She squinted at me. "Stallone?" she asked. It was like a fortress. It made me wonder what they did with the remains of people who didn't have permission to be there. Anyway, by the time I got up to the top, wheezing and gasping, I had quite the admiration for Terese. If you wanted to disappear, this was a pretty good place to do it.

A woman was standing in the doorway of Number 72 in a faded dress, bulky sweater, and canvas shoes. At first I thought she was the housekeeper, but when I got close I recognized her. There was no mistaking the perfect bones of her face and the blue eyes with their unusual square shape. You could see that this woman had suffered. There were lines beside her mouth and between her eyebrows, but she was so beautiful that she put the landscape to shame. She didn't come to greet me, just stood waiting. Then she stuck her hand out. She had a strong grip for such a fragile-looking thing, but then, she'd been one of the world's great pianists.

"Miss Stallone," she said, in a whispery, almost childish voice.

"Bess. Please."

"Then you must call me Terese." Not her first choice from the sound of it. I followed her inside. The house was airy with lots of homey touches, but I didn't see a piano anywhere.

"Would you like to sit here?" she asked, indicating a sofa by the fire. It was twenty degrees cooler than in Milan and I hadn't worn warm enough clothing.

"That would be fine, thank you," I said.

"Allow me to bring you something to drink," she said.

Whew, this woman was as formal as they

come. "I wouldn't mind a glass of wine," I said. "But only if you'll join me." Maybe if I could get her a little tanked, she'd unwind.

Terese came back carrying a little silver tray with a couple of crystal glasses. In fact, everything in the place was classy. That dress may have been faded but it was for sure out of some top designer's collection. Nardigger popped into my head — Audrey Hepburn wasn't such a stretch. And me, Courtney Love, I sat at the opposite end of the couch wondering why I'd come.

"I'm sorry for your loss," Terese said finally. She dropped her eyes but not before I saw the film of tears.

"It's everybody's loss," I said.

She nodded and folded her hands.

"I have so many questions," I said. I felt like she winced, not a good sign. But what the hell, she'd let me come. "Did you . . . was he . . . was David . . . ?" I knocked back the wine and pulled myself together. "Mr. Balaboo says that David had problems before, with depression. Did you see any evidence of it when you were performing together?"

She nodded. "David was a very troubled person." It gave me a little stab of jealousy to hear her call him by name. "But he had a sad life, a terrible childhood. His mother . . . oh, a wicked woman."

"David seemed to adore her," I said.

There was another silence. It seemed like every sentence had to travel a long way before it got to her lips.

"First he was abandoned by his father and then Aimee sold him to Beauchapel." I noticed that her wine had disappeared. She poured us both another glass.

"Sold?"

"Aimee was getting older, her beauty was fading. David was her prize, the best thing she had." Another silence, but it was getting easier. "Beauchapel paid Aimee's living expenses in exchange for David. But it was a terrible place for a child."

"At least Beauchapel was sort of a father to him."

"I will tell you about David's first Christmas in that house. No toys, no treats, only books of music. On Christmas morning, they even took away the soft toys he slept with . . . you call them . . . bears?"

"Teddy bears," I said.

"*Oui.* Because music was the greatest gift and the boy should not be distracted by foolish things. Beauchapel said David would thank him one day. For myself, I curse him."

"We're talking how old?" I asked.

"David moved in with Beauchapel when he was five. Already, he was a prodigy and performed with Aimee in two-piano concerts. She was very gifted. But also ill." Terese tapped her temple. "Here. She had terrible moods, up and down. Beauchapel finally banned her from his house. She would get David too upset."

"Is she still alive?"

"Oh, no. She died in a sanitarium several years ago. David perhaps inherited her illness, don't you think? They say these things are genetic."

I felt cold right down to the insides of my bones. "Yes, I guess so," I said.

"He was very afraid of being like her," Terese said.

"Did he tell you that?"

"Yes, quite recently."

"I don't understand. When did you see him?"

"Last year when you were in this country."

Those few days he left me to take care of "real estate" business. I was beginning to feel like I was about to get more answers than I was ready to hear. I could still get up, walk down to the ferry, and put thousands of miles between me and whatever truth was going to come out of that perfect mouth. I tried to imagine myself back in New York, lying awake at night and tortured with questions that wouldn't go away. Terese was studying me.

"You seem like a strong woman," she said.

"I thought I was, but then David died."

"Did he talk to you about me?"

Funny, I was thinking of asking her the same thing. "There were some subjects he wouldn't discuss," I said. "You were one."

"Well, he told me about you, Bess." A smile — and what a smile. She had deep dimples beside her mouth. It felt like the sun just dropped by for a visit. "He loved you very much."

I felt myself choking up but she didn't stop. "He told me you made him laugh," she said.

"Well, I guess that's true enough. Until he got so . . . sick, finally."

"The great tragedy of my life was that David was never in love with me," Terese said. "It made me so miserable that I could no longer perform."

I knew that Terese was telling me stuff that came out of a very private place. And

God knows, I understood that need for David's love.

"I don't see a piano anywhere," I said.

"The music didn't make me happy anymore. I'm more at peace without it."

A door opened. The maid came in and spoke quietly to Terese in Italian. Terese shot a look at me, hesitated, and said something back. When the maid retreated, Terese turned to me.

"Bess, I hope . . . I hope this is not a mistake, but I think not. I should perhaps prepare . . ." But before she could say any more, a boy entered the room. He was carrying a book bag in one hand and an apple in the other. He went straight to Terese, kissed her on both cheeks, and said, *"Allo, Maman. Ça va?"*

"Oui, mais nous avons une invitee. Bess, this is my son, Francois-David. Francois, this is Mademoiselle Stallone."

Francois started to shake my hand, but the half-eaten apple was still in it. He smiled and gave me a bow instead. He had his mother's dimples, but it was also that unexpected, dazzling grin, David's grin. I felt the world begin to spin around.

"Maman, elle est malade?" I heard the boy ask from a distance.

Terese was beside me, rubbing my hand.

"Oh, I'm so sorry. I should never have . . . how foolish. Yes, darling, Miss Stallone is feeling a bit weak. Would you run and ask Maria to bring us some water? Then we'll see you a little later."

After he left, the room stopped twirling and I got my head back.

"Whoa," I said. "You couldn't have given me a hint?"

"I'm so sorry," she said, and I could see she meant it. "David would be so angry with me for upsetting you. He wanted to tell you and I wouldn't let him. And now I drop it on you like a big stone."

I wanted truth, I got truth. But it wasn't so easy cramming it into my brain. It kept bouncing off.

"David wanted you to meet him. He's so proud of Francois. Was. But I was horrible." The eyes filled again. "I was jealous of you and afraid of . . . I don't know what. I'm very protective of my son, perhaps too much."

"He's beautiful," I said.

"He is intelligent and loving and happy. I wish he could have had a father all the time, but I knew how it would be before. It was perhaps very selfish of me, but I don't regret it for a moment. Francois-David is my joy. He's all the music I will ever need."

I was sitting there trying to put it all to-gether. "How old?"

"Just eight in March," Terese said. She watched me trying to absorb it. The maid came with the water, but what I really wanted was another dose of wine. I poured myself some, and Terese, too. "I loved David very much, you see," she went on, "and I knew he would never feel the same toward me. I hoped that if I had his child, it would . . . tie us. There were only the few times that we . . ."

Fucked. Believe it or not, I didn't say it. I felt as though Terese's ears would curl up and drop off if such a word passed any-where near them. "So David came to see you and Francois sometimes."

"Yes, a few times every year, but very quietly. I found this house because no one bothers to come to this village."

"Well, you've done a great job. I tried to track you down and even on the Internet, there's nothing. You've pretty much disap-peared."

We sat in silence for a while. Terese had let go of my hand, but she reached for it again. From the way she was watching me, I must have looked like shit. The truth is, I was fighting bitter envy. Terese had a de-licious, daily reminder of David, living right there in her home.

"David told me that he was losing his talent," she said. "Was this true?"

"Of course not," I shot back. But that was a lie and this was the first time I truly acknowledged it to myself. My poor David. I looked at Terese. Our poor David.

"Are you feeling any better?" Terese asked me.

I nodded.

"Permit me to give you something to eat."

I wasn't hungry, but I also didn't want to pass out on the way back to Milan. Terese showed me outside to a table that stood in a grove of olive trees. It was covered with a blue-striped tablecloth and was set for two.

"Is Francois going to join us?" I really wanted him to, and I really didn't.

"No, he has his luncheon at school."

Terese was sensitive enough to understand that I needed to be quiet for a while. We ate in silence and watched Francois play with a puppy on the hillside below. The food was so fresh and light that I found myself finishing everything, the tomatoes and mozzarella, the grilled fish, the fresh vegetables and fruit. And of course the crusty bread that we dipped in some local olive oil.

Afterward, Terese walked me to the gate.

"Wouldn't you like me to accompany you down to the ferry?"

"No, thanks," I said. "You've done enough." We stood side by side, gazing across the water to the mountains on the far shore. It was too hazy to see beyond them to the snow-covered peaks of Switzerland.

"I hope you will not be sorry that you came," Terese said.

"Why did you let me?"

"For two reasons. I believe I'm honoring David's wish. About Francois." She stopped as if she was finished.

"You said two?"

"And . . ." I saw her chin begin to quiver. "David loved only two women his entire life. I had met Aimee. I wanted to meet the other."

I don't know exactly how it happened, but the next thing I knew we were hugging. Then I left. I felt her watching me as I started down the narrow stone streets, but when I turned back to wave, she had gone.

On the plane home, I thought of a hundred questions I wished I'd asked. How recently did David see his mother? What about his father? What else did David say about me besides that I made him laugh? Then all the questions for myself. Did I really believe that David never loved Terese? Why didn't he confide in me about her and Francois? Hadn't David abandoned his son exactly as he had been abandoned by his own father? What was David's attitude toward Terese's pregnancy? Even though he'd been moved by the news of our own child coming, I couldn't help remembering how negative he was about it later. And maybe most important of all, Terese had said that loving David had silenced her musically. Maybe he didn't know this, but what if he did? And if so, was he afraid that he would eventually damage me in the same way? Could that concept have contributed to his suicide?

Time flew as we flew, as I tried to process everything I'd learned. I knew it was going to take a while. I didn't expect that I would see Terese again, or Francois. But by the time we'd crossed the Atlantic and were beginning to make our descent along the New England coastline, I'd begun to take some comfort in the memory of the two of them living on that Italian hillside. I thought of Francois's face, the shape so much like his father's, the eyes dark and sensitive, and that smile. It seemed that David's light had not gone out completely after all.

CHAPTER TWENTY

The Monday after I got back, Jake picked me up in his car and took me out to Long Island. First stop was Rocky Beach. Mumma had been such a regular in my apartment that I hadn't felt like I needed to go out there. God knows I didn't have any burning desire to see Dutch. When we pulled up to the house, I sat and looked at it for a second. It seemed unfamiliar or even fake, like a movie set. But I'd had that feeling a lot since David died. I was staring at everything through a different pair of eyeballs.

"You don't have to do this," Jake said.

"It's okay," I said.

"I'll beat him up if he gets out of line."

"He's an old fart in a wheelchair," I said, climbing out of the car. "How much damage can he do?" But we both knew the answer to that one.

The downstairs had been made into an office, with stacks of papers and posters overflowing everywhere. The plastic flower centerpiece on the dining room table had been replaced by a computer, a printer, and a fax machine. Dutch was in his wheelchair, yanking pages out of the fax. He looked up for a second.

"Jesus, go eat a banana split. You look like shit."

"Nice poem," I said. I didn't bother with the kiss. It just didn't seem necessary to go through the motions anymore. I wondered why he'd bothered to visit me in the hospital, unless maybe that was my imagination.

"Where's Angie?" he asked.

Mumma came in with a laundry basket. "She's at a lecture with her boyfriend."

Jake took the basket from her and we started folding.

"She hasn't brought him around here," Dutch said. "What's the matter with him?"

"Not a thing," Jake said, picking up an apple from the fruit bowl. My mind flashed back to Francois, the apple, that grin. "He's fine."

"What's his line of work?" Dutch asked.

"Hospital administration," Jake said.

"At least he's doing something useful."

I knew that was meant for me and so did Mumma. "Come, sit down," she said in a hurry, still trying to be the peacemaker. "I'll fix you some lunch."

But there was no smell of something delicious in the oven, no fresh bread cooling on the windowsill. Instead, she came back out of the kitchen with a platter of olives, salami, and provolone. The days of home cooking were obviously over. Wasn't I the one who was always complaining that Mumma was a pathetic housebound slave? And now I found myself wondering, Where the fuck's the ziti?

"How's the campaign, Dutch?" Jake asked.

"Catching flak from the Republican machine," he said.

I looked at the posters that plastered the dining room wall. They pictured a fireman in hat, boots, the works, seated in a wheelchair. The letters H.O.F.F. stretched across the bottom — for Honor Our Firefighters.

"Look again," Mumma said.

I did, and my eyes bugged out. The fireman on the poster was Dutch. Well, it was Dutch airbrushed into a slightly older version of Kurt Russell.

"Man, I wish I'd had that photographer for my publicity photo," I said.

"They barely touched it," Dutch grumbled.

Jake and I sat down and picked at the antipasto.

"Did you ever get an answer from Christopher Reeve?" Jake asked Dutch.

"Yeah, one of those form letters," he said.

"But it was sweet as those things go," Mumma added.

"We're not some half-ass parasite thing here," Dutch complained.

"They sent a phone number to call," Mumma said. "We'll follow up on it." I wondered how long ago she'd lost the cringing look she used to get when Dutch bitched about something in that tone.

I was more than ready to leave. It had always been a mystery how Jake could read me like I was the front page of *Newsday*. He got up and took our plates into the kitchen. Mumma followed him in and I could hear them talking at the sink. Me, I stared at Dutch. He felt my eyes on him and glanced up from his paperwork, but only for a second.

"What did you want from me?" I asked.

He kept his attention on his work. "What?"

"Why have you always been so pissed off at me?"

"Because you could have done something with your life." Said so casually.

I thought about the magazines that had done features on me and David — *People*, *Interview*, *Music Today*, and many more.

Charlie Rose. The Kennedy Center. The concert tours, the international acclaim.

"Maybe you wanted me to be a firefighter," I said.

"You had it in you to be a good one," he said.

Well, that was a surprise. "You're serious," I said. He didn't answer, just kept on stuffing envelopes.

"You don't think making music for millions of people is useful?"

"You never listened to me, that's for shit sure," he said.

"That's it, isn't it, Dutch? You just couldn't stand that I went and did what I wanted."

He looked up at me now. His eyes were faded versions of what they had once been. "You were just like me," he said.

The son you always wanted, I almost said. But at least I'd got a hint. I'd stepped outside his reach and that wasn't something he could forgive.

"Only a little like you," I said, and stood up. Jake and Mumma were loading the dishwasher. I had the feeling they were steering clear until Dutch and I had finished. I went into the kitchen, grabbed Mumma from behind, and gave her a hug. "Time to go, Jake," I said.

On the way to the wildlife preserve Jake said, "You're quiet. What's up?"

I looked out at the condominiums that had crawled almost to the water's edge. "It's kind of amazing actually. I don't care about him anymore."

"Dutch?"

"He used to get to me like nobody else. It would wake me up in the middle of the night and even make me puke sometimes, I'd get so crazed. I wasted a lot of time on that bullshit." The gulls were wheeling over the beach. They looked clean and free. "He's pretty much history. Not relevant, if you know what I mean."

He smiled at me. "I think so, yeah. That's good, Stallone, because there was a long time you kept hoping he'd turn into Father of the Year."

We drove in silence, passing through the ugly commercial area and into the preserve, where the dunes rose steeply on either side of the road. We pulled into the parking lot and up to the trail house where Jake worked.

"Come on," he said. "Exercise time."

"It's nice sitting here." I really didn't feel like doing anything, and to tell the truth, the sight of the water was getting to me. When I allowed myself to glance at it, I thought about David going under.

"You're looking at the side of a building. Water view's the other way."

I didn't answer him.

"Oh," he said, getting it. But he came around and opened the door.

"Time to move your sorry butt." And time to move on. He didn't have to say it for me to hear what he meant.

The pinewoods stretched back away from the beach. As we walked along the narrow path, there was the smell of warming earth that meant summer wasn't far off.

"Remember when we were kids," Jake said, "we'd see colonies of terns out here, maybe three hundred at a time? Well, forget about it. The drainage pipes finished that." He stopped to tear out a bush.

"Hey, what're you doing? That's pretty."

"Multiflora rose. It's too invasive, chokes out a lot of good stuff. And that's garlic mustard — we don't know where the hell that came from. But there's good news, too."

"Well, thank God for *that*," I said.

"Remember when the canals came in and the landfill squeezed out the salt marsh over toward Rocky Beach?"

"Yeah, no more frogs."

"Or clams either. Here's where we're planting new sea grass."

"It looks like hair transplants," I said.

He smiled. "Same principle, I guess." The wind suddenly kicked up. The sound in the dry grass sounded like distant waves of applause. It made me ache.

He stopped to point at a tangled pile of twigs heaped on top of a pole. "That's our newest osprey nest," Jake said. "There's three chicks. Our raptor program allows us to tag the parents and put radio transmitters on . . ."

I was smiling at him. He stopped and laughed. "Carried away?"

"It's good, Jake."

He swept his arm around. "So you like my office?"

"You're a lucky man."

His face was tanned already, and even the hairs on his wrists where he'd turned up his cuffs were bleached by the sun. A tingling like a tiny lightning bolt shot up from my crotch to my nipples. It stopped me in my tracks as if I'd never felt it before in my whole life.

"What?" Jake said.

I shook my head. I'd never believed that people are only turned on by their true loves. But that was when the one I loved happened to be alive. This was a whole different story, with David not here to defend himself against any possible infidelity on my part. It seemed so totally disloyal to be having sexual feelings for someone else. Then there was Pauline, of course.

"How's Pauline?" It just slipped out.

Fortunately, Jake hadn't noticed me eyeballing his very fine body. He'd never been much clued in to how women reacted to him anyway. Not like David, who was well aware that any woman he came within six feet of was dead meat.

"Fine. Her students are great. See this stuff?" He ran his hand across the broomlike top of a plant. It looked like a weed to me, but the tender way Jake touched it, you'd think it was the hair on the head of a newborn baby. "It's called phragmites. For years we thought it was an enemy invader, but now we find out it fights pollutants."

"Sucks them right out of the air?" I was concentrating, trying to distract myself from that buzz between my legs.

"No, deep root system that flushes the soil. Are you tired, Bess? Maybe we'd better start back."

"Yeah, okay." Actually, I was exhausted. Jake led me onto a wider path where we could walk side by side.

"This circles back to the parking lot," he said, and tucked my hand in his arm. "I've been listening to your CD," he said.

"Which one?" David and I had just managed to finish the second before he began to fall apart.

"First. I like it more."

"Why?" I was curious. Jake had no musical training at all. I suspected my CDs were the only two classical items in his collection of bluegrass and country stuff.

"The second one sounds rushed or something. Nervous. Except for that Ravel piece. That's a beautiful cut."

I was blown away. "How'd you get so smart?" I asked. In my opinion, *La Valse* was the only decent track on the whole thing. The rest of it, David had been like a demon, whipping me and the technicians into the fast lane and never letting us out. It was not a restful thing to listen to and it sure as hell hadn't been relaxing to record.

We continued along in silence through the short pines, except it wasn't exactly silence. Somewhere along the path, I began to hear music. I wasn't even aware of it at first. When I noticed that Jake was looking at me funny, that's when I realized I was humming "The Happy Farmer," the same little piece by Robert Schumann that Amanda Jones had played at the school recital back when I was a scabby-kneed brat. Jake understood the significance somehow, although I don't remember discussing how I never heard music anymore. He leaned over and kissed me on the forehead.

"Beautiful day," he said.

"Yeah," I agreed. By the time we got back to the car, the memory tape in my head had played fragments of a few of the pieces I'd learned over the years, but almost chronologically. I guess I was starting over again.

CHAPTER TWENTY-ONE

That day was the beginning of a new musical life for me. I didn't realize it at first. I was too busy worrying about feeling sexed up. But the next time Mr. Balaboo called to tell me someone wanted me to perform, I didn't go into cardiac arrest.

"Bess-dahlink? You there?"

"Yeah. I'm thinking," I said.

"You are?" He couldn't believe it.

"What's the gig?" I asked.

"The Copland Concerto for Clarinet and String Orchestra. With the Muhlenberg Orchestra."

"When?"

"The end of next month."

"Hm." The Copland was interesting because it didn't totally qualify as a solo, at least not in my head. There would be other instrumentalists onstage. The pianist plays, the clarinet plays, there's a conversation going on. "I'd be doing an Argerich," I said, referring to Martha Argerich's dislike for solo work. "It's not much time, but then nobody's around the end of July. It'd be low-key."

"Ah, yes, that's probably true," Mr. Balaboo agreed, but there was something in his voice.

"Did you cook this up, Mr. Balaboo?"

"Perhaps Harold Stein and I gave it some thought."

I imagined the two old guys sitting in a cloud of the professor's cigar smoke, plotting which piece in the vast solo repertoire would be the least likely to scare the crap out of me.

"Let me think about it."

"Certainly. Take all the time you need. I don't have to tell them until Wednesday."

That was two days away. "Gee, thanks."

We hung up and I poured myself a cup of chamomile, which I figured might calm me down. Bourbon would have worked better. I sat on the bed, hugged my pillow, and tried to imagine myself onstage. Without David. I knew one of the violinists in the Muhlenbery. He often got drunk at our postconcert jam sessions and played jazz riffs until somebody kicked him out. I liked him and he was a good solid musician. But I hadn't practiced since my injury, which was almost seven months ago. I stretched my fingers out and studied them.

"Think you could handle it?" I asked them. Then I called the concierge at David's apartment and told him I needed access right away.

I hadn't been in there since David died except to clear my stuff out — which Mr. Balaboo mostly took care of anyway. I stood outside the door with my heart doing a tap dance, pretty much the way it had that first time I came to audition with the *Scaramouche*.

"Fuck it," I said to myself, and went in. Everything looked exactly the same. The lawyers in charge of David's trust had told Mr. Balaboo that the apartment would sell more easily if it was furnished, especially given David's fame. Somebody had gone to contract on it but had been turned down by the co-op board because he only had a mere twenty gazillion dollars. A married couple passed the board but wound up getting divorced instead of moving in. Since then, there'd been a few nibbles but nobody really serious. So here I was, back in a time warp, staring at dust motes instead of David. I figured, Okay, I've gotten this far. Might as well truly torture myself. I went into the bedroom and sat down on David's side of the mattress. I couldn't feel him there, the way you can where somebody actually lives. The place seemed hollow, as if it was some historical site and we should hang velvet ropes around the rooms. But then my heel caught on something under the dust ruffle. I leaned over and pulled out a white T-shirt. The first thing I thought was, great housekeeping. Then I buried my face in it. David. I could feel him then all right. I could taste him and smell him, that lemon smell. I'd read an article that a person's odor can sometimes reflect extreme changes in body chemistry. Anxiety has a smell and so does depression. All I knew was that suddenly that familiar lemon scent made David seem real and so the loss did, too. Once I started crying, I didn't think it was ever going to end. I curled up on the bed with David's T-shirt, which seemed to be all I had left of him.

Fortunately, I'd drunk about a gallon of tea before I got there, so pretty soon I had to go to the john. I forced myself to shove the T-shirt back under the bed where I felt it should rest in peace, peed, washed my face and went to the piano. I spent half an hour doing warm-ups. It was discouraging to say the least. Everything I asked my fingers to do, they said, "Huh?" like it was all news to them, those exercises they'd done a couple million times. But after an hour, I could feel them limbering up. Then I started working through some music, getting reacquainted with old buddies like the Bach Partitas and a Schubert Sonata. By the time I quit, my spine was ready to crack in half, but now I couldn't wait to play again. I sat for a long time and watched the day fade over Central Park. "Okay, David," I said. "I'm gonna try."

Mr. Balaboo somehow kept the media off me. I didn't want the added pressure of them making a huge deal out of this concert, as in "Grieving Bess Stallone Returns to Concert Stage All Alone." As it was, the closer we got to the date, the more I started to think about how I hadn't performed solo since I teamed up with David, and we all know how pathetic those earlier gigs turned out. I tried to take deep breaths and focus on the music.

I chose the same dress from my first appearance with David at Weill. It had to be taken in here and there, but it seemed like a lucky charm. I'd insisted on being slated before intermission instead of at the end of the program. As it was, I had to warm my icy hands in the sink while the orchestra played the *Festive* Overture by Shostakovich. Then it was my turn. When

I walked out onstage, there was this huge sound from the audience, a roar that went on and on. It got me choked up and instead of the old terror and loneliness, I felt embraced out there, at home. Music was what I did, what I loved.

I hit a clinker toward the end of the first movement. Everybody does it. There's no such thing as a perfect performance. For a few scary seconds, I saw sparkles in front of my eyes. But then I thought, Oh hell, if I go down, I'll just pick myself up and start playing where we left off. It made me feel free, and it made me grateful all over again for David. And for the first time since he died, I was almost happy.

They don't usually allow anybody backstage during intermission when there's a soloist performing, but Mr. Balaboo had got them to make an exception. It was a rowdy bunch. Corny, in a truly outrageous yellow suit, brought me flowers and told me he'd never been so proud of me. Vernon was there, speechless but with liquid eyes reading poems of adoration. Mrs. Edelmeyer came all alone for once. She took my hands and said, "You've brought me so much joy, Bess. Thank you for coming back. Thank you." I put my arms around her and we had a good long squeeze. But then Jake and Pauline and Angie and her adorable and brilliant boyfriend Ben showed up. Ben was grinning from ear to ear — first of all, just being with Angie tended to make him do that, but second, he'd never been backstage before. And Pauline was overcome. "It was so beautiful, Bess," she said, "but I can hear the heartache in every note."

Jake laid his hand on my cheek for a second. "Good going, Stallone," he said. I felt that little tingle again, and thought, Oh shit, what sickness is this? I remembered him twisting the brush out of the soil in one quick motion. As strong as he was, I also knew how gentle he could be.

The musicians were there, too, David's friends. The sight of them made me feel his absence like a slug in the gut. They asked me to join them in their box for the rest of the concert, but I had to get out of there. I needed to be alone with my memories of David, all the best ones, and we'd have this night together. It really was his triumph, too.

So now I was in demand as a soloist. I didn't rush into it. After all, I'd been playing two-piano stuff exclusively for almost two years so I had plenty of brushing up to do. Professor Stein wasn't teaching anymore, but offered to give me his impressions after I'd worked through a piece. Mainly, he was too busy with his new girl-friend, a cellist, no surprise there. Robin didn't give a shit about the cigars and even let him stink up the bedroom. If you didn't have asthma before you stuck your nose in his place, you were wheezing by the time you left. But Harold Stein was one happy old dude.

I felt myself sinking deeper and deeper into the music. I practiced six hours a day, which is huge for any musician, and I started playing all over the world. If you look at my CDs from that period, the live in-concert ones, it's like Around the World with Bess Stallone — Bess in London, Bess in Amsterdam, Bess in Berlin, Bess in Madrid, Bess in fucking Sri Lanka. I'd got rid of that old cell of an apartment on West 78th and bought a one-bedroom in David's building. I told myself I was doing it to be close to Carnegie Hall, and if you believe that one, you'd better stay away from used-car salesmen.

But I'd made it through the first miserable year without David. God, those firsts were brutal. The first my birthday, the first his birthday, the first goddamn New York

City Marathon that David and I had seen approximately three minutes of on our way to a rehearsal. Everything was an anniversary. But even on an ordinary day, I could be walking down Madison Avenue looking in a store window and suddenly I'd feel like somebody suddenly jammed a baseball bat into my stomach. I'd double over and groan, the missing him was so intense. Those moments became less frequent as time passed, but on the anniversary of his death in November, I locked myself in the apartment and went to bed. It was strictly fetal position for twenty-four hours. Then once that was behind me, there was a sense of relief. I'd never have to go through those firsts again.

So I racked up the frequent-flyer miles and got richer from giving concerts and cutting CDs and making appearances all over the world. I got to see myself on the front cover of a lot of magazines in funny-looking languages. I'm not quite sure why, but I got to go to the Academy Awards. What I didn't get was laid. When you're famous, your sex life becomes everybody's business . . . well, duh, just ask Bill Clinton. There were some pretty attractive candidates — you'd laugh if I told you some of them — especially the rock stars and the movie actors, but they're still alive, sometimes just barely (as in drug abuse), so I won't go into it. But hard as it might be to believe, given my prior history, I steered clear. I figured that life had finally beaten those overactive hormones into submission.

But then I got a surprise. A biggie. God-damn it, but life is one strange ride. I was minding my own business, attending a combination New Year's Day and engagement party for Angie and Ben at a funky joint on the Lower East Side. All their friends were there — wearing black, of course, because the management throws you out of those downtown joints if you've got color anywhere on your person. I'd just gotten back from a trip to Tokyo so I was pretty spaced out. At the particular moment Jake and Pauline came over to say hello, I was hovering somewhere over the Pacific. I took one look at Jake from thirty thousand feet up and realized, *Uh* oh, I'm into this man. A guy I've known my entire life, who's practically a brother — well, okay, setting aside one-and-a-half rolls in the sack in the distant past — and someone who is totally committed to my oldest girlfriend. Thank God it was dark in there because I felt myself turning pink as a smoked salmon. It was simply too ridiculous. When Jake hugged me, my blood started pumping overtime. I squirmed out of his arms in a big hurry, pretending I couldn't wait one more second to snag a passing cracker with caviar on it. The place was kind of a dive — Angie's choice — but since I was paying for the party, I figured we might as well have great food.

I tossed back some champagne and started chattering away like a nutcase. I couldn't admit even to myself these scary feelings for Jake. The consequences were too scary and sad. No more best friends — I'd lose him and Pauline at one crack. I was petrified of Pauline's ESP. She was giving me one of her brain-drilling looks, excavating for my deepest thoughts. My only recourse was to start going through every bloody note of Beethoven's *Tempest* Sonata in my head so maybe I could throw her off the track. Last movement, tadadaDAH, tadadaDAH, tadadaDAH, tadadaDUM. Down, Bess. Down, girl.

When I got home, I stayed up the entire night practicing on my silent keyboard that has earphones so I don't torture the neighbors. And it wasn't just on account of jet lag.

I startled Mr. Balaboo the next morning

by calling to tell him I'd take the gig in London.

"But you said you were worn out from traveling."

"That was yesterday. I got a good night's sleep," I lied.

"You were complaining that you were just in London last month."

"Not a complaint. An observation. I'd like to go. Do you think they still want me?"

"Of course they want you, but Bess-dahlink, should I be worrying about this? I think I'm worrying."

But he booked me and off I went to Europe for another month, hoping I was suffering from temporary insanity and that when I came home again, I'd remember that Jake was my co-best friend and nothing more.

It turned out, however, that Pauline's spooky vibes were transatlantic. The day I got back, she called to say that we were going to have a girl's lunch — command performance, not a request. She'd already made a reservation at Ricky's, a couple of blocks from my apartment. I was feeling queasy about the whole thing because the fantasies I'd been having about Jake were not suitable for her radar screen.

Pauline was sitting in a booth when I showed up. I only got my butt halfway down toward the seat when she said, "You're in love with Jake, aren't you?" She was pouring me a glass of bottled water at the time. I wished with all my heart that it was vodka. "Don't look away, Bess," she said. "I want to see your eyes."

I sat all the way down and obeyed. To my disgust, I could feel tears starting up. "Nope, nope," she said. "Bess, it's okay. I was only borrowing him anyway."

"Pauline, what the fuck . . . ?"

"Shut up and listen," she said. "I've been rehearsing this speech all the way in from the island."

I nodded. What else could I do?

"Jake Minello has been crazy about you his entire life." I started to protest but she held up her hand. "Shut *up*, Bess. He's even still got that stupid tattoo."

"What, the Rocky Beach one?"

"You're such a dumbass," Pauline said. "Rocky B isn't for Rocky Beach, even if that's what he told you. Remember how we were all so obsessed with the Rocky movies back then? The guys liked the gore and we girls talked about how they were so deep but really we just wanted to look at Sly's body."

"I remember," I said, still clueless.

"Rocky stands for Stallone — inside the heart in Jake's tattoo. That's you. Stallone. And just in case there's any doubt, he stuck the 'B' in for Bess."

"You're crazy," I said. She just sat there. "He told you this?"

"Yeah. Ask Angie. She knows."

"But we were just kids."

"So why hasn't he had it sanded off?" Pauline asked.

"A dozen good reasons. It would hurt, for instance."

Pauline sighed. "You will always be his one true love."

Oh, man, I thought. Here we go with the soap-opera stuff.

"I knew it when I moved in with him," she went on, "but I figured it was never going to work out with you. You were with David and he was resigned. So what the hell, I figured since he was never going to get his dream, I'd make him happier than most, and I think I have."

I was speechless. "I don't see how you know this. Has he said anything?"

"Jake never says anything. But I know. Trust me."

I thought about her antennae. It was hard to argue.

"I'm not over losing David."

"That's going to take a lifetime, honey. But it doesn't mean you don't love Jake." She reached across the table and took my hands. "Listen to me. David was the love of your life, but Jake is your destiny."

"How do you think those things up, Pauline?"

"It's the truth. And take it from me, you stand in the way of destiny, you wind up as roadkill."

We sat holding hands across the table. "Assuming you're right about Jake's feelings . . ." I said.

She rolled her eyes at me.

"Then what about you, Pauls?"

"Look, I'm not saying this is the easiest thing I've ever done, but this is how it was supposed to come out. I'll be all right."

"I can't stand for you to be sad."

"Don't feel sorry for me." She kissed my hand, put it back on my side of the table, and signaled the waiter. "My story isn't over," she said. "I promise."

"No, you are *not* paying for this," I said, grabbing the check. Pauline was in a big hurry to put on her coat and stuck her arm in the wrong hole. I could see she was close to losing it but when I stood and reached for her, she waved me off.

"Gotta go," she croaked. I stood out in front of the restaurant and watched her walk down Seventh Avenue toward Penn Station. Every now and then, she'd stop to dig a tissue out of her pocket. I couldn't bear to think what her face looked like.

After that, I went into a kind of paralysis. I mean, what was I supposed to do, call up Jake and ask him for a date? Also, I couldn't stop thinking about Pauline. She'd left a message on my machine that she'd moved into an apartment in Riverhead. I called her several times after that, but our conversations were mainly me asking if she was all right and her reassuring me that she was fine. What I was still waiting to hear was, I'm over him. My heart is not broken.

Jake phoned one Sunday in early March. "Hey, Stallone, feel like a little trip to the country?" he asked.

"Sure," I said.

"What?"

"I said *sure*," but I was gagging on a huge lump of nerves that had established squatting rights in my throat. Hey, Bess, this is Jake we're talking about, not the frigging pope, I told myself. But under the circumstances, it felt like an audience with His

Eminence might be a breeze compared to an afternoon with my old buddy Mister Minello.

"Can Phillip drive you to my house?" he asked.

"I'll take the train," I said. Phillip had been too much a part of my life with David to include him in this weirdness. "Is the two-forty okay?"

"I'll pick you up at the station."

"Bye." I knew I sounded like I'd swallowed a gym sock but Jake wasn't exactly normal either. There was a funny wrinkled quality in his voice, like it needed to be smoothed out.

I had an hour on the train to think about seeing him but my brain was in a jumble. My blood had heated up to about two hundred degrees. I caught hell from the old guy across the aisle because I kept having to open my window until I cooled down enough not to faint.

I saw him on the platform when we pulled in. Hands in pockets, jacket collar pulled up, jeans torn at one knee. I wondered what his heart was doing, that good heart, because mine was revved up like an Aston Martin. I stepped out of the train and straight into his arms. He kissed me, a long tender one. When we came up for air, nobody was left on the platform and the train was long gone.

"What the fuck is going on here?" I asked him.

His eyes looked like blue jewels. "I've been asking myself that question for twenty-two years," he said.

"Exactly?"

"We were eight, in Betsy Smilowitz's basement."

"The birthday party we all got caught playing sex games."

"That's the one." Jake put his arm around me and we started walking. "I can't answer for you, Stallone."

"Do you . . . how's Pauline?" I didn't even know if he was in touch with her, but I had to ask.

He didn't answer right away. I figured he was remembering a bunch of bad days. "She met someone this week, another teacher," he said finally. "She'll be okay." Spoken like a man who consistently underestimates his unique and wonderful self.

Then he kissed me again. I knew he was trying to remind me that things were not the same between us. We weren't old pals anymore, and life had dealt us both some ugly blows. When something sweet and good was offered, you'd damn well better reach out and grab it. All of it was in that kiss and I got the point. When we finally came up for air, he started propelling me up his driveway instead of the front walk.

"Where are we going?" I asked him.

"To the garage."

"What for?"

"You'll see." There was that wrinkled sound again. He was hiding something inside his voice but I knew he wasn't going to tell me a bloody thing until he was ready.

We stopped at the garage door, which was pulled shut. I could feel the tension in his arm.

"You're a nervous wreck, Jake. What's in the garage? There better not be a surprise party or something. You know I hate those things and it's not my birthday . . ." I had to stop and think. No, it wasn't my birthday.

"Shut up, Stallone."

Jake's pickup truck was parked in front of the door. He squeezed around it and reached down for the handle. "Cover your eyes," he said.

"Oh, for Christ's sake," I said, but I did as he said. I heard the door slide up. "Okay? Now? Can I look?"

"Yes," Jake said.

I opened my eyes, and there in the middle of Jake's garage on a square of old blue carpet stood Amadoofus.

I closed my eyes. Then I opened them again. Then I blinked a couple of times to make sure I wasn't seeing things. There it was, a jigsaw version of the old piano, with hairline cracks covering almost every square inch, but it was Amadoofus all right.

"Oh, Jake," I said. "Oh, Jake."

He strolled over and pressed down a key. "Took me a while," he said.

"I can't. I can't believe it." I ran my hands over every inch. "How did you? It was totally shattered. You took it away in your truck."

"Yeah, but I got to the dump and I just couldn't do it. So I turned around and brought it all back here. It was a good project. I learned a lot about how pianos are put together." He put his finger into a gap on the keyboard. "There's just this one piece I couldn't find."

"Middle C. It's in my safe-deposit box. Jake. Oh, Jake."

"You said that."

I put my arms around him. "Nobody ever had such a perfect friend."

He didn't look so happy.

"But that's okay, Jake," I said. "It's good that we've been friends forever."

"First."

"Yeah, I mean before."

"Before what, Bess?"

I was so used to the "Stallone" treatment, it always freaked me out on those rare occasions when he called me Bess. It felt very sexy. In fact, all of a sudden I was feeling pretty sexy in general.

"It's kind of chilly out here," I said, leaning back in his arms.

"You need to put some of that weight back," he said. "I've got doughnuts."

I followed him inside the house, but when we went into the kitchen, I said, "Jake, I'm actually not all that hungry."

He kissed me again, and then again for good measure.

"Let's go in here for a while," he said, leading me toward the bedroom.

Jake unbuttoned my sweater, very slowly, letting his knuckles brush lightly against my breasts. When did this old buddy of mine learn to be so maddeningly tantalizing?

"Do you ever wear a bra?" he asked.

"Now and then," I said, letting my sweater drop to the floor. "Take this off," I said, unzipping his sweatshirt. His flesh felt smooth and warm against me.

"I wish we could bring Amadoofus with us," I said.

"Let's not get carried away," Jake said.

But I did get carried away, and so did he. I felt the need to explain. "I want you to know it can actually take me longer than two minutes," I said.

"You'll have to prove it," he said.

"Maybe I should take my socks off for the next round."

He moved down to the end of the bed and peeled them off. Then he put my toes in his mouth one by one. That was one I'd forgotten about. It made me a little wild. But even so, this time it did take longer, mainly because there were other people in bed with us — David and Pauline and even my baby, who would have been a toddler by now. As usual, Jake knew.

"I'm sorry," I said. "I guess I'm still not over everything." I didn't want to say David's name.

"I don't expect that," Jake said. "Not now. Not ever."

I had to kiss him again for that.

"Pauline's here, too," I said.

"Not for me," Jake said. "You were always in this bed, no matter what other body was lying here."

"Don't you think it's kind of ridiculous, us two old cronies from the sandbox?"

"No," he said.

The funny thing was, even with everybody else hanging around in here, I still had the feeling of being exactly where I belonged and even that David and Pauline and my little girl agreed with me.

Jake gave me the keys to the place, and the following week I came back out with a suitcase so we could have a sleepover before I had to fly off to Belgium. I brought the middle C for Amadoofus. Jake slipped it into place and set up a heater before he left for work so I wouldn't freeze to death in the garage before he got back.

I sat there at the keyboard just messing around and before I knew it I was playing the Bach Prelude in C major. I felt like it was my own private memorial to David and that I was telling him that I'd heard what he was trying to say on my answering machine. Finally, after all the months of grief, I thought I understood. Just like he'd helped me up every time I fell on my butt onstage and sat me back down at the piano and told me I could do it, he was saying with every sweet, singing note, "Yes, it's sad. I know you'll miss me. But you have to move on. And when you play especially well, you'll think of me because I'm in the music. I am the music, and as long as you keep playing you will never, ever lose me."

I finished the Prelude. Then I dropped the cracked and battered lid, laid my head down on it, and stretched my arms out to hug that old piano. It wasn't exactly like holding Jake, or David either, but I have to say, at that particular moment, it felt damn close.

The employees of Thorndike Press hope you
have enjoyed this Large Print book. All our
Large Print titles are designed for easy
reading, and all our books are made to last.
Other Thorndike Press Large Print books
are available at your library, through selected
bookstores, or directly from us.

For information about titles, please call:

(800) 223-1244

To share your comments, please write:

Publisher
Thorndike Press
295 Kennedy Memorial Drive
Waterville, ME 04901